Authors thrive best where people leave deserving reviews, or pass on the feeling that remains with them after they finish the book. Beside telling all your friends about it, please, if you can spare the time, leave a review of

MAGPIE

Wherever you purchased it from.

Thank you,

Cybermouse Books

Copyrights

Text:	© Bill Allerton 2021
Cover & Graphics:	© Cybermouse Books 2021
Cover Image	© Cybermouse Books 2021
Typeset & Layout:	© Cybermouse Books 2021
Font:	Garamond 12pt.

ISBN:978-0-9930424-5-4

Cybermouse MultiMedia
101 Cross Lane
Sheffield S10 1WN

www.cybermouse-multimedia.com

First published by Cybermouse Books 2021

In the design of this book, Cybermouse Multimedia have
made every effort to avoid infringement of any established copyright.
If anyone has valid concern re any unintended infringement please contact
us first at the above address.

On the Author:

'I am very jealous of your skill with dialogue. The economy of it and the precise way you catch all kinds of talk from all sorts of people...

I love the way things and people recur in the book; but I love the range and the surprises too...

I like the 'you' who emerges from these stories, with this alertness to language and a sense of the odd...

I think your stories are kind, while dealing with loneliness and death and loss and madness and funny love and time and all the mess that usually gets people to be unkind...

Your stories tease me to keep going back...'

Rony Robinson, Sony Award-winning BBC Radio presenter and Playwright

'Your writing is so original and the dialogue so inventive and funny it cracks me up. It's brilliant, clever and lyrical. You have one hell of a talent...'

Clem Cairns, Fish Publishing, organizer of the International 'Fish Prize'

By the same Author;

The Fox & The Fish (A Novel 2013)
Firelight on Dark Water (Short Fiction 2015)
A Day for Tigers (Short Science Fiction 2015)
Watch & Wait (A Collaboration of Short Fiction)
Urban Tiger Radio (Internet Podcast on all platforms)
Urban Tiger Radio Childrens Hour (Podcast for children)

This book is dedicated to

Arabella

A Great-Granddaughter

Who,

Thanks to the Pandemic,

I have yet to meet

To DOROTHY

MAGPIE

Not All Souls Catch Fire…

BUT YOURS DID!

Bill Allerton

BEST WISHES

Chapters:

Chairs

Huron Drive
Spring Grove
Chain O'Lakes
Illinois

2018

'Maggie? Have you borrowed my chair? You know… the one I tuck under the shade at the back. I don't mind if you have… I just need to…'

'Whoa, Maybelline. Backtrack a minute.' Maggie put the phone on speaker and picked up her teacup. 'What chair?'

'The old rattan one. We poked some of the loose strands back in last summer.'

'Maybelline Watson… where are you? That was…' Maggie counted summers loosely in her head then guessed three more. '…eight years ago if it was a day. You still got that old thing?'

'No.'

'Then what you going on about it for?'

'I did have it. Until this morning.'

'Is that 'this morning' as in 'this morning', or as in sometime during the last eight years?'

'Maggie. Don't be terrible to me…'

'Get off it, Maybelline, this is Reality Hall. Sympathy House is over the way.'

'Do you have to be so abrasive?'

1

'How long you known me, Maybelline Watson?

'Thanks... I'm sure. Only I do wonder...'

'About what?'

'Well... when I moved in, Louise over the way was your friend.'

'So?'

'So... I only came over after Sam died and I don't remember the last time you spoke about Louise. I hope I haven't... you know... driven a wedge...'

'You wouldn't make much of a wedge, Maybelline. But the drift began a way before that.'

'Oh... I'm glad to hear that, Maggie.'

'What? That I'm losing friends?'

'No, I didn't mean it that way. I just...'

'Maybelline? The reset button?'

'I don't know what you... Oh.'

'So, okay, when did this chair go missing... and there can't have been much of it left anyway.'

'I told you... this morning.'

'You see it yesterday?'

'Sat in it.'

'That's pretty conclusive.'

'Maggie. You agreed with me. That's not like you at all. I'm coming right over.'

Maggie lit the gas, dropped the kettle on the stove and waited while it sang. Slipping on her cardigan and muffling her feet with an old pair of slippers, she crept slowly out to her porch door.

Maybelline Watson, her neighbor from down the road apiece, lay sideways along the wooden glider, skinny old legs overlapping under a full skirt, one foot tracing the floor as the seat swung.

'Maybee!'

Maybelline's eyes sparked open wide. 'Oh, Maggie. I made it. I thought for a moment there I was going to faint. Did I hear the kettle?'

'It won't be a minute, May.'

'Did I also hear the biscuit barrel?'

'I guess not, May.'

'Oh…'

Maggie levered Maybelline upright in the glider and went back inside. She kicked around a few things in the kitchen, slid oddments into drawers that had jammed open, put cups and saucers on a tray along with a jar of sliced lemon then wet the inside of the cups with a long shot of clear vodka while she waited for the Earl Grey to settle out.

'Inside or outside, Maybelline?'

Maybelline settled more comfortably into the cushion. 'Oh. Outside, I think.' She swayed into the pattern of the glider's swing… sashaying… remembering what that meant with a giggle.

'What you laughing at, May?'

'I was just remembering.'

'Go for it while you got it, Maybelline.'

'I was remembering what it was like to leave the Theater after a show. Those beaus waiting outside in the foyer lights… just to watch me walk…'

'They not get enough from looking up your skirt while you was on stage?'

'You can be so crude, Maggie Gray… Oh God! Biscuits! Thought you said…'

'Nope. Just said you didn't hear 'em.'

'I thought you'd given up…'

'Given up looking in the cupboard is what I did.'

'Well, I wouldn't know what I'd hear these days. Didn't hear a thing last night when the chair went.'

'You think burglars should blow a horn, Maybelline?'

Maybelline eyed the biscuit barrel, pretending to shake the worry out of her crisp, grey hair, but secretly glad that the chair had at last gone… glad that she no longer had to pretend to be keeping it for if Sam came back, which she knew he wouldn't, having planted him six feet deep going on fifteen years ago.

Maggie dropped the biscuit barrel into her lap. 'Take it with you when you go.'

'Maggie. I couldn't. You must have had it years?'

'Yeah, and look at me.'

'You look fine! A couple of pounds here and there that's all…'

'Once upon a time the wind blew right through me.'

'Maggie Gray. Don't josh with me. You always been… kind of… solid… ever since I known you.'

'You think size zero is thin? We could've shown these supermodels a thing.'

Maybelline sat up straight, a childlike caul descending over her. 'You have pictures? I can see them?'

'No, May. It's the memories they bring I don't want.'

'Can I hear them? Please?'

'No, May.'

'You gave me the biscuits…'

'I'm keeping the memories. I can't get fat on what once was.'

'Don't know 'bout that. Sam got fat on what once was a pig. I had to pay extra for the plot.'

Maggie slid herself into the full depth of the glider and lifted her feet from the floor.

'Maybelline Watson! It's not right to speak ill of the dead.'

'You mean the pig… right?'

Maybelline's hand found its way into the biscuits time and again. Maggie's feet swung the glider back and forth until the laughter dried from their eyes.

'Oh God, Maybelline. The man's twice the fun now he's dead. Do you remember…'

Maybelline's hand took her arm. 'Perhaps I don't want to, either.'

'Okay… we don't have to go there.' Maggie placed her cup and saucer on the little side table, topping it up from the pot. 'By the way, have you seen a yellow plastic dustpan and broom anywhere?'

Maybelline looked quickly over to the corner to find the rickety broom and rusty pan that had always lived there. 'When did you lose them?'

'This morning.'

'Is that 'this morning' as in…'

'Maybelline Watson, that biscuit barrel looks kind of heavy, I think you should…'

Maybelline clutched it to her gaunt chest. 'No! It's mine now! You gave it!'

'Well, when you get fat you can always blame me.'

'I do so hope so, but I promised myself to eat only the broken ones.' Maybelline cramped the lid firmly on then gave the enameled tin a violent shake. 'Say, Maggie… this dustpan and broom… are you sure you had one?'

'Sure, Maybelline. Came by post. Bright yellow… plastic… couldn't miss it.'

Maybelline tightened her grip on the biscuit barrel. 'You surprise me some days, Maggie.'

'Huh?'

'Thought you had more taste than that…'

Bill Allerton

Magpie

Maggie dangled her legs over the edge of the porch, the soles of her feet brushing the tips of grass that spurted along the rim of the flower patch. Out by the street a small yellow flatbed truck drove slowly past. Three children walked across the entrance to her yard, two carrying schoolbooks and one with a violin case tucked under her arm. Maggie watched the tops of their heads float above the fence towards the corner where they would be picked up by the school bus. She envied them the certainty she hoped their small lives would have.

Ben next door rolled his car to the slope of his drive and began to wash it.

'Hey, Ben.'

'Hey, Maggie.'

'Electricity gone off again?'

'Nope. Just felt like washing tin. It's a nice day.'

'Not like you to notice.'

'Well… yes… okay. I guess since I took that computer course I've been a little absorbed.'

'Buried, Ben. Some would say buried.'

'Yes, Maggie, I guess you would.'

'So what exhumed you? The sunshine… or Louise?'

The yellow flatbed drove slowly past in the opposite direction. Ben paused to watch as it hesitated a moment, then picked up the hose and chased drying soap off the roof of the car.

'Neither, Maggie.'

'So what was it?'

'A virus.'

'Had your Flu jab?'

'Yes… but…'

'Should be okay then.'

In the shed at the bottom of the yard, Maggie set out a row of earthenware pots. She shook a handful of gravel into the bottom of each, lined them with potting compost and carefully pressed in a Geranium seedling.

She pushed the rusting bike back in, closed the door and turned around to pick up her old dustpan and broom. They were gone, but the new yellow ones were leaning against a corner of the porch. She picked them up. They were clean as a whistle.

She used them to sweep the edge of the yard then spaced out the pots where the seedlings would get the best of the sun from early to noon.

Overnight, half the pots disappeared.

\#

The police officer stood at the bottom of Ben's drive. Maggie watched him from the top of her curtains, hoping he would just turn and walk away.

Maybelline's voice shrilled on the other end of the phone.

'Maggie? You still there?'

Maggie winced a little, craning her neck so she could see over the rim of the curtain. 'I'm here, May. I'm just watching Ben in the next yard.'

'What's he doing?'

'Looking…'

'What at?'

'Not at… for.'

'Maggie Gray! Stop trying to be charismatic!'

'That's enigmatic, Maybelline.'

'Anymatic automatic. What's he doing?'

'He's looking for his barbecue.'

'It's a little early… but do you think he'll invite us over?'

'No, Maybelline. He's looking for it. It's missing.'

The officer folded his notebook into his pocket and looked up.

Their eyes met.

Maggie climbed down from the stool, hung up the phone and counted the footsteps out across the yard until she heard the knock. She opened the inner door and left the screen shut. The officer outside was young, somewhere around forty, tall, fading slim, marginally athletic even… and with a warm smile. If it hadn't been for the uniform, Maggie could have allowed herself to enjoy the strong oval of his face.

He took out his notebook and shook it open in one hand. 'Mrs… Gray?'

'Hmm… yes?'

'Can I talk to you for a minute?'

'I only have a minute. I'm expecting company.'

'It won't take long. Can I come in?'

Maggie picked up her old cardigan from the chair. 'Wait a minute. I'll let you in.'

'We can do it out here if you like? Been years since I sat in one of these old wooden gliders. Mine's all mold and rust.'

'No, no, Officer. Come in. Can I make you tea?'

'That won't be necessary… but if you're having some yourself, then…'

He stepped into the room.

With every step he took, Maggie retreated towards the kitchen, never taking her eyes from his boots. 'Earl Grey? With lemon?'

'Be real good, Ma'am.'

'There's a comfortable chair by the fireplace.'

'One at the table's fine, Ma'am.'

'Sit down, Officer...'

'Gradzynski, Ma'am.'

Maggie went into the kitchen and heaved a sigh. She rattled cups into saucers using both hands and filled them with tea.

Gradzynski stood up as she brought them through. 'Here, let me take those off of you.'

Maggie passed the cup she'd poured for him and offered the jar of lemon slices.

'Sit down, Mrs Gray.'

'Maggie.'

'Alright… Maggie. I didn't mean to frighten you.'

'I'm not… you didn't… it's just that…' Maggie curled her fingers around the cup, warming a sudden chill from them. Gradzynski spooned two slices of lemon from the jar and slid them into her tea.

'How'd you know how much lemon I take?'

Gradzynski smiled at the sudden memory her question evoked. 'Two's company, three's a crowd.'

'Who said that?'

'My grandmother, bless her soul.'

'Sounds like a wise woman.'

'She said that about everything.'

'You don't need to be complicated to be wise.'

Gradzynski screwed the lid back on the jar. 'You're not related by any chance?'

'No, I'm too complicated.'

'Well, in that case I'll keep this simple. Did you hear anyone out back last night?'

'No. Why?'

'Your neighbor had his new barbecue stolen.'

'What? That old thing? Did he also tell you he hasn't used it since he bought a computer? And that it has rust holes in the bottom and the coals drop out and scorch his grass. Did he tell you that?'

'No, he didn't. But there are other things happening around the neighborhood. Looks like we got ourselves a magpie.'

'Magpie?'

'Opportunist thief. Have you had anything taken?'

Maggie thought back to the broom and pan set, then remembered how the new one had come back cleaner than it went and how the old one, much as she'd loved it, as much as one can love an old piece of equipment... well, they'd been worn out... and a few plants?

'No... not really. Not anything worth a mention.'

'Any reason why the neighbor might lie about the condition of his barbecue?'

'So he can get his computer fixed on the insurance, I 'spect.'

Officer Gradzynski put down his cup, smiled at her again in the way that she wished he wouldn't. 'What about Mrs Watson?'

Maggie sat up to the table. 'What about her?'

'She says she lost a new rattan chair. Said you'd vouch for her.'

'Hah! She did, did she? Wait 'til I see her.'

'You saying she hasn't had her chair stolen?'

'If you could call it a chair…'

The officer flicked over a page in his notebook. 'I'd call three hundred dollars some kind of a chair.'

'Yeah…' Maggie sat back into the cushions as the vodka beneath the lemon in her teacup kicked through her old veins. '…it was some kind of a chair alright.'

Beetles

'Hey Maybelline. You still got that old car of yours? Sure you haven't traded it in for a new rattan chair?'

'Now Maggie Gray, there's no reason to be unkind. I was just trying to recover something on that plot we talked about.'

'May, you already lost it. About the car... can I borrow it?'

'Couldn't you just have come around instead of phoning like this? Especially when it's something... you know... important?'

'You getting lonely over there, Maybee? I can send you a nice police officer. He has some questions about your ratty chair...'

'Maggie. What did you tell him?'

'I told him it was some kind of a chair. And you were some kind of a friend to put me on a spot like that.'

'Just come over. I have something else to show you.'

'I hope that kettle's on.'

Maggie banged in through Maybelline's screen door and let it slam shut behind her. Maybelline took her arm and swung her around.

Maggie looked quickly over her shoulder. 'What you doing, May?'

'I'm just looking to see if you brought in any of those nasty ticks on that old cardigan of yours.'

'Where you think I've been? Out hunting Sasquatch?'

'I just don't like them. I was once… you know… bitten.'

'My God, Maybelline. It must have had stamina, that's all I can say. Here…' She plunged her hand deep into the expansive pocket of her cardigan and pulled out a pack of biscuits.

Maybelline snatched them from her outstretched hand.

'My favorites. Just a minute…' She turned the pack around, reading the label. '…how long have these been in your cupboard?'

Maggie held out her hand again. 'If you're going to complain…'

Maybelline drew back quickly. 'I didn't say it was a problem.'

'But who would steal your broom?'

'Who would take your ratty chair?'

'Rattan.'

'Don't correct me when I'm right, May. And put more water in this tea. I can stand the spoon…'

'… and your smelly old Geraniums.'

'They were smelly new Geraniums.' Maggie took the kettle from her and topped up the half-empty cup. 'Aren't you even the slightest bit interested in what happened to your chair?'

'Well… now you mention it… I think it was past its best.'

'It was past its best in nineteen eighty-nine, May. Show me the car.'

In the middle of Maybelline's garage, a misshapen lump lurked under a grey cloth. Maggie took one corner and dragged it clear. Maybelline sneezed in the cloud of dust now hovering above the car.

'Gesundheit, Maybelline…'

'No, Maggie. It's a Volkswagen.'

'Yes, May, I can see that but… Lime Green?'

'It was fashionable at the time.'

'So were Burns and Allen.' Maggie tried the door with no success. She held out her hand.

Maybelline reached down the keys from a hook and gave them to her. 'It won't start.'

'How do you know that?'

'The battery's over there on the bench.'

Maggie took the keys and opened the door, examining the inside of the car. 'Not much room in the back.'

Maybelline held out her hand for the keys. 'If you're going to complain…'

Maggie pulled the door closed behind her and wound down the window. 'I didn't say it was a problem…' She settled into the driving seat and shuffled the controls and gearshift around. She triggered the release on the passenger door. 'Get in, May.'

Maybelline climbed in beside her. 'Where are we going?'

'We're not. I am.'

'You don't even have a license.'

'I will have.'

'Maggie Gray, not once in twenty years have I ever seen you drive a car!'

'When was your last visit to the Optometrist, May?'

Maybelline swung her feet back to the garage floor. 'I thought you wanted me to lend you the car?'

'No. I just wanted to borrow it.'

15

'There's a difference?'

'Sort of. Well, no... I guess not.'

'Then you better be nice to me for a change.'

'How many biscuits will that take? Here... show me how to open the hood.'

Maybelline reached into the foot well and pulled a hidden lever. The hood popped up a couple of inches. 'There's a catch underneath. Right at the front.'

Maggie's fingers travelled along the folded steel rim. 'I got it.' She lifted the hood and propped it with one hand. 'Here, May. I think you should take a look at this...'

Maybelline came around to the front of the car. 'Take a look at what?'

'Someone's stolen your motor.'

#

Ben put the newly charged battery on the car and re-inflated the tires with a little humming gizmo that plugged into a socket. He ran a reminiscent finger along the curve of the Beetle's fender. 'Used to have one of these at college.'

Maggie stuck the ring of keys in his hand. 'Then you'll know how it goes.'

Ben studied the perished leather tag. 'Maybelline? How long's it been stood?'

'Why, Ben. Can't be no more than, say... five years?'

Maggie nudged him towards the car. 'Make that fifteen... Come on, Ben. Let's hear her fire up.'

'I can try...' Ben climbed into the driver's seat. He dipped the clutch and found neutral, pumped the gas pedal and turned the key. The meagre dashboard lights winked on and the gauge showed half full. 'There's plenty of gas in it.'

Maggie slid into the passenger seat beside him. 'It was only fifteen cents a gallon back then.'

Maybelline banged on the side window. 'I know you're talking about me in there.'

Maggie wound down the window and leaned out. 'The Hell we were. Well... maybe... Ben did say it had a lot of gas.'

The motor turned over sluggishly at first then gradually sped up until the starter was whirring away in back.

Ben let go of the key. 'Told you it wouldn't work.'

Maggie nudged him firmly in the ribs. 'Try again. Imagine it's your computer...'

Ben turned the key and again the motor turned over and over. A smell of raw gasoline and hot wiring began rising through the car. He let go of the key.

Maggie nudged him again. 'One more try...'

This time the motor caught, first on two cylinders, then three, then four. The whole car shook violently and the garage filled with smoke.

Maggie yelled out of the window. 'For God's sake Maybelline get that door open!'

The garage door shuddered upwards, smoke and noise pouring out into the street.

Ben allowed the motor to subside into a rattling roar. 'Hope you weren't thinking of going anywhere quietly?'

'Only as far as my drive. Think you can get it there?'

Ben dipped the clutch and eased the car into first gear. 'You ever drive a stick shift, Maggie?'

'Yeah, once. How hard can it be?' She got out and stood by Maybelline as the car lurched down the short incline, trailing smoke in its wake. They heard a crunch of gears as Ben turned it into Maggie's drive and parked up. Maybelline pressed the button that closed the door.

Maggie followed her back into the kitchen. 'So what was it you wanted to show me?'

Maybelline waltzed over to the window and pointed out

back.

Maggie stood beside her and peered into the shade.

'What? What? What am I looking for?'

'Over there…' Maybelline pointed over to where the shade was darker still, where a projection from an upstairs room cast a deeper shadow that seemed to stay most of mid-summer. 'There…'

'You bought another chair. Thought you were glad to be rid of the last one.'

'Yes, but this is my chair. Not Sam's. Mine.' She clasped her hands together with glee. 'Mine! And there's something else. I'll show you…'

Maggie followed her to the cupboard over the sink. 'You got the check from the insurance?'

Maybelline flung open the doors. 'Don't be silly. Takes an age. Here… take a look.' She reached down the biscuit tin and proudly presented it to Maggie. Maggie turned it around in her hands. Stuck to the front was a small piece of appliqué with bright red cross-stitching. 'What's this? I don't have my glasses.'

Maybelline snatched it from her. 'Here… it says… 'Presented by Maggie Gray to her Best Friend Maybelline Eugenie Watson'.'

'Eugenie, hmm?'

Maybelline snatched the biscuit tin away, trying to decipher the look on Maggie's face. 'Is that a problem?

Rockets

'Maggie, you will never believe what I have to tell you…'

'After 'Eugenie' you might have to stretch a little for that, May.'

'It's my chair.'

'I know. You said yesterday. The old one was Sam's. How senile do you think I am?'

Maybelline held her clenched fists together, shaking them at the air in frustration. 'No. No… It's gone.'

'It's probably the insurance. They're hot on scamsters…'

'But it's not just gone… the old one… Sam's. It's back… and it's been mended.'

'Mended?' Maggie looked around her house to where pelmets hung loose and drapes drooped. 'I should meet this person. Any idea who it is?'

'I thought you might.'

'Not yet, but I'm working on it. Drink?'

'Yes, please.'

'Lemon?'

'Three.'

'Rocket fuel?'

'Just a little…'

Maggie splashed vodka into the cups before adding the lemon and a small amount of Earl Grey. 'Here, Eugenie… this'll make you forget the chair.'

#

Maggie selected her best down quilt and stowed it in the back seat of the Volkswagen. Ben had left the car with the tail-end sticking out and from there the tiny rear window commanded a view of most of the street. By her feet was the two-foot section of lead pipe she kept under her bed. At nine the streetlights ticked on, until around four a.m. when they ticked off again, one by one. A few minutes after, from the edge of her vision, a small yellow flatbed coasted silently down the street and stopped on the incline fifty yards away. In the dark she couldn't see who was in the cab but movement suggested two people. She rolled the section of pipe under her foot, but decided to stay put and watch.

A figure climbed out of the cab of the truck and walked quickly up the drive two doors down from Maybelline's. Maggie shuffled and rubbed her eyes clear, waiting for whoever it was to return. A few moments later she saw them creep down the path, slide a long box onto the back of the truck and get back in. Brake lights blazed red into the dawn darkness, then faded out as the truck coasted off silently.

Maggie climbed stiffly out of the car and shrugged off the quilt. It was warmer outside. Within seconds she heard a light screech of tires and the sudden cough of a motor… the note picking up as the truck drove away.

#

'You'll never believe this, Maggie!'
'So what's new, May, apart from the fact that I've been

freezing my ass off all night in the back of your old car and just managed to get off to…'

'What is it with you, Maggie Gray? I ring up to be neighborly and tell you what happened last night and you just grouch at me.'

'What time is it anyway?'

'Eight o'clock.'

'Maybelline Watson you never got up at eight o'clock. You never knew there was two eight o'clocks in one day.'

'If you're going to take that tone of voice with me… I won't tell you about the rabbit.'

'May?… May… May!'

'You should've seen it Maggie! It had the cutest whitest face and the longest floppiest ears… Little boy, three plots down… loved it so.'

'Did they feed it on biscuits?'

'I don't know, Maggie. I shouldn't think so. Wouldn't that have been too expensive?'

'Perhaps I should've made friends with the rabbit.'

'Maggie! Why did you come over if you're going to be…?'

'To bring you these…' Maggie held out the pack of biscuits from the back of her cupboard.

Maybelline turned them over in her hand. 'Arrowroot. So that's what's making you grouchy.'

'It is not. I'm as regular as your lapses of memory.'

'I don't have…'

'You forgot to put the kettle on.'

'Oh.'

#

The car motor fired first time. Maggie let go of

everything to think for a moment about what she was doing. On top of the gear lever was an arcane symbol that she remembered should show the gear positions. Reverse was through the middle, off to one side and up. She attempted to push it in that direction. The gearbox shrieked in protest. She stopped and looked around the controls, tried the pedal under her left foot next to the brake. It pressed down easily at first then sprang up again under her foot. She held it in again and tried the gear lever. This time it went where she pushed it. She pressed the brake pedal with her other foot and let off the handbrake. The car held still on the incline of her drive, motor chugging sluggishly. Maggie took a deep breath and began a five second countdown. At zero, she took her foot off the clutch and pushed hard on the accelerator. The car hurtled backwards down the incline, across the road and up the drive opposite, where Maggie remembered the brake pedal. The car shuddered violently and stalled. She looked around quickly, hoping she hadn't killed, maimed or bent anything, and pulled up the handbrake.

Smoke wreathed outside the windows. She sat back in the seat and gathered a deep breath.

'Okay. Houston? We've had a problem here…'

Maggie sat beside Ben and studied him carefully as he turned the car around in the road and reversed it up her own drive.

He threw the keys at her. 'See how easy it is?'

'Oh yeah. Can't think why they make us wait until we're fourteen to learn.'

'Next time you want to move it, send me an e-mail.'

'First or Second class?'

#

Maggie waited until the light had fallen then quietly moved the remaining Geranium pots to one side and dragged the old glider out to the edge of the porch where it could be plainly seen from the bottom of the drive. Back in the kitchen she banged the kettle on the stove, sorted two slices of lemon and a generous helping of rocket fuel into a clean cup. The clock showed ten p.m. and that was far too early. She turned off the light and settled down in front of the silent TV.

A noise outside woke her at three a.m. At the foot of the drive was a small flatbed truck, faint yellow in the streetlight. In the back was the striped seat from her glider. She drew back the edge of the drape a little more to see a man, tee-shirt, jeans, young and lean-looking in the not-quite dark, carefully lifting the glider frame from the edge of the porch. She watched him carry it to the truck and single-handedly struggle it onto the back. Maggie thought she could see the shape of someone else in the cab and considered why they hadn't come out to give him a hand. The man opened the cab door wide and gave the truck a push. As it gathered momentum he jumped in behind the wheel.

Maggie threw herself into the Volkswagen. The motor fired uproariously in the quiet of the early morning. She thought about that for half a second then switched it back off. She slipped off the parking brake, allowing the car to free-wheel out onto the road, swinging it hard to the left, following the direction of the truck down the incline. The truck was two hundred yards away, parked in the edge. Maggie stopped and kept her distance. She could see someone beside it, tying the glider down to the bed. They jumped back in the cab and rolled off down the street. Maggie took her foot off the brake and followed.

Silent and dark, they wove their way downhill, never

stopping or slowing for junctions until they hit the flat down by the river. Before the slope ran out, Maggie saw the truck jerk suddenly and through her open window she heard the snarl and catch of the motor. The tail lights came on and it drove quickly over the bridge and out into the green belt beyond the river.

As the Volkswagen drifted to a halt, Maggie turned the key. The motor caught and she revved it quickly to make sure it wouldn't stall. In the dark she couldn't read the diagram on the gearshift so she pushed it directly forwards. There was a loud grating sound. The car threw her back in the seat, leapt forwards six feet and stopped. Maggie couldn't remember which had appeared first, the pain in her back, the blue light, or the sharp, menacing snarl of the siren.

'Step out of the car please.'

Maggie climbed awkwardly from the old Beetle. Her back was developing a vague insistence that she knew by tomorrow lunch would be building a fire in her lower vertebrae.

'Can I help you, Officer...' She looked up into his face. '...Gradzynski?'

'Mrs Gray? What are you doing out here at this time of the a.m.?'

'I was taking the air. The town smells different this time of night, don't you think?'

'Ma'am... Mrs Gray... get back in the car. Wait there a minute...' He reached in and took the keys from the ignition then walked over to the patrol car. He leaned in the window and spoke to his partner. A moment later, the driver's door opened in the Volkswagen.

'Move over, Ma'am. I'm taking you home.'

Maggie nodded sleepily, watching houses flash past,

hearing the echo of the car exhaust diminish as they rumbled past empty lots and street corners. The Volkswagen swung into her drive and the patrol car swept in behind them, blocking the exit.

Gradzynski turned sideways in the seat to look at her. 'Mrs Gray, do you even have a license?'

'You better come in.'

'I think I better. I want to hear this…'

'Mrs Gray… this license…' Gradzynski fluttered the piece of paper back across the table. '…says it's forty years old if it's a day but looks brand new. I can't quite make out the name on it, though. You ever renewed it?'

'Didn't seem worth the trouble. If you've done it once, shouldn't that be enough?'

Maggie tipped the pot of tea she'd brought in from the kitchen, filling three already wet cups to a little short of the brim. She passed one to the younger cop sat by the fire.

'Here…?'

'Officer Hunter, Ma'am.' The officer took off her cap and a ponytail dropped to her shoulder. She looked quizzically at the jar of sliced lemon that Maggie had passed, then up again at Gradzynski.

'Take two, Shirley… It's a Polish thing.'

Shirley spooned two slices of lemon and a little of the syrup into her cup, lifted it slowly and took a sip. 'Jeezus Christ!' She spit the tea back into the cup. 'What you got in here, Ma'am?'

Gradzynski took back the jar and sniffed the contents. 'Hell, Shirl… it's only lemon and sugar.' He spooned two slices into his own cup, took a leisurely sip then stopped and stared at Maggie. He gulped, once, and loudly. 'Mrs Gray. Show me the bottle.'

Maggie passed him a quarter-full bottle. He turned it

over to read the label. It was in Cyrillic script but there was one little symbol in the corner that he recognized.

'Hundred per cent proof! What do you call this?'

'Rocket fuel.'

'You trying to get me fired?'

Maggie shrugged. 'It keeps out the night air.'

Shirley stood up and put the cup back on the table. 'How many of these cups of tea did you have before getting in the car, Ma'am?'

'Oh, two… or three or four. Can't remember. Fell asleep at some point.'

'I'm surprised you ever woke up.'

'It has less effect as you get older.'

Shirley took out her notebook. 'Ma'am, you know this is an offense, don't you?'

Gradzynski put out a hand. 'Which offense are you talking about, Shirl? The no-license, the no-lights, the driving-under-the-influence or the no-insurance? Sit down, there's a story here I haven't heard yet.' He switched off his radio and stretched his legs under the table. 'Alright, Mrs Gray. Let's have it.'

'Well… I was thinking of taking up driving again. The bus service has gone now. Can't get into town in less than an hour and that…'

Gradzynski shook his head. 'No, Mrs Gray, that's not the one.'

Maggie took a long drink of tea. 'My friend Maybelline… it's her car by the way… needed to take it to the shop for repairs and I said I'd help and as I hadn't driven a car with a stick shift in forty years, I thought I'd practice while there was no-one…'

Gradzynski stopped her with a glance. 'Start at the beginning. Where's the glider? It wasn't on your porch when we came in.'

'Oh! That old thing? I sent it off to be…' She stopped when she saw his head begin to shake. 'Someone must have stolen it.'

'Who took it? You saw them, didn't you.'

'I didn't see a thing. It was dark… and what was I supposed to do about four big men with a huge panel truck?'

Shirley reached for her notebook again. 'What you were supposed to do is ring the police.'

'It all happened too quickly.'

'Things usually do in an alcoholic haze, Ma'am.'

Shirley slipped the notebook back in her pocket at a glance from Gradzynski. He leaned up to the table. 'Mrs Gray? What am I going to do about you?'

'I don't know. Whatever you have to.'

'I'll come by tomorrow after my shift. You be here.'

'I'll be here. Probably be asleep.'

'I won't make it too early… Oh… and I'm impounding the car. Explain that to Mrs Watson.'

#

'Stolen, Maggie? Off your own drive? How could you let them? The insurance won't cover me over there. I just know they won't. Any excuse and they…'

'Shut up, May. It's a car. You hadn't seen it for years until I took the cover off. Oh yes, and while you're asking… I'm okay. They never laid a finger on me. So you won't need it for hospital visits or anything.'

'I'm coming right over… this very minute.'

'Okay, May. I'll put the kettle on.'

'Have you got any of that… that… lemon tea?'

'I think so, May. I'll take a look.' Maggie fetched the bottle from the cupboard. There was a half-inch of clear liquid remaining. She decided to save it.

Maybelline stormed in through the porch door. 'Maggie! Your glider has gone!'

'Yeah, May. They tied it to the top of your car and just drove away.'

'I hope they haven't scratched the car.'

'They wouldn't care about that, May. It was the glider they were after.'

'That old thing?'

'That old thing? As opposed to a lime green Beetle? Listen May, I told you a lie.'

'Oh, that's not like you at all, Maggie Gray.'

'Maybelline Watson, now is not the time to get cute on me. I'm having a rare moment of honesty here...'

'So where is the car? Maggie, don't tell me you totaled my car.'

'It's being held to ransom.'

'Oh Maggie, don't go there. Can you not just tell me straight where it is?'

'It's true, May... but it's not the thieves. It's in the Police Pound.'

'Why? What's it done?'

'Maybelline you're priceless. I was driving it.'

'But I never seen you in a car. I thought you just wanted to put it on your drive so it looked like there was a man in the house.'

'I was following the people who stole my glider... and probably your chair.'

'Maggie, what're you doing following desperate people like that? They could've killed you or worse.'

'Maybelline, they can't be all bad, or they wouldn't mend things before bringing them back, and anyway, I know they have taste.'

'Why?'

'They didn't want the yellow broom and pan.' She poured tea into two cups. 'Sorry May, I'm out of rocket fuel. Tea straight up this morning.'

Maybelline placed the cup carefully back on the saucer. 'Oh…'

'Maybelline, I'm sorry about your car, too, but the police won't let anything happen to it… unless…'

'Unless what?'

'Unless I don't come up with fifty dollars by the end of the month.'

'And if you don't?'

'That's when they crush it.'

Bill Allerton

Unblessed Fruit

'Hey Ben!' Maggie banged her fist on Ben's front door. 'Hey! Hey! Cyberspace!'

From deep inside the house came the sound of slow footsteps ascending a staircase. Ben's face appeared behind the mesh screen. 'Hi, Maggie. Where's the fire?'

'Nowhere 'round you these days, Ben. I want to borrow your gizmo.'

Ben opened the screen wider but still didn't ask her inside.

Maggie shuffled her feet on the bare boards of the porch. 'You going to ask me in so I can talk to Louise while I'm waiting?'

'Not right now, Maggie, she's busy... which 'gizmo' anyway?'

'The one with the wires... for the tires.'

'Oh... you got Mrs Watson's car back?'

'No, not yet. I need to get the money first. Anyway, what do you know about that?'

'The e-mails are just scorching around the neighborhood.'

'I guess that'll keep the Mailman in a job.'

'Hang on. I'll get you the inflator.'

He closed the door in Maggie's face and she stood back, wondering which panel to back-heel right through.

It opened again and Ben passed her the little gizmo wrapped tightly in its own wires. 'Here… how long do want to borrow it for?'

'Couple of hours… minutes maybe.'

'Okay. Just don't forget what day it is. I might want to use it myself.'

'Does it deflate things too?'

'Sure. You just push this little button on the side once you're connected up.'

'Doesn't work on egos, then…'

#

A couple of day's rain had left the shed lock stiff to open so Maggie went to the kitchen and dipped the key in margarine, leaving behind a rusty slur in the tub. Once in the shed, she wiped her hands on the garden apron that hung behind the door and wrestled the bike out into the yard. The tires were flat to the rims. She wiped the front wheel with the greasy apron and the rust came off easily. On a whim, she went back to fetch the rest of the margarine.

An hour later she returned the gizmo to Ben's front porch, banged on his door and walked away. She turned the now shiny bike around, pushed it backwards into the shed and clicked the lock.

As night fell, Maggie carried out an old cardboard box and sat it in the middle of her drive. Inside it she put the unused crockery from the back of her cupboard, the cooking pans she had been keeping in case she ever got a creative urge and a spare set of mismatched cutlery. She threw in a boxed carving set she'd inherited from the previous tenant and never used. He wouldn't be back to ask for it, she knew where he'd gone.

Around three a.m., a small, yellow, flatbed truck pulled up alongside the drive. A young man got out, leaving the door hanging open. He looked around, then walked up to the box and lifted it easily. As he lifted it, the bottom of the box opened and some of the pans tumbled noisily through onto the drive.

Maggie watched through the crack of the shed door as he struggled it onto the back of the truck and calmly returned for the fallen items. He pushed these onto the seat of the cab and a pale hand reached across to draw them in. He climbed back into the truck and it rolled off down the road, gathering momentum on the incline.

Maggie butted the shed door open with the front wheel of the bike. Way down the street she saw the truck light up yellow as it passed beneath a streetlight. She placed one foot firmly on a pedal, took a deep breath and pushed off. She pedaled once or twice to remind herself of the way it went, then the incline took over. The slope was gentle here on Huron Drive, but falling steeper as Maggie got close to the corner beyond Maybelline's. As she passed May's house she noticed a pale blue glow from the bedroom window then returned her attention to the rushing of air across her ears and the feel of the road through her rear end. In front of her, the truck continued to pull away.

Maggie caught up with the speed of the chain and pedaled as vigorously as her seventy-eight-year-old legs would allow. The road began to hum beneath her, changing pitch as the tires passed from blacktop to cement and back again. Under the lights at the junction the truck swung sharp left and headed for the hill that would wind it down through the estate to the river. Not wanting to lose sight of it, she left it to the last moment to brake.

No matter how hard she squeezed the brakes, the bike continued to accelerate. Splashes of oil burned her skin as it flew from the brakes to spatter her legs. A strong scent of hot margarine followed as she swung the bike desperately around the bend. The incline was steeper now, and Maggie found herself following the route she had taken before in the Volkswagen, past Vineyard and Breezy Lawn, weaving, abusing signs and signals, flouting junctions that in the daytime would have had her killed instantly. Her hair whipped out in a tangled white stream. The wind blew tears into eyes that she daren't let go of the bars long enough to wipe clear.

Halfway down the estate she realized she was gaining on the truck. She didn't notice it pull up until the brake lights registered on her brain. The door swung open and Maggie managed to pull over enough to miss the driver as he climbed out.

She whipped down through the rest of the estate, just making the bumpy right and from there accelerating onto Michigan Drive, enjoying the straights, terrifying herself on the bends until the road began to level off towards Kenosha. She recognized the intersection that led away left to the bridge and tried to guess whether her speed was too high to make it. She edged the bike into the bend, tires thrumming as she forced it around the junction. Kenosha slid grudgingly downhill from here to the river, rising as it approached the bridge. As the bike slowed, Maggie caught up with the pedals. She rolled up the crest of the bridge and sped off again down the other side.

Two hundred yards further and the road became flat as a pancake. The bike slowed and came to a halt. Maggie stepped off it and turned around. In the distance she saw the loom of headlights approaching the far side of the bridge. She wheeled the bike out into the road and laid it down, then arranged herself on the grass verge where she hoped it would appear she'd been thrown.

Headlights approached. She heard the truck swerve as the driver saw the bike. He went past her then stopped. The first thing she heard was the bike being thrown onto the back of the truck and thought she was going to be left by the road. Then she felt a hand under her head, another adrift across her body, feeling this, checking that bone or joint, fingers searching for a pulse in the soft skin at the side of her throat.

A man's voice… young-sounding… close by her ear. 'She's alive.'

A voice from the cab, a girl's voice. 'What can we do? We cain't take her into town.'

'We'll have to take her with us.'

Maggie felt the pressure of the hand under her head increase. Her legs were swung into the air and she marveled at the strength of the arms that lowered her with great sensitivity onto the back of the truck.

The girl's voice again. 'She'd be better in the cab. It's warmer in here.'

'Cain't sit her up. First rule. Here… give me a… hand… to put her legs…'

The girl's next words cost Maggie an involuntary smile.

'I cain't. What if Kid wriggles off the seat again?'

The truck set off slowly. Whatever happened now, this was safer than being on the bike. Maggie worked her way around until from the corner of one eye she could see a tiny face peering at her through the rear cab window. Some minutes later, the truck lurched off the road onto a rutted track. The bike spun on one pedal and the old box beside her split wide open with the movement. Maggie found herself surrounded by her old plates and cups, chinking and grating against each other. Cutlery slid across the bed of the truck, knife handles warming themselves against her. She caught a hold of one, just in case, feeling the night chill pass into her fingers, then recalled the face at the window and pushed it away. After a while, the truck made a sudden turn and stopped.

Maggie opened one eye. In the east a star shone, and only the slightest hint of glow on the horizon. She reckoned they'd travelled slowly for quarter of an hour... twenty minutes at most. She felt the arms cradle her with their strength again. This time she rolled against him, enjoying the safety of his broad chest.

'She's waking up. Where shall I put her?'

'There... it's the most comfortable thing we got.'

Maggie allowed herself to be laid onto a soft, cloth surface... and recognized the feel of it immediately. She heard heels twist in dry earth as the youth spun around to check the stars.

'She'll be fine here 'til sunup. Put a blanket over her.'

#

The sun peered between two alders at the edge of the clearing and lanced Maggie with its warmth. A light breeze chafed her cheek. She didn't remember leaving the window open on the back but she must have done. She pulled up the blanket around her neck and turned over.

A slight shuffling sound made her open one eye. Staring at her were the huge brown eyes of a child. Behind the child Maggie could see a bare dirt yard, with holes where someone had scratched with a stick and planted Geraniums. The plants seemed to be thriving.

Maggie sat up and tugged the blanket free, held out a

hand to the child. The child backed away along the glider. Maggie's fingers beckoned. 'Hey there! Come to Maggie.'

The child stopped, regarding her curiously then, with a great smile, scrambled herself onto Maggie. Her head fitted neatly into Maggie's shoulder as she hung on, tiny arms stretching as far as they could reach. Maggie looked down into the tangle of short, wiry hair... fine and filigreed as black cotton lace. The color of her own skin seemed pale beside the soft brown of the child. She pushed her nose into the child's hair and inhaled deeply the scent of milk and dirt and flowers and beneath it all, something a little more human. She lifted the child up and held her at arm's length.

'Have we been introduced?'

The child giggled and Maggie sat her on her lap and turned her around so she could pull the tiny body under the blanket and into the warmth of her belly where they could both sit and watch the sun. She closed her eyes and let the light and the warmth of the child seep into her bones.

'Now this is Mister Sun. He says, 'Hello' to us every morning. Except those days when he gets up all grumpy, like your Aunt Maybelline. You don't know her yet? Well, child... you got a treat coming. Now... your Aunt Maybelline... she's cross with me because I can't buy back her car from the pound and I just know that when she wakes up this morning she'll be looking like a big old storm cloud...'

The child began to kick her bare feet against Maggie. Maggie tightened her grip. 'Hey... hold on there. This is Aunt Maggie. You don't kick Aunt Maggie.'

A wide grin broke the child's face, followed by a loud gurgle.

The child was looking beyond her now, over her shoulder. Maggie turned around to where a young girl stood in the doorway watching them silently. She had a smile on her face and a cup of what smelled like coffee warming her hands. Her skin, even in this soft light, seemed pale and patchy. From around her throat, stretching downwards into the bodice of her simple dress were lines that Maggie knew stemmed from a lack of proper nourishment.

'Hi, Aunt Maggie… 'd you like a coffee?'

'Do birds fly south for the winter?'

'Not all of us, Maggie.' The girl turned away from the door and went inside.

Maggie bounced the child on her knee. The child laughed at her, reached out a hand and poked at Maggie's nose, laughed again.

'Ok, kid. You wouldn't be the first… and probably not the last. It's some honker… right? Not like yours… yours will be pretty as a button, but don't you go poking it where it shouldn't or you'll end up with one like mine.'

'Here y'are Aunt Maggie.'

Maggie took the mug of warm coffee and put it on the floor beside the glider out of harm's way. 'I'm glad I found you.'

The girl dropped seamlessly into the sway of the glider. 'What makes you say that, Maggie? You don't even know who I am. An' if you'd been a better cycle rider we'd never have met.'

'You think so?'

Something about the look in Maggie's eye made the girl hesitate. 'How come I feel like I'm not in control here?'

'Because you're not. Been trying to work out how to meet you for days.'

Fear flickered in the girl's face. 'How'd you know where I was?'

'I didn't. I just knew what you was.'

'Who sent you to find me?'

Maggie stroked the child's hair gently. 'Are you scared of me?'

'Should I be?'

'I guess so.'

'Why? What you goin' to do?'

'Listen… What did you say your name was?'

'I didn't.'

'Then how'm I going to post a card come Christmas?'

'Leave Christmas out of this, Maggie. My name's Æppel.'

'Æppel… Okay… Spell it…'

'It's kinda funny. It starts with an A and an E but they're kinda mixed together. Æ.p.p.e.l. Eppell, my mother said, but it don't matter much.'

'Well… kind of… yes, it does.'

'Don't let it bother you none, Maggie.'

'Oh, but it does. For a start… that's not your real name.'

'It is so… Mother said…'

'Mothers say a lot of things… most times they don't know what they're saying… and sometimes they do but can't bring themselves to say it right. It sounds like Appell… not Eppell.

'Did my mother send you?'

'No… no, not your mother.'

'Then who?' Gradually, Æppel's face softened as the child moved snugly against her, fingers twisting in the holes of the thin cloth.

Maggie sat back and allowed the glider to swing them all at the same pace. 'I guess… nobody. Call it providence.'

'I had enough of that to last me a lifetime.'

Maggie watched them, sensing the delicacies flowing between mother and child. 'This is such a happy child… What's her name?'

'Kid.'

'Kid? What kind of a name is that? What's it short for?'

'Nothin'. We couldn't agree on a name for her.'

'How old is she?'

'Year and a half.'

'What sort of names did you argue about?'

'Oh… the usual… this and that…'

'Well, I have a fine and dandy one just going begging. But first I need two things…'

'No rituals, Maggie… don't want no ritual. No ceremony neither.'

Maggie laughed out loud. 'No rituals, honey. Just a toilet and breakfast. In that order.'

#

Maggie shuffled one of her own old plates around on the bare table. 'Well, this is a first. I never had lettuce and raw carrot for breakfast before.'

'It's good for you.'

'It don't make rabbits live any longer.'

'It's all I got, Maggie.'

'Then I guess it's a banquet.'

Æppel got up from the table, rinsed her plate in a big old stone sink and peered out of the window towards the roadway. 'Maggie? How did you know 'bout my name?'

'The Venerable Bede.'

Æppel turned around, resting her back against the sink. 'Sounds kinda like… Clergy.'

'And then some. He was…'

'Was?'

'Yeah…was. Many years ago.'

'How many years ago?'

'Let's see… something like… thirteen hundred years? Is that enough?' She could tell by the smile that skirted around Æppel's eyes that it was.

'What did he do?'

'He was a writer. And a good one.'

'I never heard of him.'

'No… but I think your mother did.'

'Mother never hears nothing much. Only woman I know can turn off her ears at a switch.'

'I know one can turn off her sense at a biscuit.'

'So… Bede? What did he write?'

'About other people, mostly. And Cædmon especially. Come here… sit down…'

'Just a minute…' Æppel squeezed Kid into a homemade upright chair with a little table fixed to the front. Kid squirmed but couldn't get loose. Maggie waited for her to yell but instead she just kicked and gurgled, banging the flat of her hands on the little table. Maggie coughed loudly and Kid stopped her drumming.

'How'd you do that?'

'Don't know. Works on Maybelline too. They're about the same age. Anyway… Cædmon… first recorded English Poet. Lived and worked in Whitby Abbey… that's in England, you know. Translated tracts from the Bible into poetic Old English. Bede called it Metrical Paraphrase.'

'What's that got to do with me?'

'I'm getting there. He wrote: Æppel unsceþful, deaþbeames ofett.'

'What kind of a language is that?'

'Old English. It sort of means 'Apple, free from sin, fruit of the tree of death.''

'You mean 'free from love', don't you?'

Maggie laughed out loud. 'Hell, no. Kids are always loved… maybe not at first sight, but always one way or another.'

'And the 'tree of death'?'

'You just fell a little far from it. Don't worry, you'll make your way back there in around… oh… say, how old are you?'

Æppel gathered her hair into a dark twist at the back, slid an elastic band from her wrist to hold it in place. 'Twenty-one.'

Maggie stared her straight in the eye. Æppel looked away out of the window, unable to match the dark brown intensity.

'Eighteen.'

'Again?'

'…and a half.'

Maggie leaned over to tease Kid's hair. 'Halves are so important.'

Gizmos

Maybelline Watson walked across to Maggie's house. She'd left her phone off the hook and could hear her own call ringing plain as day on the wall in Maggie's kitchen. She banged noisily on the door.

'Maggie. Maggie? You in there?'

She put her face up to the screen and peered through the mesh panel. The door opened at a touch. The house looked tidy enough... for Maggie. She went up into the bedroom. Maggie's usual day clothes, grey twill trousers with a patched hem and a long-sleeved shirt with a paisley motif, were thrown over a rail-backed chair. She opened the cupboard door to see if Maggie's gardening clothes were lying adrift in the bottom but it was empty. She pulled back a corner of the bed but the sheets were so rumpled it was impossible to tell if someone had left it today or the week before. She slid a hand further down between the sheets, feeling for warmth. The bed was stone cold.

Maybelline stepped off the porch into an open tub of rust-streaked margarine. It filled her sandal, squeezing out between her toes like a yellow rash. She wiped her foot in the grass by the flowerbed and shouted back at the closed door.

'Maggie Gray! You know I only like butter.'

Met with silence, she turned and sat down on the porch step. Inside the house the phone had stopped ringing. She looked around for evidence of Maggie having been out in the garden that morning and found none. She walked up the drive to the back and noticed the shed door hanging open. It was empty inside, apart from the bench and a few Geranium seedlings.

'Ben? Ben! Come to the door…'

Ben slid half his lean face around the door. 'Hi, Maybelline.'

'Say, Ben. Have you seen Maggie today?'

'Nope.' He looked past Maybelline to a bundle of wires out on the porch. 'But she was here either last night or this morning.' He held his hand out of the gap between the door and frame. 'Can you pass me that… that… gizmo as Maggie calls it?'

Maybelline looked around. 'I'm sure I don't know what you mean, Ben. Maggie has a language all of her own, I don't understand her half the…'

Ben pointed again. 'Maybelline… the thing with the wires?'

'Oh! That old thing. It's an inflator. Come on, Ben. Surely you knew that?'

Ben took the gizmo from her hand and slid it behind him onto the hall table.

Maybelline tried to peer in as the door opened a fraction wider. 'You're sure you haven't seen Maggie at all? She hasn't been home all day and the door and the shed are wide open and I swear her bed's not been slept in.'

'No, Maybelline. I haven't seen her. Anyway, she's a

grown woman. Can stay out all night if she wants to. Doesn't need our permission.'

'Ben. Aren't you the least bit concerned? How long have you known Maggie? Ever know her stay out? Ever know her go anywhere without telling me?'

'Ah. So that's it, Maybelline. You think she's cut you out of the loop.'

'Loop… poop… I'm sure I don't know what you're talking about. Maggie and I are just old friends.'

'And old enough to look after yourselves, too. Stop chewing on it, Maybelline. She'll turn up… and if she knows you've been fussing around in her bedroom, she'll cuss you out good and proper.'

'I only ever have her best interests at heart. You know that, Ben. And anyway, I wouldn't ever tell her… and I don't suppose you would, either?'

She smiled up at him and tried to sashay a little.

'Maybelline, I have important things to do. I'll let you know soon as I hear her come back.'

'Oh… Well… I guess I have important things to do, too.'

'I guess you do, Maybelline. So now might be a good time?'

'Oh… right.'

The door closed in her face. From the porch she heard Ben's footsteps running up the stairs and the slamming of a door.

Ben launched himself into the chair in front of his laptop. His avatar, Jack the Black, lurked in a corner of the hotel bedroom he'd rented at fifty Linden per hour. He could barely afford five minutes at that rate since he'd traded some of his pension last month to buy a new outfit.

He spun his avatar around, admiring the new threads. Cool… but where was Madeleine? He'd sent her a message ten minutes ago to let her know where he was. The special room was to be a surprise. He could see she was still logged on... the cursor was flashing up on an empty message line. He fidgeted in his chair, wondering what she would make of the fur handcuffs on the bed.

After a few minutes a line of type twinkled across the screen...

allo Jaques, give me ze co-ordinates again, vill you?

Ben watched the Linden counter in the corner ticking down, typed back...

Hell, Madeleine... they're still on the screen... six lines up...

There was a pause before the flashing cursor flicked carefully across the dialogue screen...

Oh... so zey are... be wiz you in seconds... keep it hot...

There was a knock at the hotel room door. Jack the Black lurched across the room as quickly as Ben could move him, grasped the knob and pulled. Outside was a Bellhop avatar.

Sorry Jack, you're out of credit.

Canoes

'I'm not sure what to say, Officer. Other than you can see she's not been back all day.'

'Does she do this often, Mrs Watson?'

Maybelline shuffled her feet on Maggie's carpet, straightening the corner of the fireplace rug with her toe. 'Well no… not in the last fifteen years… not that I can think of.'

Shirley pushed her way between them. 'Probably got lost on the way back from the liquor store.'

Gradzynski pulled a face at her. 'Guess we'll take a look around while we're here.'

He went over to the cupboard by the side of the fire and swung the doors wide. He scanned the shelves but didn't find what he was looking for. 'Any idea where she keeps it these days, Mrs Watson?'

'Keeps what? I'm sure I don't know what you mean…'

'The rocket fuel.'

'Oh! I don't know. It's always been in that cupboard far as I know. She said she was out of it last time I came around for tea.'

Shirley nudged her aside so she could get through into

the kitchen. 'Sure you weren't both out of it?'

'Shirl…'

'Okay, Pav. I'll take a look in the shed.'

'I think you'll find it's empty.'

'That's alright, Mrs Watson. Even the fact that it's empty might give us something to go on.' Shirley went out through the door, closing it behind her.

Maybelline looked up shyly at Gradzynski. 'I'm not sure I like that young lady.'

'Join the club. Let's talk about Maggie. Sit down Mrs…'

'Maybelline.'

'Right. Maybelline. That's a pretty old-fashioned kind of a name.'

Maybelline tugged at a strand of overly-permed hair until it stretched across her mouth. 'I'm an old-fashioned kind of a girl.'

'Let's talk about Maggie.'

The hair snapped back into a tightly rolled curl. 'What do you want to know?'

'Well… who is she, for a start?'

'Maggie? She's Maggie Gray. But then you knew that.'

'Yes, Maybelline, but I want to know who Maggie Gray is. What does she do, apart from make the most lethal cup of Earl Grey I ever tasted?'

'I'd need time to think about that one. Maggie's kind of chaotic. Does what she wants when she wants. Usually tells me later, like the time she went canoe fishing out of season down by Chain O'Lakes Park.'

'Why would she go out of season?'

'Maggie says Rules and Regulations are to keep Rulers and Regulators in salary. Say… she won't get into trouble now I've told you that?'

'I've more to do than chase fishing permits. There's a whole other bunch of Rulers and Regulators for that.'

'That's what Maggie said. She'd been walking down there and found this old plywood canoe hidden up in some reeds. Looked like it had been there a while, she said, and anyway, she only wanted to borrow it for an hour or two.'

Gradzynski stretched his legs out under the table and switched off his radio. It was going to be a slow day. 'Sounds reasonable to me. Any reason to think she might have gone back there?'

'Oh no, I doubt that. You see, when she tried to get back to shore with the old spade she was using as a paddle, she couldn't get it far enough up the bank to get it out of the water.'

Shirley banged in through the door. 'Shed's empty. Apart from a few smelly old flowers.'

'Geraniums...'

'Gesundheit, Mrs Watson.'

Gradzynski closed his eyes in despair and leaned back into the cushions. 'Shirley. Try the bedroom, please?'

Maybelline turned to watch her pass through the hall and begin the climb to Maggie's loft bedroom. 'I don't know why she doesn't use the downstairs one.'

'Downstairs what, Maybelline?'

'Bedroom. Climbs those creaky old stairs every night. I ask her, she says it'll make it just that bit harder for the undertaker one of these mornings. I can hear her saying it now. I don't know what to believe half the t...'

Gradzynski tapped the table with a finger. 'Canoe?'

'Shame about that girl...'

'Who? Maggie?'

'No.' Maybelline shook her head and rotated her eyes upwards to the ceiling.

From above them came the shriek of drawers opening, the protest of a tortured wardrobe hinge, footsteps across the short landing and down the stairs.

Shirley swung around indecisively between the hall and the kitchen then came through into the sitting room. 'Nothing much up there. No sign of Versace... or Jimmy Choo.'

Maybelline sat bolt upright. 'Maggie never has visitors. Never known anybody stay over. Not in fifteen years.'

Gradzynski reached out and touched her arm gently. 'She didn't mean that, Maybelline, calm down. Shirley? Was there anything in the bedroom? Anything at all?'

'Oh, there was plenty. It was all over the place... either a tornado or a burglar... you choose.'

Maybelline bristled visibly and turned a grip on Gradzynski's hand. 'That's just Maggie!'

Gradzynski tried to loosen her fingers, flushed a little as he caught Shirley smirking at him before she went out the door.

Maybelline let go and allowed her shoulders to relax.

Sitting back, she now seemed to Gradzynski much older and far less robust than she'd first appeared. 'Have you got friends on the street, Maybelline? Is there anyone I can...?'

'No-one. Only Maggie, and if she's gone I...' Maybelline took a hankie out of the end of her sleeve. 'Why do you put up with that girl?'

Gradzynski massaged life back into his fingers. 'Because I have to, Maybelline. Rulers and Regulators, as Maggie would have said.'

'Did you have to say that?'

'What?'

'Would have...?'

'I'm sorry, Maybelline. I didn't mean it that way. Is there anything else you can tell me that might be important?'

'I don't think so. I can't think of a thing right now. That girl...'

'Okay, okay, Maybelline. Then tell me about the canoe.'

'Don't think I can right now. I don't want to speak ill of her. Just in case she's... you know...'

Elements

'I need the toilet again. It's an age thing. More regular than the Chicago bus…'

Æppel reached the spade from the corner. 'Here… you already found the path.'

'And the bush… never thought to grow bushes… might start one off when I get home. That sensation of fresh air is remarkable.'

'Not in winter, Maggie.'

Maggie stepped out the rear door of the shack. By her feet were spare shingles in a neat pile stacked on the bare boards. Slivers of new wood, white as milk teeth, had been slid in to repair the steps down to the dirt. She took a few paces across the yard and turned back to examine the place.

Æppel's face appeared at the door. 'You all right out there?'

Maggie leaned back into the light. 'Yeah. I'm just admiring someone's handiwork up on the roof.' She narrowed her eyes against the sun, seeking out the places where shingles had been expertly refitted, peeling ones turned downside to the weather, angles cut and square… unlike the rest of the roof. She lowered her gaze, turned around and found she couldn't see a thing but a huge, fuzzy ball of latent sunlight. She stumbled forward a step and tripped over a shallow wire fence. The dirt came up to hit her side-on. She rolled onto her back and gasped for air, closing her eyes tight shut until the glow behind the lids subsided.

Æppel ran out from the house. 'Maggie! Maggie? You okay?'

Maggie's senses reached out along her body, searching for aches and breaks.

'Yeah, I'm alright.' She opened her eyes. A large white rabbit was staring intently at her. 'Unless my name's Alice...'

She'd been lucky again. Didn't know how many more times she would get away with this.

'Stay there a minute, Maggie. Get your breath. I need to get Kid. I left her on her own.'

'It's alright. I'm going nowhere... besides... I want to keep an eye on this feller over here. If he goes for his pocket watch I'm in trouble.'

Æppel hurried back carrying Kid.

Maggie lifted her head to look. 'She okay?'

Æppel nodded and put Kid down. The rabbit instinctively hopped into the farthest corner. Kid watched it for a disinterested moment, then scrambled headlong on top of Maggie. Æppel reached over to pull her off but Maggie had already folded her arms around Kid and was hugging her, making her giggle.

'Maggie... you might be hurt.'

'Pride, Kid.' Maggie spoke to the laughing infant in her arms. 'Only pride.'

'I don't want to move you on my own, Maggie. Do you still need the toilet?'

'Little late for that.'

'Oh, Maggie...'

'Don't suppose you have a shower.'

'You'd be wrong.'

Maggie sat up and sniffed at the child squirming in her arms. 'Then get the water on. Kid and me are sharing.'

A small structure made of three old doors hooked together leaned against the end wall of the shack. Æppel moved one so Maggie could see the cement floor inside. The cement had been properly smoothed and a channel led from the center into the mud at one edge.

Maggie looked around for the shower. Above her head hung a small bucket with holes punched through the bottom by a sharp nail.

'How's the water get in there?'

Æppel reached behind the doors and dragged out a rattan chair. 'I kick off my shoes and stand on this with a bucket of water.'

Maggie looked her in the eye. 'I know someone who would be very interested in that chair.'

Æppel pushed it back. 'You do…?'

Maggie nodded slowly. 'Yeah…'

'Well… it's not for sale.'

'Drag it back out again.'

Æppel lifted the chair back out of the shadow and pushed its feet square in the dirt. Maggie sat in it and reclined, letting the sun wash over her. 'Chair like this ought to fetch… oh… three hundred dollars or so?'

'D'you think? Three hundred dollars…'

'At least. Bet you could do with the money too.'

'Like I said, it's not for sale.'

'You sure?'

Æppel turned away from Maggie's steady gaze, watching Kid playing in the soft mud outside the shower.

Maggie watched her too, noticing the threads showing in the short pants that covered Kid's loosely slung diaper.

'You could use the money. I can see that.'

'Okay, Maggie. You got me there. We could use that kind of money. But the chair's not for sale.'

'Good.'

'Good? I thought you wanted it?'

'Heck no, I don't want that monstrosity. But I know a woman who does.'

'Like I said. It's not for sale. We only borrowed it. We've had it a week already. Leroy says that's enough and it has to go back.'

Maggie rose from the chair and turned to study it. 'Enough for what?'

'Payment.'

'Excuse me here, I may be old and ignorant, but payment for what?'

'For mending the other one. Leroy says that's fair. We mend the old things, or look after things that nobody seems to care about any more, use them for a while, make them better, then take them back... like the rabbit.'

'The rabbit?'

'Sure. How long do you think it's been since that poor old thing got let out of its cage to run and dig?'

'I guess its owner loved it, in their own way.'

'Is that love, Maggie?'

Down by Maggie's feet, Kid had discovered a small stick and was digging. Maggie reached down and pulled the vest over Kid's head. Kid giggled and patted her bare chest with muddy hands.

Maggie handed the vest to Æppel. 'Love comes in all shapes and sizes. Strange looking packages, too. Is that water ready yet?'

'Any time you are...'

'I like it hot...'

'So do I... but we only have cold.'

'How come?'

'I daren't have a fire until after dark, Maggie. This is a State Park. We're not supposed to be here.'

'Then how'd you make the coffee?'

'Sat it in the ashes all night.'

Maggie stared at the ring of trees that surrounded the dirt yards either side of the cabin, cut through only by the narrow thread of tire ruts.

'How'd you find this place?'

'Leroy found it. Came to the lakes with his folks once when he was a kid. Kept it a secret, even from them. He reckons it was an old Fire Ranger's station. Used to have a wooden tower, he says, right over there.'

Æppel pointed to four short, sturdy posts about three yards apart. Chicken wire had been wrapped around them and inside it the rabbit was nibbling happily at forage greens.

'You all right with this, Maggie?'

Maggie was shivering visibly. 'With what?'

'The water's really cold.'

'What about Kid?'

'She's used to it.'

'Might wake me up.'

'D'you need that much waking up?'

'Depends what kind of a dream I'm in… I'll let you know when it's over.'

'Tell you what, Maggie… I'll clean up Kid. You stand on the chair and pour in the water.'

Maggie climbed unsteadily into the seat of the new, blonde, rattan chair, aware that her worn old gardening shoes were scuffing the seat bottom and that she wasn't sure how she would square that with Maybelline.

Æppel grabbed the bottom of her tee-shirt and slipped it over her head. Where the shirt had kept her skin from the sun she was bone white except for a large, badly drawn tattoo over her left shoulder.

'What's that?' Maggie steadied the bucket with one hand on top of the doors and pointed.

Æppel shrugged. 'Tattoo.'

'Yeah, but what is it?' Maggie watched Æppel's fingers trace the fuzzy rays of light from a blue sun at the point of her shoulder. The spread of the ink suggested that it had been applied while Æppel was still very small. 'Did it hurt?'

Æppel picked up Kid from the mud and placed her in the center of the shower.

'Was too young to remember... hurts now, though. Let her rip, Maggie.'

Maggie tipped a little of the water into the shower bucket. Within the doors it began to rain. Kid shivered, then looked up and began to squirm around under the gently falling water, laughing and gurgling. Maggie tipped in more.

Æppel leaned in with a small bar of soap then rinsed Kid clean. 'That'll do, Maggie.' She picked Kid up and carried her through into the shack. Maggie followed her into the single room. Æppel had thrown Kid onto a make-up bed in the corner and was rolling her in the sheets as Kid kicked and squealed.

Maggie smiled, sharing the delight. 'Such a happy child... you are so lucky.' She handed Æppel the t-shirt she had brought in from outside. 'Cover that thing up if it hurts so much.'

'What... Oh.' Æppel pulled the shirt over her head, picked a clean vest and diaper for Kid from a pile by the bed and handed them to Maggie. 'Here, I reckon you'll know how to do this? I'll fill the bucket again.'

Maggie looked at the diaper in one hand, the vest in the other. 'You're not going to believe this... but I never...'

'What, never?'

'Never.'

'How come?'

'Long story... wrong time.'

'But you're a natural, Maggie. I watched you with Kid. Was sure you had a dozen of your own.'

'I reckon I can manage the vest... and I've seen diapers put on... just never done one myself.'

Æppel took the diaper and with one twist of her fingers dropped it on the bed as a triangle. 'Here... I'll show you... take hold of both feet in one hand...'

Maggie tried to catch hold of Kid but she kicked and played around.

Æppel caught her deftly in one hand. 'Like this... like you was about to gut a chicken. You ever gutted a chicken?' She lifted Kid's rear high in the air and slid her over the diaper. With one deft hand she pushed it into place and wrapped over the ends.

'Hold that...'

Kid sat quietly, watching Maggie with huge dark eyes.

Æppel slid the clip on the pin. 'I cain't believe you never did up a diaper...'

'Never had a reason.'

'You do now.' Æppel picked up Kid and pushed her into Maggie's arms. 'Yours is the next one.'

'Look, Æppel. I better be getting off home 'bout now. Maybelline will have the Army, Navy and the Fire Service out looking for me.'

'They won't find you here.'

'Maybe not. But if they do, they find you, too.'

'Maggie... stay a while, please?'

'I can come back whenever you like.'

'Yes, but... we might not be here.'

Just outside the door, Maggie's old glider sat still as the breathless day. A few yards beyond it the old rabbit hutch sat up on bricks in the dirt, new leather flap hinges screwed to its door. Along the step stood a row of familiar plant pots.

'Looks like you got yourselves dug right in.'

'This is the third place in a year, Maggie… and I'm tired. Kid needs somewhere we can stay for a while.'

'Is that why you need me? You think I got someplace you can stay?'

'No, Maggie. But you know a lot of things I don't.'

'Like what?'

Æppel came up beside her and pointed over the treetops where they fringed the blue of the sky. 'Like what's out there.'

'You don't need me to know that. You done all right for yourself up to now.'

'I ain't never been allowed out there, Maggie.'

'Not ever?'

'Never. Tell me what it's like.'

'Well… I guess out there it…' Maggie thought for a moment then laughed out loud. 'I guess it kind of wraps itself around you… like a diaper… but not the fresh one.'

'So how do you make sense of it?'

'You can't ever. The only sense is that there's no sense in trying. Give me a minute to freshen up. You got a dry towel or do I roll around on the bed like Kid?'

'Here…' Æppel threw her a stretch of peach-colored toweling from under the sink.

Maggie caught it mid-flight and held it up. All the loose threads had been gathered together at one end and finished with a new hem. 'Thought I recognized this… It's from my shed, right? Under the bench? Wrapped around the shears?'

'If you say so, Maggie. When I got it, looked like it had been thrown out.'

'Well it had… sort of…'

Maggie held it to the light. 'Where'd you learn to hem like this? Think you can teach me?'

'Where'd you learn about the world?'

'From liv… Okay, I get it. Give me five minutes. I'll be okay in the yard on my own. You look after Kid here.'

'Who's going to pour the water?'

'Nobody. Okay?'

Maggie picked up a half-empty bucket as she crossed the yard to the shower. She peeled back a door and stepped in, dragging it closed behind her. The space was small, barely large enough to turn around in. She put down the bucket, pulled up the sleeves of her cardigan and took off her underwear, slinging it over the edge of a door to keep it out of the way. She dipped a corner of the towel into the bucket and wrung out some of the water.

'You okay in there, Maggie?'

'Yes. Go away. Look after Kid.'

Æppel's footsteps came closer. Maggie's underwear was whipped from the top of the door where she'd hung it. '

Are you sure you're okay in there, Maggie?'

From outside the shower came the scrape of the rattan chair being moved closer.

'Sure you wouldn't like a little more water?'

'No. I'm all done.'

The chair creaked as it took weight. Maggie pulled down her sleeves as Æppel's face appeared above the doors. Beside it was a full bucket of water.

'Sure you won't stay for a while?'

'Have some respect. Can't you see how old I am?'

'You're not old, Maggie. Just think you are, is all.'

'And how would you know?'

'I know some things… you know others.' She smiled down at Maggie. 'How 'bout we trade?'

'How 'bout my underwear?'

'After I wash it, shouldn't take more than say… oh… three or four hours to dry?'

The air began to cool as the sun brushed against the westerly trees.

Maggie shivered a little. 'Be getting dark soon.'

'Don't worry 'bout that, Maggie. That's how we get you home.'

'Then I guess we use that time to talk about 'We'.'

Maggie sat up to the table, wrapped in as many scraps of dry towel as Æppel could find. She wrapped her hands around the cold coffee cup, trying to instill warmth into it.

'Nobody ever teach you to make tea?'

Æppel mushed up half a banana in some milk for Kid, ate the other half herself and passed a whole one across to Maggie.

'Never made coffee with cold water before we got here neither. Still trying to get used to it.'

'You can waste your entire life trying to get used to things. Only way to do anything is to meet it head-on and ignore the noise.'

Kid twisted around in Æppel's lap, straining to see out of the window. Maggie glanced that way but couldn't see anything other than the glider.

'But what's it sayin', Maggie? All that noise.'

'You must have heard it.'

'Nope. Never done more than hide from it.'

'I'm not really sure what it's about... mostly it's like hearing an argument from half a block away... you get all the anger but none of the sense... I suppose when you filter it down it's mostly folks shouting 'Here I am'.'

'Who they shouting at, Maggie?'

'Damned if I know. Well... themselves, I guess.'

Æppel shifted her grip, winding her fingers into the loose material at the back of Kid's vest.

Maggie twisted around to see where Kid was looking.

'What's the matter with her?'

'Trucks going by on the highway.'

Maggie held a breath to listen. 'Can't hear a thing.'

'Neither can I, but she can. Does it all the time... 'course, she's only ever listening for one in particular.'

'Diesel... yellow... flatbed... hole in the muffler...'

'That's the one.'

'When's it due?'

Kid kicked her feet hard against Æppel's legs until she set her down on the floor. Maggie instinctively took a hold of Kid's vest.

Æppel opened the door to the front of the shack. 'Let her go, Maggie. He's here.'

Outside, the dappled light showed Maggie the glider in a light she hadn't seen before. She ran a hand across it. The fabric was still faded but now the cushions were full and plumped, even the little hollow place that Maybelline always made a beeline for, where Maggie said it fit her skinny old ass.

'At last...'

'Maggie... be kind.'

'Why should I be anything else?'

'I... I don't know.' Æppel glanced through the door at the glider sat out on the dusty porch. 'We only borrowed it.'

'I know that... and you mended May's old chair... not that it doesn't serve her right, mind.'

'Then you won't... Maggie... he's not a thief. We always take things back. We only use the things other people don't...'

'...deserve.' Maggie watched Kid scramble onto the glider. She kicked her legs in the air and the freshly oiled seat slid back and forth.

Æppel came over to stand by the door, blocking Maggie's view. 'I'm not sure what you mean by that, Maggie but... please... you can help me by being kind of open here.'

'Have we got a problem?'

'How many do you want, Maggie? We got plenty of those.'

'No... I mean... Oh Hell... does he hit you or something?'

'No, Maggie. Not ever. Nothing like that at all. He's just different to me... and you. That's all.'

'He has two heads?'

'Maggie...'

'He has two of something else? Jeez... I used to know a man ran a Sideshow. Still owes me a favor, come to think. If he's still alive...'

'Maggie...'

'Listen... how different can he be? Does he look like a man? Sure is strong... picked me up last night like I was Maybelline Watson.'

'Who? What? We thought you were unconscious.'

'Not since New Year's Eve nineteen-eighty-four. That was one hell of a night.' Maggie pushed Æppel away from the door and stepped out onto the porch. 'Excuse me, but this is something I got to see.'

She gave the glider a push that set Kid gurgling. From down the tire tracks between the trees she heard the sound of worn metal making its way, bouncing and jostling something hard on the flatbed.

Æppel took hold of Maggie's arm and spun her around. 'Maggie... before he gets here... I have to tell you...'

Maggie shook Æppel's hand loose and turned back to watch the opening at the edge of the clearing.

'Maggie!'

'What, for Heaven's sake?'

'Maggie... he... he's...'

Maggie reached down and lifted Kid from the glider, running her fingers through the wire-curled mop of hair. 'You think I'm stupid... as well as old?'

The yellow flatbed jostled the tracks into the clearing, swung a hard right and came to a halt by the cabin steps. A young man of around twenty climbed from the cab. He was little taller than Maggie herself but his shoulders were broad and the faded white tee-shirt brimmed at the collar and sleeve with toned muscle. He left the door swinging wide and with a smile lifted Kid easily from Maggie's arms.

'Hi Kid! Hi, Ma'am.'

'I'm Maggie.'

'Okay...' He swung Kid effortlessly by one hand into Æppel's reach. She caught the end of the swing and Kid clung on tight, twisting to watch his every move. He wiped his hand down the side of his jeans and offered it to Maggie.

'I'm Leroy. Pleased to meet you.'

Maggie took his hand in hers and turned it before letting go. The skin of the palm was hard from work and still warm from the wheel of the truck, nails pale and pink against the brown sheen of his skin, hair pulled tight above his handsome face in corn-rows tipped with small, brightly-colored beads.

'See now what Æppel meant about different.'

While Maggie watched from the shack doorway, Leroy gripped Ben's old barbecue by one of its legs and sat it upright in the dirt. He gathered the griddle and the irons off the truck and turned to find Maggie poking around in the base plate of the thing.

'Neat bit of welding in there, Leroy.'

'Took my time.' Leroy handed her the irons and set it up the way Maggie remembered it being stood out in Ben's yard for the last five years. 'Worth doin'... worth doin' well.'

Maggie poked him with a handle. 'Especially Anarchy.'

'That what you are, Ma'am? One of them Anarchists?'

'For one I'm not your Ma'am. For two I am The Anarchist.'

'How d'you get away with that?'

'Because I'm old. I can spit in the street, too.'

'Is that official?'

'What's official? I'm an Anarchist!'

'Can Anarchists grill steak?'

'You betcha. Where are the coals?'

Leroy reached into the cab and lifted out a small paper sack, tipped a few briquettes into the bottom of the barbecue. 'I have some lighter fuel here somewhere…' He took the top off a small jar of clear fluid and sprinkled it liberally on the coals.

Maggie nudged him. 'Give me the matches, there's nothing an anarchist likes better than a good fire. Especially if it's under someone they don't like.'

'I'll stand back then.'

'Don't be stupid… I like you.'

The burst of flame took the wool nap off her cardigan sleeve. She jumped back into the waiting arms of Æppel, who hugged her from behind.

'Hey, Maggie. Your knickers are nearly dry.'

Leroy glanced from one to the other. 'You barbecuing without knickers?'

Maggie shrugged at him. 'It helps with the draught.'

Emeralda

allo Jaques... allo... are you zere?

Ben watched the line of type vibrate across his screen. As his fingers hovered over the keys, another line flickered into being.

Jaques? I went to ze place but you were not zere. I could not get in.

The Madeleine avatar came closer to the screen. Ben could plainly see her pouting, angular lips. Bright, emerald eyes scorched and smoldered behind the glass.

allo?

Ben pounded on the keys.

Heaven Sakes Madeleine how long does it take you to get ready? Do you know how much that room cost me? I'm all out of Linden now. I thought you wanted this as much as I do.

The reply stitched lazily across the dialogue panel.

Of course I want zis too, but vous cannot rush a Lady.

Ben sat back in thought, then opened a new browser window and logged in to his bank account. If he didn't drive the car for the rest of the month… if he didn't pay the Golf Club fees, and anyway he hadn't been for the last twelve months… then maybe… He logged out of the browser to find Madeleine still waiting, eyes burning into his soul...

Madeleine... It's been three months now. What more do you want from me?

On screen, the avatar of Madeleine turned and swayed over to a nearby bench. Ben watched the suggestive motion, edging closer to his screen all the while. The black diamond-encrusted cat suit he'd paid for clung to each and every swooping curve of her body.

Behind her, the park opened up and away, spanning the full depth of the screen. In the distance other avatars floated against the blue sky, passing with angelic grace in front of cotton-white clouds, swooping low over fountains playing in a wide, central paved area. Ben found himself falling into the complete illusion until a new line of type clattered into life.

Ohh Jaques... vous are a man of many passions. I vant only zat it is more... parfait... more... powairful... zan in vou's wildest dreams. I do not vant anysing from vous... I vant only to geeve.

Ben sat back and considered the last months he'd spent online... the missed assignations... the clothes he had bought for her avatar... the physically-enhanced body for his own... the rooms, this last one being the third on that score. On screen, Madeleine's avatar stood and turned, profile on. Ben's stare followed the curve down from the ski-slope of her perfect nose, the promontory escarpment of breasts, the slight but enticing roundness of her stomach, a place where he knew his avatar's head would fit comfortable as on a down-filled cushion, to her derriere, rounded but tight, muscles rippling the Lycra as she shifted her weight calculatingly from one foot to the other. Her fingers toyed with the huge zip tab at the neckline of her suit. Ben traced the clasps of it all the way down to her crotch as she turned again to face him. He held his breath for a moment, then began to type.

Dearest Madeleine... You and I want each other so much it

seems cruel that such a paltry thing as a few Linden should stand between us.

Madeleine's avatar pulled down the zip tab until it was level with her nipples. Her breasts began to spill slowly towards the gap in the center, creating a cleavage the like of which Ben had never witnessed in This Life… or any other. The screen refreshed.

I am zo glad vous agree. I vould sink vous are being mean to a girl eef vous vill not zbend a leetle of vou's Lindens on a girl like mois. I 'ave zeen a emerald clip pour my zipper. Eet fassens jus 'ere…

Her avatar pulled the zipper down another inch or two. From either side of the metal track a crescent of dark brown aureole slid tantalizingly into view. A smile spread on her face and her lips parted as she moved into camera. Ben found himself staring, trapped as a rabbit in headlights, into the warm dark spaces between her breasts until fresh typeface interrupted his descent.

Eet iz not zo beeg. Eet vill fit in ze palm of vou's 'and. Eet makes eezy ze pulling, yes?

Ben replied quickly, revisiting the bank balances in his head as he typed.

How much is it?

Madeleine's avatar froze on screen until she'd considered the reply.

Dear, dear Jaques… do not truffle wiz my affections. Mois Papa zed zat if a man 'ad to ask 'ow much I cozt, zen 'e could not afford me…

The avatar began to fade from sight. Ben punched the keys dramatically.

Madeleine, wait! I have a small problem, but we can resolve it. If you could just lend me five hundred Linden until the end of the month I can book another room.

The fading of the avatar stopped. She moved closer to

the screen so that Ben took the full force of the disturbingly translucent glare.

And vot about zee emerald?

His fingers caressed the keys.

Madeleine... I also have something to give, but right now all I have left is my desire for you. It burns like hot fat on my skin. It blinds me like the whiplash of a tornado at the thought of peeling back the layers of your suit. One gaze into your eyes and my soul melts like a bacon and mozzarella panini...

He paused a moment, then hit the 'enter' key. His text flashed up on screen. A moment later came her reply.

Dearezt Jaques... vous zayz zer zveetest sings. Ow can a girl rezizt?

Raymond

Ben shut down the computer and made his way slowly to the basement stairs. In the lower bedroom the drapes were drawn closed and he sat quietly on the edge of Louise's bed. He patted her hand where it lay across the cover, exactly where he had left it an hour ago.

Her eyes flickered open, vacant and un-focused, her mouth thick with words. 'Is that you, Raymond?'

'No, Louise. I'm Ben... remember?'

She took away her hand as he flicked on the bedside lamp. The shade lit the room in pink, gentled by the low-wattage bulb inside.

Louise sat up. 'I don't want Ben. I want Raymond. When is Raymond coming? He said he was coming.'

'He won't come until you get up, Louise. You have to have a bath first. Then we'll get you some nice clean clothes. Would you like that?'

'I don't know.'

'That's fine. I'll run the bath. Do you think you can get out of bed on your own?'

Ben took away the stuffed rabbit she held close by her side. Louise snatched it back.

'No. No.'

'Alright. But you'll have to put her down to get undressed.'

'No. You'll take Lucy away.'

Ben went through into the en-suite bathroom and set the water running. 'I won't. Not today.'

'You promise?'

'Yes, Louise. I promise. Scout's Honor and all that.'

Louise placed the rabbit gently on the pillow, arranging her ears so they spread all the way across. 'Isn't she lovely?'

Ben made a point of staring at the rabbit. 'Yes, dear. Just like you…'

From the bathroom behind him, the sound of water gushing into the tub seemed sharp and vicious as a squall.

Louise bounced on her toes. 'Help me. Help me. Help me.'

Ben took the hem of her nightdress and lifted it high over her head. Louise suddenly widened her elbows and jammed it so that her face was hidden. She started to giggle from inside the soft cotton. Ben pushed his hands inside and struggled it over her elbows but Louise ran away across the bedroom, nightdress wrapped around her face, neither seeing nor caring where she went. Ben lurched after her, caught her before she hit the wall and wrapped his arms safely around her.

Louise panted breathlessly in his ear, bouncing. 'This is fun! This is fun!'

Ben held her in his arms until she quietened down. She heaved one huge sigh as he lifted the nightdress carefully the rest of the way.

Her face was beaming, wreathed in smiles, careless and wanton until she noticed the look on his face. 'You're not having fun.'

'Yes, Louise. This is fun.'

'Is it really? Is it really? You don't sound as if you're having fun.'

'Oh yes, Louise. I'm having fun.'

He threw the nightdress into a corner. There was a clean one in the drawer, the one with the embroidered birds that he knew she liked. He led her through into the bathroom, took her hand and helped her into the tub.

Louise sat back into the warmth, squeaking her feet against the enamel. 'This is fun.' She looked up into his face, saw the worry lines furrowing his forehead. 'You're not having fun.'

'I am, Louise. Honestly. This is always fun. Bath times especially.'

Her face folded into a scowl that blurred her features with age and confusion. Ben handed her the bar of soap and watched from the chair as she played with it, dropping and finding it again with glee, always the scowl returning as she looked at him.

'You're not having fun.'

Ben watched the soap slide easily through her hands, the way her memory had slipped beyond her grasp, at times an implosive collapse, at other times a steady erosion, a dissolution of self into what, this child of seventy-two years?

'I am having fun, Louise. I always like to watch you having a bath.'

'No you don't. You think I'm ugly.'

'I don't think that, Louise. Whatever gave you that idea?'

'You said to Lucy I was old and fat and ugly.'

Ben opened a small bottle of her favorite shampoo. 'I wouldn't say that about you, Louise. And you shouldn't believe everything that rabbit tells you. Shall we wash your hair today?'

'You would say that.'

'No I wouldn't, Louise.'

She bent her neck so that he could direct the shower head onto her wiry grey hair.

'Yes you would. And don't you lie to me, Raymond.'

Naming of Names

Maggie wiped her chin with the back of her hand. 'Who did you borrow the steak from? I hope they don't want it back. That was good.'

'Farm over by Twin Lakes. Grazes a few head in a corner. Works mostly arable land but keeps these for himself. Ought to be good. Hung three weeks before he has them cut.'

'And you know the butcher…'

Leroy pushed away his plate. 'Should do. He's my Pa.'

'The farmer too?'

'No. Pa's just the butcher… and the slaughter-man… handyman, too.'

'I guess you won't ever starve while he's around.'

'That's my problem. Pa wants to move back South. Says the weather's better for his joints. Grandma's real old now and forgets where she is, so Ma's been back there a while already. They have this big wreck of a house with a sizable spread at the back that Pa says he can work enough out of to keep going. Everybody likes good beef, he says, an' what you cain't sell you eat.'

'Taking these two with you?'

Æppel stood up abruptly and scooped the dishes from the table. Kid watched her wide-eyed from the high chair. Leroy leaned back against the wall behind. 'That's another problem…'

'Another solution opportunity?'

'Jesus, Maggie…'

Æppel snapped at him without turning from the sink. 'Leroy don't you use that word!'

Leroy shrugged it off. 'Maggie, you sound like a teacher.'

Æppel pulled the window shut with a slam, came back to the table and lifted Kid from the chair. 'Knew it… that's why you was… with Kid. I seen it before… that way.'

Leroy's eyes lit with admiration. 'What'd you teach, Maggie? First… second grade? …College? You a Professor?'

Maggie shook her head. 'Only thing I ever professed to know was less than most other folks. I guess you could say I played around with language most of my life. Here, pass Kid over. Let's set one thing straight right now.'

Maggie scooped Kid into her lap. Kid twisted until she could see Leroy before she settled down. Maggie felt moist warmth seep through the fibers into her skin.

Leroy reached over and gently poked at Kid who pushed her face deeper into Maggie's cardigan. 'You all right, Maggie?'

'More alright than I can remember. You ready to take me home?'

Leroy peered out the window into the gloaming dark. An umbrella of cloud showed up yellow in the street-lamps a mile beyond the trees. 'Another couple of hours would be better.'

Maggie hid her eyes, burying her nose in Kid's hair. 'Got things to do first anyway. I feel a sense of occasion coming on.' She looked up and wiped her face on the cardigan sleeve. 'So… names… Who was the one behind the door when they gave out imagination?'

Leroy picked at the nails of one hand with the other. 'Both of us, I guess. Started off when she was just a bump. We didn't know what she was going to be... just a kid... 'the' kid at first. Later on it was 'Hey' kid then she was 'Our' kid and somewhere along the line it turned into just plain 'Kid'. Neither of us seemed to want to do anything about it after that. I reckon you could say we've been too busy moving around.'

'So you registered her as...'

Leroy glanced quickly at Æppel. 'We couldn't. We moved away straight after she was born. No-one around here knows about her. Not even my Pa.'

'Doctor?'

Æppel fetched out a kerosene lantern from the cupboard over the sink. The beads in Leroy's hair flicked with color in the light from a match.

'It's just another bridge, Maggie. We haven't reached to cross it yet.'

'Shots. She has to have her shots. Even I know that.'

Leroy trimmed the wick and the shadows settled in comfort against the walls.

'She'll get them, Maggie. We just haven't worked out how.'

Æppel lifted the sleeve of her tee-shirt. 'Never had mine.'

'Well, you should've.' Maggie swept her hand to encompass the world beyond the window. 'What if you caught something out there?'

'You forget, Maggie. I never been out there.'

'Then where have you been, girl?'

'Good question, Maggie.'

Maggie shivered a little and drew the cardigan tighter around her. 'Then it deserves a better answer.'

Æppel reached across to Leroy, who sat absorbed by the way Kid was trying to twist the stray flickers of light around her tiny fingers. 'Leroy? Can we have a fire yet? Maggie's cold.'

'Sure... hang on to this little heater, Maggie, while I sort it out.'

Kid twisted in Maggie's grasp so that she could watch Leroy's every move. He picked up Maggie's old dustpan and went out the door. He returned with a pan full of glowing coals from the barbecue and tossed them in the hearth. Æppel passed him a small bundle of dried brushwood and the fire leapt into life then died away into a crackle that looked like it was set for hours.

Maggie held Kid up to watch the flickering flames. 'Good fire.'

Leroy turned and smiled. 'Does that make me an anarchist, too?'

'I think that might take a little more work.'

Æppel lifted Kid and sat her in the high chair. 'You said earlier, Maggie... you might have a name? Is it a pretty one?'

'Oh, it's pretty alright. Fit for a Princess even. Like the sound of that?'

Leroy swung a large pan of water over the burning firewood. 'Who wouldn't like the sound of that?'

'Well... let me tell you. This name has belonged to an Empress and two Princesses... maybe more but these are the only three that spring to mind.'

Leroy came back to the table. 'Don't be modest, Maggie. I think you know everything.'

'Maybelline says that too. But I'm not sure she means it right...'

'So what's the name, Maggie?'

'Okay, Leroy. You asked for it... are you ready for this?'

'Fire away, Maggie.'

'Ok… it's Eugenie.'

Leroy laughed out loud. 'You mean, like… You Janie, Me Tarzanie?'

'For an Anarchist, you're a remarkably trivial young man.'

'Sorry, Maggie. Couldn't help it. You have to admit…'

'Admit nothing. First Rule of Anarchy.'

Æppel cut into the quick of the conversation. 'I like it. It has something… something better than 'Kid' anyway.'

Maggie sat back in the chair. Beside her, Kid had found banana mush in a corner of the tray and was tracing patterns in the wood grain.

'First one I know of was Eugenie Montijo. Born round about eighteen something or other. Married a Bonaparte, Napoleon, though he was only the third by that name, became Empress of the French Empire.'

She leaned over to the high chair and tapped on the little tray. 'How does that grab you, Kid?' Kid caught her finger and used it to make the patterns bigger. 'Second was Victoria Eugenie, Granddaughter of good old Queen Victoria of the British Empire. Let's see… she was around eighteen eighty and a bit…'

Leroy poured water into a big old coffee pot and set it on the fire. 'These are all dead people, Maggie. Got any live ones?'

'I haven't finished yet. Third one is 'Princess Eugenie. Somewhere in the UK.'

'Now when did she die?'

'She isn't… hasn't… not yet anyway. She's only young. Just starting out. No reason for her to be dead yet. Hang on… I forgot the fourth. In fact, she was the whole reason for this conversation.'

'And that is..?'

'Maybelline… Eugenie… Watson.'

'Doesn't sound like a Princess.'

'Oh, believe me. She's a legend in her own lunchtime.'

Æppel pushed a small bag of coffee across the table. 'I like it.' She picked up Kid from the high-chair and wrapped her in her arms. 'Yes... I do like it. It's soft... new and old at the same time.'

Leroy pushed a few more sticks under the simmering coffee pot. 'Okay. So how do we seal it? Cain't have her Christened.'

Æppel swung round abruptly. 'Cain't we just... say it? Cain't we all just say it? Won't that make it so?'

Maggie drew them both to the table. 'I guess it just might. So let's all say it together. After me... okay? In the sight of each other...' She waited for them to catch up. '... all present today... we name this child 'Eugenie'. How about that?'

'Eugenie' laid her head on Æppel's shoulder, let out a long, bubbling sigh and promptly went to sleep.

Calling Home

'Is Raymond here yet?'

'No, Louise. He's not here yet.'

'Are you Raymond?'

'No, Louise, I'm Ben. Remember?'

'Are you sure you're not Raymond. You don't look like Raymond. Was he here yesterday?'

Ben lifted the cover over her hands to keep them warm. While the lighting in the room was kept subdued, he knew Louise was happy to stay in bed, getting out only occasionally for a bath or the toilet. He had set up a trip beam, cobbled together from an old intruder alarm, so that if Louise put one foot out of bed while he was upstairs a small light glowed above his computer. He could then direct her to the bathroom and back to bed where she felt safe. Sleep had thankfully become the largest part of her life. Ben wasn't happy to feel that way but the years of her slowly decaying consciousness had taken their toll. Only at the computer could he shake himself free.

'Yes, Louise, Raymond was here yesterday.'

Louise shuffled the bedding away from her chest. 'He doesn't stay long. Why doesn't he stay long?'

'I don't know, my love. Perhaps you can remember to ask him next time?'

'I'll try.'

Ben reached to pull back the covers and caught the warmth of her body radiating through the fresh cotton nightdress. He wasn't sure any longer what his fingers were touching. There was no electricity tingling the tips like there had been in previous years. He could remember it leaving, like a passenger waving from a slowly receding train.

Louise giggled, clasped his hand with hers. 'Your hand is cold, Raymond. Don't be naughty... you know where I like you to hold me.' She tugged Ben's hand down the bed and pushed it under her nightdress.

Her skin felt old beneath his fingers, short hair bristling between them from surfaces turned soft, sagging, distorting as she pushed him downwards. He pulled his hand free but the feeling of that skin stuck with him, still clammy from the bath, the scent of violets rushing out from the gap in the bedding. He gagged... took a deep breath and held it for as long as he dared.

Louise turned away from him onto her side, the shape of her shoulders showing that her face would now be set against him. Slowly, she drew her knees upwards, arching her back into foetal position.

Ben went into the bathroom, carefully washed his hands and closed the door quietly on his way out. The click of the latch stirred Louise into a moment of wakefulness.

'Is that you, Raymond?'

Ben stood over her, hands on hips. 'No. It's me. Ben.'

'Ben?'

'Yes, Louise. Ben.'

'Is Raymond coming?'

Ben ran his fingers through his sparse, grey hair, streaming it back forty years to their wedding day. His eyes filled to the brim. A piece of his throat shrank, making it hard for him to breathe. He lifted a hand to his face. His skin still held the scent of violets, though now more strongly than before. He had used her soap.

'I hear the phone ringing, Louise. That might be him now.'

Louise turned over, a smile running the width of her pale, pink lips. 'I can't hear the phone. I never hear the phone. Why don't I hear the phone?'

'Because it's in the bedroom, Louise. So it doesn't disturb you.'

'But I'm in the bedroom.'

'Sorry, my love. My mistake. The phone is in the study.'

'Where's the study?'

'That's where the phone is.'

'Oh.'

'I'll go answer it soon.'

'Ask him where he's calling from.'

Ben reached under the shade and turned on the lamp by the bathroom door. The table beside him was small, oak-veneered with a semi-circular inlaid marquetry top. It had been a wedding present from Louise's mother. He should have realized thirty years back when Lilian was committed to a home that Louise might be in danger, but they were all younger then... and the world was just a big place and all the time in it to explore... and now... how little of it they had managed to find.

Louise had recognized it... he could see that now. That was why she had begun this inward spiral, narrowing the boundaries of her world so that all the patterns within it would remain familiar and so deeply entrenched as to be unforgettable... well... that hadn't worked, either. He pushed aside the coaster he'd had for his coffee the night before and laid down the book.

In the bed, pushed safely up against the other wall, Louise stirred and turned to look at him. The lamp lit the randomly opened page of the book on his lap, casting his face in shadow.

'Raymond? Is that you, Raymond?'

Ben recalled a time when he had choked on his next words, a time when it seemed important that he pushed her hard to the limits of her own recall so that he could still exist, if only within the disappearing tendrils of her mind... and now... outside of his own head, he seemed to have no presence at all.

'Yes, Louise. I'm Raymond.'

'Oh, Raymond, where have you been? I knew you would call today. But I'm never sure. Is it still dark outside?'

Ben glanced up at the window where a faint chink of light shone in through the overlap of the drapes. 'Yes Louise. It's dark today. It's always dark today.'

'I don't mind if you're here, Raymond.'

'I'm always here, Louise.'

She turned over in the bed, eyes bright in the dim light from the lamp. 'Is that a good thing?'

'Yes, Louise. That's a good thing.'

'Raymond? Where are you calling from today?'

Ben riffled the worn paper of the book, stopping at titles, blank spaces. 'I'm not sure, Louise. I'll take a look...' His fingers stopped the flight of pages, turned two or three back. 'Did I tell you about the time I went to get a haircut?'

'No, I don't think so...'

Ben settled back in the chair, slipped his spectacles from his forehead to rest on the bridge of his nose. 'Good. Hold onto your seat, Louise. This is exciting...'

Louise closed her eyes to listen as Ben fingered the first words into life.

'I was getting a haircut. I was in the chair...'

Bears

Pawel Gradzynski pulled into Maggie's drive on his way home and stepped out into late evening. It was coming cool now and a zephyr of breeze bent slowly around him, bringing with it a faint scent of Geraniums. He hadn't known what that was until he'd called in Maggie's shed earlier that afternoon. He walked around back to it now. The door swung open easily. Inside, the timbers were so impregnated with the scent that with your eyes closed you could imagine it filled with blossom.

Mrs Watson had said it was the only thing Maggie ever grew in there. Hours spent pricking out seedlings into pots, arranging them along the porch where she could see them from the window. It was a strange scent... biting and peppery. Not one he particularly cared for, either. Still, it took all kinds.

He closed the door and made his way to the porch. Along the edge were a few remaining pots of Geraniums in early bloom... fragile and colorful as butterflies. There were no lights showing from inside the house so, on a whim, he plucked a small spray of flowers, opened his notebook, laid them on an empty page and refastened the elastic strap.

Stepping up onto the porch he tried the screen door. It was stuck in the frame. He tugged harder and the whole thing came away in his hand. He lifted it clear of the doorway and propped it against the wall, opened the door into the sitting room and called out.

'Maggie?'

He closed the door behind him and moved quietly through the house, tipping the edge of drawers, cracking open doors. He took the liberty of Maggie's absence and went up into the bedroom. Shirley had been right. He just hadn't liked her turn of phrase, was all… that disrespect of age and the right to live how you please. It would come to her, too… if she was lucky. A thought of the freshly pressed Geranium in his notebook sparked his memory. What was it his grandmother had once quoted at him? 'I shall go out in my slippers in the rain and pick the flowers in other people's gardens.'

He chuckled to the darkness in the crook of the stairs as he made his way back down into the sitting room. He checked the cupboard high in the corner for any evidence of rocket fuel he might have missed. There were bottles of various spirits in there, mostly set well back from the edge of the shelf. He lifted them down one at a time. Their caps were dusted, settled a long time… ten… maybe twenty Christmases at a guess. He replaced them exactly on their ring marks and softly closed the doors.

The cushions on Maggie's favorite chair were already crumpled. He helped himself to a moment of comfort, shrugged off his boots and relaxed. His eyes closed as he ran through the details of the last few days, trying to make sense out of Maggie.

There was something that the situation had been telling him, but he couldn't quite see it. Like Maggie, whatever it was seemed to be hurtling around in the dark, jumping in and out of gear, lurching almost to the front of his brain and then tumbling away behind him out of sight.

Perhaps Shirley had been right all along but, no matter how he tried, he couldn't see Maggie as an 'alcohol-raddled, demented old psychopath'. He could think of a few things to say about Shirley... but Maggie? No. She reminded him too much of his grandmother.

#

Gradzynski opened his eyes into pitch dark. His legs were aching and stiff and his feet were cold. He sat still a moment, trying to make sense of where he might be. Straining his eyes to the limit he recognized the window in Maggie's sitting room.

Across the yards a shard of light fell from the neighbor's bedroom. It flickered blue, limning the edges of the table and chairs close by him. As he stared into the gloom, still barely awake, a shadow flitted across the window. The shadow loomed larger, closer, until it became a presence emanating heat in the chill of early morning. He had the unmistakable sensation that someone was watching him very closely... and that his gun was in the glove-box of the car. The light came on.

'God sake's, Gradzynski. What are you doing here? It's four a.m. Do you have any idea what this will do to my reputation?'

Gradzynski slumped back into the chair, tension draining from him in a flood of relief. 'Or mine, Maggie. What you think my wife's going to say?'

'Who cares? She'll probably blame Shirley.'

'Give me a break, Maggie. There's twenty years between me and Shirley. What makes you think I'd even...'

'Most of the day, Gradzynski, there's less than two feet

between you. Bet that's closer than you ever get to your wife… even in bed.'

'What would you know…?'

'You got that look.'

'Even in the dark?'

'Especially in the dark. Now if you don't mind, I'd like to go to bed.'

Gradzynski fumbled for his shoes. Maggie stopped him with a touch. 'I'll throw you a blanket. Stay there. The world will look better tomorrow.'

'It will?'

Maggie took off upstairs and turned on the light in her bedroom. 'Gradzynski! Who's been doing the Three Bears through my drawers?' Her footsteps padded quickly over the floor above. 'An' who's been in my wardrobe? My laundry basket, even?'

Gradzynski snuggled into the rumpled cushions. 'How's about that blanket?'

Her steps came down the stairs, steady, even, threatening. A blanket dropped out of the air to cover his head. 'I know who it was and it wasn't you, Goldilocks… you would've put things back. You were brought up… not dragged.'

Gradzynski held tight to a corner of the blanket, glad of the cover. The creaking of the door in the infrequent breeze kept asking him what in God's name he was doing here. He dozed fitfully, knowing that Mariel would ask the same question.

#

A slow brilliance began to hurt Gradzynski's eyes, pushing him up towards the surface. The low battery signal on his cell phone was bleeping. He tried to reach his hip pocket to turn it off. His neck locked. His hand and most of his arm seemed to be still asleep. A single muscle just below the middle of his back caught like a barb. 'Oh, God.'

'Fame at last...'

Gradzynski pulled back the edge of the blanket to see Maggie standing over him, kitchen slice in hand. 'God, Maggie... don't hit me with that... already feel like I went ten rounds.'

'There's been a lot of debate about that, from time to time... people burned at the stake, too.'

'What?' Gradzynski sat up and shook out some of the creases of sleep.

'About God being a woman.'

'Might explain a lot of... Maggie, I can't believe I'm debating religi...'

'With God?'

'No. At this time in the morning.'

Maggie hovered over him with the slice. 'You saying I'm not God?'

'I don't know, Maggie. Maybe you are...'

'That's fine. Just remember which end of this slice you're on. One egg or two...'

Gradzynski shook his head and went out to the car, grabbed his radio and his gun and went back into the house.

'Bullets don't work on God, Gradzynski. Just thought I'd let you know... in case.'

'In case of what?'

'You lost the debate and resorted to violence.'

'What comes with the eggs, Maggie? Waterboarding?'

'No. A phone call to your wife.'

Gradzynski flicked the screen of his cell phone. It was dead.

Maggie waved the slice at him. 'It's on the wall over here behind me.'

He came through into the kitchen where Maggie was

busily turning the eggs. 'Sunny-side up, Maggie.'

'Remember that when you phone…'

Maggie slid the eggs onto a plate already warmed and put them back in the oven. She came to stand beside Gradzynski as he took the phone off the hook. He keyed in his home number then hung up the handset before it rang. He elbowed his way around to face her. 'Maggie! Could I have a little..?'

'You can have anything you like except privacy, Gradzynski. I wouldn't miss this for the world.'

'Hang on, Maggie. Maybe I ought to radio in first. See how the land lies.'

'See how you lie, you mean. Tell the woman the truth.'

'You mean… how I went to visit another woman… and fell asleep?'

'Yeah, she can take it. She's a grown-up. You just don't understand women.'

'Fine, Maggie… and which part of 'she'll have my nuts in a jar' don't you understand?'

'From what I see right now they wouldn't feed the birds.'

'Can I have my eggs first? I promise I'll ring her straight after.'

Maggie dropped a plate in front of him and threw him a fork. 'It's hot.'

He glared back at her over the table. 'What isn't around here?' His eggs were perfect. The four pancakes swimming in butter. 'No bacon, Maggie?'

'Never got the taste for it. When your wife rings, what shall I tell her?'

'Don't you tell her anything, Maggie. Let me… damn. You get me every time. How would she know where…'

Maggie broke open the yolk of her egg. 'I could get used to being God.'

The radio crackled into life on the table between them.

Before Gradzynski could move, Maggie picked it up and pressed the button on the side. 'Hi, Shirley.'

'Who the hell is this?'

'The woman whose cupboards you tipped out.'

'Oh, yeah. The drunk-at-the-wheel. What you doing with Pawel's radio? Is he there or have you killed him in some rocket-fuelled orgy?'

Gradzynski grabbed the set from Maggie. 'Hi Shirl...'

'I've been waiting outside the station for half an hour, Gradzynski.'

'Give me an hour. I have to go home first for a shower and a change.'

'Did that old witch get you drunk last night?'

Maggie leaned across the table. 'Tell her the old witch is listening.'

He let go of the button and Shirley came back sharp as a razor. 'How does he like his eggs of a morning, Mrs Gray?'

Maggie took the radio out of his hand. 'Unfertilized. Like yours are thanks to that smart mouth.'

Gradzynski snatched the radio clear.

Maggie cut her pancake into small pieces and forked them over the remains of her egg. 'What did you do that for? It isn't every day I get to play God.'

'Not on my radio, Maggie. I have to work with these people... and you two fighting like hens in a farmyard ain't exactly entertainment at this time of a morning.'

'Worked out what you're going to tell your wife yet?'

Gradzynski stared down blankly at his plate.

'What are you thinking about that's stopping you eating?'

'What to say when I get home that won't end up stopping me breathing.'

'Then tell her you spent the night with another woman.'

'Oh, yeah? I'm not sure whether it's safer to tell her I was with you or Shirley.'

'Shirley. Definitely Shirley.'

'Are you crazy?'

'Of course I am, but what's that got to do with it. She knows you wouldn't go for such a hard-assed bitch as that. You're too sensitive a soul.'

'Behave, Maggie.'

'…whereas one look at me and she'll see I'm anybody's after two cups of tea. Give hard-ass another call and see what she knows.'

Maggie got up and went into the kitchen for the tea. When she returned with the tray, Gradzynski was on the radio.

'Hi Joseph, did you take any calls for me last night?'

'Mariel called about nine thirty. Wondering where you were.'

'What did you tell her?'

'Nothing much… Police business… said I'd get back to her when I knew more.'

'Did she ask about Shirley?'

'No, but Shirley was here. Called back in to go through some paperwork. Needs to get a life. She talked to Mariel for a while. Where you been, Pav?'

'You wouldn't believe me. I thought I'd stake a place out for a while and just… fell asleep.'

'Don't try that one on Mariel when you get home.'

'Thanks, Joseph. I'll be there in a while. Let you know how I get on.'

'Don't worry. We'll see the bruises.'

Gradzynski turned off the radio and picked up the tea that Maggie had poured for him. He sniffed at the rim of the cup. 'Is this safe?'

'Safe as I was when you shared my bed last night.'

'Maggie, don't do that to me. Why would you say that?'

'Depends what tone of voice Mariel uses when I ring.'

'Why would you ring her?'

'So I can tell her where you spent the night.'

'Maggie, what are you after?'

'I want a favor, Pawel. I'll tell you what it is later.'

'Can't you tell me now?'

'No. I want to play God a while longer.'

Bill Allerton

Ransom

Maybelline was in the bedroom when the phone rang. She rushed down into the kitchen and snatched it from the hook. 'Hello?'

'Maybelline…'

'Maggie! Is that really you? Where are you calling from? Why didn't you ring?'

'Sorry, May. I got carried away and…'

'You were carried away?'

'Sort of.'

'Maggie… tell me… quietly… is there anyone listening to this call?'

Maggie turned around. Through the doorway she could see Gradzynski slipping the radio into his belt pocket, the gun hidden away inside its black leather holster.

'Yes, May. They've been here all night, why?'

'Then don't give anything away, Maggie. Just answer yes or no, okay?'

'Hmm… okay.'

Maggie pressed the button that switched on the speaker.

Maybelline's voice squeaked loudly into the kitchen. 'Are they bigger than you?'

Gradzynski filled the kitchen doorway with his frame and stood to watch.

Maggie glanced in his direction. 'You could say that, May.'

'Yes or No, Maggie. Yes… or No.'

'Yes, May. They're bigger than me and they're listening.'

'Do you think they might be violent?'

'Don't know, May.'

'Yes or No, Maggie.'

Maggie watched the expression slowly changing on Gradzynski's face. 'Yes, May.'

'Do they have a gun?'

'Yes, May.'

Maybelline's heart fluttered behind her ribs. 'Do they want a ransom? Is that what this is all about?'

'Yes, May.'

'How much do they want?'

'Yes, May.'

'Sorry Maggie, of course you can't answer that. Is it less than fifty dollars?'

'How cheap do you think I am, Maybelline Watson?'

'Oh Maggie! Now they know my name!'

'Look, May. If you have fifty dollars handy, just bring it over.'

'Where do I bring it? Is there a hollow tree or some…'

Gradzynski took the phone off Maggie. 'Mrs Watson?'

'Oh Heavens!' Maybelline's voice shook in the air around them. 'She shouldn't have given… told you my name.'

'Mrs Watson.'

Maybelline went quiet for a moment.

'Mrs Watson. This is Officer Gradzynski…'

'Oh My! That was quick. Have you caught them all?'

In Maggie's kitchen they listened to the sound of a biscuit barrel hitting the table, the rustle of the contents settling into crumbs and the pieces of the jigsaw dropping into place in Maybelline's mind.

'Maggie Gray you are wicked. What will his wife say?'

'Don't know, May. But if you come round in half an hour and you get lucky, you'll be here when she rings. Right, Pawel?'

'Pawel! Oh, Maggie. I'm coming round there right now!'

'No, May. Give us half an hour. We need to tidy ourselves up a little first.'

'Oh! Maggie Gray! Oh! Oh! Oh!'

'Half an hour, Maybelline.'

#

'Maggie? What happened to your screen door?' Maybelline stood out on the porch examining the places where the screws had ripped from the frame.

Maggie came out to the front, dishcloth in hand. 'Police brutality, May. Never seen anything like it. One minute quiet as a lamb, the next…'

Maybelline peered closely at the torn wood and bent metal of the screen.

'Officer Gradzynski couldn't do that? Could he?'

'Would I lie to you, Maybelline?'

'Well, yes.'

'How would you tell?'

'Your lips would be moving.'

'I thank you for your support, Maybelline Watson, and wish you good day.'

'Now hold on, Maggie. I only said you would lie to me… I didn't say you had.' She fingered the splinters protruding from the wooden edge of the door. 'Oh my…'

'Doesn't let anything get between him and what he wants… you should see my…'

'Perhaps I should report my chair again... does he eat biscuits?'

'Biscuits, Maybelline? He'd have you for breakfast.'

'And what about you, Maggie, what are you..?'

'Too late Maybelline. Had him for breakfast myself this morning.'

'You can be so crude, Maggie Gray.'

'And you can be so naive, Maybelline Watson. Just what do you think he was doing here all night?'

'All night?'

'Every minute of it. Just gone off now to explain our relationship to his wife.'

'Maggie! How could you? That poor woman...'

Maggie put down the dishcloth and held out her arms. Her old cardigan sagged at the pockets from long misuse with garden implements, loose change and a bunch of keys she no longer remembered what they fit but felt comforting somehow under her fingers on a slow day. Her felt slippers eased out at the sides like a pair of settled carpet bags. 'May? Take a good look. Is this the picture of a Jezebel that you carry around in your head?'

'I've seen stranger things...'

'Name me five...'

'Well... there was Onassis and that Kennedy woman...'

'Case proven. Perhaps I'd better buy a mirror next time I'm in town.'

'Do you think he'd come over if I rang and said my chair was missing again?'

'He'd be over like a shot.'

'He would?'

'Yes, and while you're buying him biscuits make sure they're chocolate ones. He likes to dip them in his tea and lick it off real slow...'

'Oh Maggie. Do you think he would... if I...'

'Of course he would, May. If you don't mind my cast-offs.'

'Sam was never ashamed of going in a second-hand shop. Took me all my time to keep him out.'

'Then you might have to visit one yourself before Gradzynski comes over.'

'Why's that, Maggie?'

'Otherwise it might be difficult to explain why there are now two chairs in your back yard.'

'Two?'

'Yes, May. Two.'

'Have you been in my back yard?'

'Who do you think put them there, Maybelline? The Rattan Fairy?'

Maybelline clutched at the neck of her blouse with one hand. 'Maggie! Did you bring those desperate men in my back yard while I was sleeping?'

'Okay, May. I promise I'll wake you up next time so we can share the defibrillator. Just make sure it's on your insurance…'

Maybelline sat heavily into the chair by the table. 'Are you sure… really sure… you haven't any of that rocket fuel left?'

Maggie turned out the logs from the large box by the side of the fire, lifted out a full bottle of perfectly translucent vodka. 'I may just have a drop… but first… I want to hear about that blue light.'

Maybelline's fingers tugged at a large emerald locket. 'Blue light?'

'And you can stop playing with that thing, too, Maybelline. I know you took Sam's hair out of there and put in some of the cat's.'

'I'm sure I don't know what you mean, Maggie Gray.'

'Yes you do, Maybelline. I rode past your house the other

night and in your bedroom window there was this blue light. Don't tell me you don't know what I mean. And I know it wasn't Gradzynski. He leaves his blue light on the car. Does when he stays here, anyway.'

'Oh… Oh… I remember now…' Maybelline held out her cup for Maggie to splash rocket fuel into. 'It was my 'Insect-O-Cutor' lamp.'

'May, we are so far above the lakes here the mosquitoes would have to file a flight plan.'

Maggie splashed a liberal measure into her own cup, tipped a fraction of it into Maybelline's. Maybelline kept her cup in the air.

'You know it's not the mosquitoes, Maggie. I told you before. It's to keep away those nasty ticks. Can't be doing with them at all.'

'When was the last time you saw a tick up here, May? I never seen a single one, myself.'

'There you are, then… got any lemon, Maggie?'

'Sure you need it?'

Shot of Earl Grey

'Pawel? Is that you?'

Gradzynski took off his jacket and hung it in the closet by the door. He swung his belt beside it on a hook, slid the gun from its holster and slipped it into his pocket. It would spend the night in the drawer beside their bed.

'What's for supper?'

'Bigos…'

'Bigos? You getting Polish on me after all these years?'

'No. I'm turning into your grandmother.'

'You mean you're drunk?'

'Your grandmother wasn't always drunk.'

'And how could you tell?' He reached out for her as she walked into the kitchen. Mariel sidestepped him in a way that still surprised him. He thought he knew her by now, but there was always one move, one word…

'Sit down, Pawel. Supper won't be more than a minute but I want to talk.'

'Uh-oh.'

'How do you mean 'Uh-oh'?'

'Sounds like a woman thing.'

'What's a woman thing? Some days I could fall out with you, you're so... so.'

'This kind of talking. That's a woman thing.'

'What kind of talking? What do you mean?'

'I mean the kind that starts off with me being in trouble and not knowing why and I end up apologizing for something I was never aware of.'

'See... you're in denial already.'

'It's a man thing.'

'Okay, Man-Thing. Tell me about this other woman.'

Pawel shook his head and rested his forearms on the tablecloth. 'Okay. Which one?'

Mariel got up from the table and turned the power off on the oven. Supper would be a while in coming. 'I don't know. How many are there?'

'Let's see...' He held up his fingers and pretended to count.

Mariel swatted the back of his hand with a wooden spoon. 'What's this? Community Policing? I meant the one you spent the night with.'

Gradzynski reclined in his chair, the front feet hovering above the linoleum floor.

Mariel knocked him forward again. 'Don't do that...'

He smiled to himself as he lowered the chair. Whatever happened now would not be terminal. There were small familiarities, things that would never cross the mind of someone tipping the edge into something permanent. 'You mean Maggie.'

Mariel slid her hands from the oven gloves, straightened her hair and took off the apron. Behind him, out of sight, she touched herself in places where a pound or two less might make a difference... if only to the way she saw herself. 'I had heard.'

'And so you might. Who was it? Which damn fool couldn't mind their own business?'

'I can't tell you. She asked me never to say... oh.'

Gradzynski stood up from the chair and reached for the phone. 'Shirley... It was Shirley. That girl will be...'

'It wasn't Shirley.'

'Then who was it?'

'I told you... I can't tell you.'

Gradzynski let the phone drop back into the cradle. 'Now... hang on a minute. Does that even make sense?'

'Does to me... But I 'spect you're different. Always you're different. Don't get all Polish on me. You've never even been there.'

'What does being Polish have to do with it?'

'That's what she said... it's in your blood... being Polish and all.'

'Who said?'

Mariel turned on the power of the oven, peered in at the dish and slammed the door shut again.

'Now don't go trying to drag this conversation around to it being my fault 'cause I don't understand. I don't care if you're Polish... fact is I don't care if you're from Timbuktu or one of them other places... or even if you go back there. She said you can't help it and that's good enough for me.'

'Who said?'

'There you go again. You know damn fine who said.'

'I have no idea what you're talking about.'

'Yes you do! Why else would she ring up to tell me that unless I looked after you properly she would see to it herself?'

Gradzynski propped his elbows on the table and lowered his face slowly into his hands. A smile hung around the corners of his lips as he stared into the curved abstract pattern of the tablecloth. 'Did you make a dessert?'

'Of course I made a dessert. Stop trying to wriggle. Just be honest with me.'

'Szarlotka?'

'How did you know?'

'You think I made detective grade for nothing?'

'Then how come you're still on patrol?'

'This way I get the money and the excitement.'

'And the women.'

Gradzynski reached out with one tentative finger and touched her. She stood immobile, wrapped in thought in the center of the kitchen. She didn't brush him away or sidestep. He withdrew the finger and pulled out the chair beside him. 'Sit down.'

She hesitated. He took her hand. It was limp and cold, like it was looking for somewhere to belong. His fingers closed over it. 'Mariel, sit down.'

#

'Where did you get the recipe?'

The remains of the main course sat cooling on top of the stove. The szarlotka graced a glass salver in the middle of the table, the scent of hot apple and spices competing with the bright pungent smell of the Bigos stew. Gradzynski watched molten sugar trickle slowly down the side nearest him and knew it would take the skin straight off his tongue if he tried it.

Mariel poured cream into a jug and set it by his dish. 'We'll have to wait... while you tell me about Maggie.'

'That's the damndest thing... I looked into her and she only goes back twenty years. It's like she stepped out of nowhere.'

'Think she's an alien?'

'You been talking to Shirley?'

'No, why?'

'No matter. Have we got a drink around here while we're waiting?'

'In all the excitement I forgot to get you a beer. I'll make you something. Go through and switch on the TV. The szarlotka will be a while yet.'

With one last, lingering look at the sugar still making its way down the side of the dish, Gradzynski went through into the sitting room. Mariel followed him in to push the side table up against his chair. He listened to her moving around in the kitchen, making those little noises that he'd never usually notice, the dull clack of porcelain in heated water, the jangle of cutlery, the boiling of a long-spouted kettle, the scrape and slide of pans. By the time the TV warmed up and he'd found the least worst channel, Mariel came back in.

She handed him a jar. 'I can't open this.'

There was lemon sliding around in syrup behind the clear glass. He twisted the top and it came clean off in his hand. She took it from him and spooned two slices into the cup she'd placed on the table beside him before filling it with tea.

'Earl Grey. I hear this is how you like it.'

Gradzynski began to flick through the channels again, hoping for something half-way intelligent. He found a news channel, put down the remote and picked up the tea. It hit the back of his throat like the through train.

#

Gradzynski woke into darkness with the sudden sensation that something was dreadfully wrong. He allowed his mind to settle slowly around the hard, pressing sensation in his ear and reached up slowly to find the barrel of a gun.

Without moving his head, he reached into the drawer beside him. His fingers rummaged around until they found the ammunition clip.

He relaxed back onto the bed. 'Mariel. For God's sake. Give me the gun.'

'Maggie…'

'What?'

'Tell me again about Maggie.'

'I told you all I know.'

'Then how come when she rang, she said she was only seventeen?'

'Mariel, give me the gun and stop playing around.'

'It'll cost you…'

Home to Roast

Maggie clung to the door frame with one hand and reached out with her voice.

'Go Witness Jehovah with somebody else. Can't you see the sign?'

Under the headscarf, the face out on the porch was a little softer than Maggie had expected. The woman's eyes searched the bleached timbers.

'What sign?'

'The one that oughta be there.'

'What did it oughta say?'

'No… to whatever you got to sell.'

'I'm not here to sell you anything, Mrs Gray.'

'You got my name too. This Hotline to God… He got broadband now?'

'Mrs Gray, I got your name from my husband. I'm here to see Maggie, your daughter.'

'She's not here right now. She's at school. Won't be back until late and then there's all the homework thing… What do you want her for anyway?'

'Mrs Gray. I think she's having an affair with my husband.'

'Right... come on in Mrs Gradzynski. You look like you could use a drink.'

Mariel waited patiently in the chair by the table. She was so quiet Maggie kept returning to the door to make sure she was still there. Finally the kettle began to chatter and Maggie no longer had an excuse to hide. She lifted the laundry basket lid and selected a bottle from the necks poking through the washing. She dropped a splash into the second cup... then another one... a good one.

'Right, Mrs Gradzynski...'

'Call me Mariel.'

'That's a sight informal for now... maybe when you've had your tea.'

Mariel lifted the cup and drank half the contents in one go. 'That's good, Mrs Gray.'

Maggie waited, calculating the exact moment when the vodka would kick... and waited.

Mariel smiled and put the cup down. 'That's real good.'

Maggie sat down slowly in the opposite chair. 'That stuff would kick the ass off a mule. You some kind of a mutant?'

'How old were you when your daughter was born, Mrs Gray?'

Maggie downed her tea in one gulp. The vodka chased all the way to her socks. 'Let me see... if she's in twelfth grade that makes her... and take that away from... would make me... somewhere around sixty-two. Does that answer your question?'

'I guess it does... Maggie.'

Maggie watched as the worry lines dropped from Mariel's face. She tipped up the pot and went into the kitchen for the bottle. 'Want more lemon?'

Mariel's laugh shook Maggie more than anything. 'No thanks. It takes up vodka space.'

'Mrs Gradzynski? Have you got a problem?'

'Only you, Maggie. Only you.'

'Then, boy… are you in trouble.'

'Maggie… what are you doing with my husband? He's gone all Polish on me since he met you. It's like when we lived at his mother's house.'

'You lived with a Polish mother-in-law?'

'She was Yonkers, but his pa had an accent you could cut with a knife and when they got to fighting… Maggie… I don't want him to turn into his pa.'

'Then we better do something about it.'

'Like what?'

'Like you.'

Without warning, Maggie leaned forward and grabbed Mariel's shoulder. She twisted away but Maggie held tight, burying her nose into the bound hair at the nape of her neck.

'Chicken…'

'What did you call me?'

'I didn't… I just told you what Pawel's having for supper. If you go around smelling like a fried chicken dinner how do you expect him to look at you? Come with me.' Maggie grabbed her by the arm and led her upstairs. 'Don't look at the bedroom…' Mariel's face was a picture. '…I said don't look at the bedroom.'

Maggie swung open the door to a box room. There was a large cupboard fixed to the wall. She fished along the top ledge for a key and opened the door. 'Now… let me see… No, maybe you should pick one. Here…' She dragged Mariel forward so she could see into the shelves.

In neat rows were more bottles of perfume than Mariel had ever seen outside of a store. She glanced back into the disorder of the bedroom, then back at the rows of bottles.

Maggie pushed her hands into the pockets of her cardigan. 'Yeah. Hard to reckon, I guess. Never had much use for them myself.'

'Then whatever made you buy them?'

'I never did. Nary a one. They followed me around the country until I was fifty years old, turning up wherever I was at the rate of one a year.'

Mariel reached out then hesitated. 'May I?'

'Course you may… which one?'

'I don't know… I don't recognize most of them. Except that one. My mother wore that one.'

Maggie reached it from the shelf. 'How old are you Mariel?'

'Thirty-two.'

'This one's older than you. But then, they all are.'

Mariel unscrewed the stopper and breathed in the drift of fumes.

Maggie took a sniff and put it back on the shelf. 'A woman didn't ought to smell like her mother. Try this one…'

'Maggie… that's a classic. I seen it in magazines at the hairdresser. You should put this stuff on E-bay.'

'What's an E-bay?'

'It's…'

'I know what an E-bay is… just don't ever tell my neighbor I said that.' She unscrewed the stopper and took a sniff. 'I don't know…' She dabbed the neck of the bottle on Mariel's wrist and took another sniff. 'Don't smell much like 'stay home errant husband' to me.'

'You think that's what he is, Maggie?'

'No, not yet.'

'Who do you think I should worry about, Maggie. You think it might be that Shirley?'

'What? Hard-ass? Girls like that are all the same. They never take away your husband, they just screw him up inside and leave it for you to sort out. No, I mean a real woman.'

'Like you, Maggie?'

'Yeah… like me. Let's see… how bad has the problem got?'

Mariel lifted down another bottle. The contents made her eyes water. Maggie snatched it off her and put it back.

'Talk to me, Mariel. When was the last time you had sex?'

'Maggie! How can you ask…'

'Listen… if you'd asked me, I'd have to get out the almanac. Yours should at least be within living memory.'

'I think it was… Oh hell, Maggie… it was last night.'

'That's some feat for a woman who smells like a fried chicken. What did you do… starve him first?'

'No, Maggie… I…'

'You what? Told him you were Colonel Sanders?'

'No, Maggie. I pulled a gun on him.'

Intermittent Communication

'Come in, Mrs Gray. Take a seat.'

The doctor was unbelievably young, it seemed to Maggie. His face was angular, his hair a shock of black above the pale forehead. His shaven cheeks carried an all-day blue and his eyes were almost as dark as hers. Maggie took a chair across the desk from him. The seat was hard, the backrest upright and designed to keep conversation short.

She leaned forward to peer at him. 'Are you the doctor or are we waiting for your father?'

The doctor took off his dark-rimmed glasses and peered back. 'Mrs Gray. I assure you...'

'Don't bristle. Take the compliment.'

The doctor slid his glasses back on and stared at Maggie over the desk. 'Mrs Gray? Are you new to this practice?'

'Do you mean... have I tried this before?'

'No, Mrs Gray. I mean, have you been examined by a doctor at this practice before today.'

'Yes.'

The doctor shuffled papers on his desk in a vain attempt to find anything with her name on. 'Can you remember when that was?'

'You were probably in fifth grade. Does that help?'

The doctor pushed aside his paperwork. 'Strangely enough, it does. Can you remember what it was for?'

'It was a small sailing problem I had.'

'Motion sickness?'

'No, Doc. You don't get sea-sick on a lake. It was more of a… physical problem.'

'And what kind of treatment did you get?'

'I got two paramedics… no, the jogger and a dog came first. They're the ones found me. The paramedics came later.'

'Then how did you end up here?'

'It was the artery. I nicked it. Wasn't much of a bleed but the water was red around me for quite some way. The jogger fixed that with his dog lead and a stick and a rock.'

'Tourniquet?'

'Can't remember his name. It was a while ago. But the dog was cute… 'cept the Fire Tender scared it off and I don't know if he ever got it back.'

'Fire Tender?'

'Well, the ambulance came first but I couldn't fit through the doors. So they called 911.'

The doctor studied Maggie over the top of his glasses. 'You don't look like someone who's been that far overweight, Mrs Gray. You've made a remarkable recovery.'

'Doc, you ever tried to get a canoe into an ambulance?'

'Why would I want to do that, Mrs Gray?'

'Look, Doc, don't be obtuse here. I'm explaining it the best I can.'

'And the sailing problem?'

'My leg was through the canoe right up to my… derriere.'

'Why would you do that?'

'I was trying to walk home… the water levels were dropping… the tide was going out…'

'In a lake, Mrs Gray?'

'Doc. I'm not stupid. But if you want to know what stupid feels like, try riding through the center of town in rush hour strapped to the back of a Fire Tender with a plywood canoe up to your ass.'

'But the doctor sorted you out ok?'

'Yeah, he called the carpenter. But he said it was out of hours and he'd charge double rate. I said I'd wait 'til morning but the doc said I was bed blocking and he'd charge me mooring for the canoe.'

The doctor sat back and took off his glasses. Out in back was a pile of records going back half a century. He'd heard the odd story about old Doc Kelly. Now he knew what he was going to be reading for a while. 'Now what seems to be the problem?'

'Well… it's sort of intermittent.'

'Did you mean… intimate?'

'Listen Doc, when I say intermittent, I mean intermittent.' She pointed at the heavily wrinkled skin of her face. 'Don't let this disguise fool you.'

The doctor threw his glasses onto his paperwork and blinked across the desk at Maggie. 'Alright Mrs Gray. Now you can be whoever you want.'

'I have a question first.'

'Fire away.'

'It's about Patient Confidentiality.'

'What do you want to know?'

'Well… what I want to know is… under what circumstances can you be made to reveal something a patient tells you.'

The doctor polished his glasses thoughtfully on the sleeve of his house coat, slid them back on. 'Well… I guess a combination of pliers, toenails and a red-hot poker would be a good place to start. Short of that, what comes here stays here.' He checked the clock on the wall. '...but if you don't mind?'

'Like I said... it's intermittent. First I get this rash...'

'Where?'

'On my derriere.'

'So you did mean intimate.'

Maggie scowled at him. 'I'm trying to be serious here.'

'I can see where that might be a problem, Mrs Gray.'

'Then I get this cough, right back in my throat. You ever hear the seals in the Bay Area?'

'Anything else?'

'A temperature. Don't know what but it sure feels high. And breathing. Breathing like an old steam loco. Comes and goes, though.'

'There's a medical term for that.'

'Yeah?'

'Intermittent. Let me look at your throat.'

'What for? You've seen throats before. Can't you give me a scrip for some pills or something?'

'Okay, Mrs Gray. As you're paying for this, I'll give you my considered diagnosis. One. You are aged between one and two years old. Two. You have Croup. Three. It is infectious and it sounds like it's at the worst stage right now. Four. The breathing sounds you have indicated tell me that unless you are treated immediately there is a danger of the airway into your lungs becoming blocked. Five. If the condition remains untreated it may result in death by asphyxiation. So tell me which hospital you would prefer to be admitted to and I will make the arrangements.'

Maggie sat back in the chair, face ashen. 'Doc? About that confidentiality thing? Well... it's not me that's ill.'

The doctor took off his house coat and picked up his

bag and stethoscope.

'Don't let this disguise fool you, Mrs Gray. Where's the patient?'

#

The doctor's car was small and red with an open roof. Maggie looked up to watch the boughs of trees passing overhead. She felt detached somehow, like her feet had left the earth and now it was spinning by without her. She closed her eyes, hoping the sensation would go away. The next bend pressed her against the door with a great urgency. She opened her eyes as the brakes took a hold and a tractor appeared, using up the road. The Porsche dipped and kicked and then they were around it and speeding up. Maggie leaned across to watch the doctor's hands and feet on the pedals and stick shift.

'What are you doing, Mrs Gray?'

'Learning to drive, Doc. Could be useful. In fact, could've saved me a whole lot of trouble up to now.'

'How have you been getting around? There's no bus runs through that estate anymore.'

'I used to cycle.'

'When was that?'

'When I had a bike. Take a right here… over the bridge.'

The bridge rose up before them and Maggie watched the co-ordination of hands and feet that took them down through the gears, spinning up the motor noise from the rear. The low growl was somehow reassuring. Her eyes kept wanting to close. She propped them up with a finger.

'You okay in there, Mrs Gray?'

'I'm okay. Just tired. Too many late nights. Left here…'

'Up this track?'

'Would I lie to you?'

The doctor slowed to a crawl so the car wouldn't ground in the potholes. 'It wouldn't be a first, Mrs Gray.' He stopped the car alongside a set of cabin steps. 'Looks deserted. Sure this is the right place?'

Maggie tugged at the door handle but her fingers were not strong enough to pull it out of the recess.

'Let me out of here, will you? It's supposed to look like this.' She leaned against the side of the car and caught her breath. She closed her eyes and the tightness eased while other parts of her took up the slack until she made a reasonable stab at feeling human again.

Across the yard the rabbit sat in a corner of the netting, nibbling fresh shoots. They were still here. She pushed herself away from the side of the car and climbed the steps to sit in the glider on the porch. 'Hey Æppel, come on out of there.'

The doors shifted on the shower by the side of the shack. Æppel peered cautiously out, Eugenie cradled in her arms. 'Maggie... why did you bring someone here? You know we'll have to move now.'

'Don't worry about the doc. He has a very patient confidentiality.'

Æppel was trembling. The doctor took Eugenie from her and laid her down on the glider next to Maggie. Maggie teased her gently with a finger.

The doctor took off his stethoscope and shook his head at her. 'You know I have to report this, Mrs Gray. This child needs some real care and attention.'

'And this child is getting it, or what else are you doing here? Is she going to die from this or what?'

'Without the proper medical care...'

'Which she is getting.'

'And better accommodation.' He nodded up at the shack. 'I bet there isn't any heating in there... or even fresh water.'

'The coffee's good, if a little cold. You like some? Æppel. Give me and the doctor here some space.'

Maggie sat up to the edge of the glider and stared the doctor in the eye. 'Listen Doc, this is where your patient confidentially cuts in.'

'Mrs Gray, you aren't my patient, and neither is this child.'

'What if I register her?'

'As?'

'My daughter.'

'How old are you, Mrs Gray?'

'What's that got to do with the price of bread?'

'You mean I can't report this miracle? You'd get a hell of a spread in the Journal. Seriously though, it's an infectious disease and I have a responsibility to report this.'

'Who says? You have a responsibility to heal the sick, that's all. So do it.'

'I wish it were that simple, Mrs Gray. The law…'

'Just be patiently confidential until the child is cured and they've moved on. Then discharge your responsibility to the law next time you take a leak.'

The doctor sat down beside her. He gently pressed the end of the stethoscope against Maggie's wrist. Apart from a sensation of coolness she barely felt a thing.

'I have a proposition, Mrs Gray.'

'I'm spoken for… and you should see him… he's a Police Officer this tall…' Her head fell back against the glider's stripes.

'Mrs Gray, do you have a spare room in your house?'

'Your wife throw you out? Been taking your own pills?'

'Mrs Gray, if you can take this child and her mother…' He looked up as Æppel held out a coffee cup. Her hands were fine if a little calloused by work. Her clothes were mended but clean and her face, turned towards him, held a great fear of him, yet at the same time her eyes brimmed with hope. 'Mrs Gray… if you can take Æppel and…'

'Eugenie.'

'…if they can stay with you awhile, I can register you as my patient and then my visits will be legitimate.'

'How's that, doc?'

'Mrs Gray… I need to see you again.'

Maggie lifted Eugenie into her lap where she began to cough, face turning swollen and blue. She patted her gently on the back until her airways cleared.

'I'm flattered, doc. But it's the child I'm worried about.'

'So am I, Mrs Gray. So am I.'

He wrote out a prescription.

'Doctor?'

'Yes, Æppel?'

'Doctor… we ain't got no money for prescriptions.'

'Don't worry about that. It'll be booked to Mrs Gray's account. Just get it filled today. Eugenie will be fine with a little more…' He looked around the shack but lost the words… the shingles were tight… the yard was clean and clear… the wood sides all mended… 'I was going to say a little more homely care… but I see it now.'

Maggie lifted Eugenie from her lap and sat her up in the glider. 'You mean they don't have to come to me?'

'Oh no, Mrs Gray. They do. That's the deal.'

'Why do I feel like Faust?'

'Don't push it Mrs Gray. Æppel? Will you carry my bag to the car?'

Buttons

'Hey Ben, I want to talk to Louise.'

'Can't do that right now, Maggie, she's busy.'

'She's been busy this last year, Ben. What's she doing in there, building a Golem? You the prototype?'

'Maggie… I got to go out.' Ben shook his car keys at her. 'Anything you want from the Mall? Spyglass? Listening Device? How about a Bug?'

'I'll have a look at the one you got when you're done with it.'

'Which one's that, Maggie?'

'The one stuck up your ass…'

Maggie couldn't remember a time when her fingers had ever felt so clumsy. Louise's spare keys were a fumble of brass and steel rings that she was struggling to separate out. Just when she thought that Ben must have changed the lock, she found the one that fitted. She opened the door and stepped quietly into the hallway.

It was dark inside, but even with Maggie's eyes it was plain that nothing had been done in here for years, not since Ben put in that basement bedroom for the friends who never showed. There was a pathway marked into the carpet by the dust that had settled each side of it in a way that Louise would never have allowed.

Somewhere below her an edge of light shone... a faint, pink, barely discernible stripe across faded wallpaper. She took a few steps down the basement stairwell, more scared now than ever about what she might find. Ben didn't look the type... but you never knew... and it was over a year since she'd caught a glimpse of Louise. The bedroom door was locked... but the key was in the handle.

From where she stood in the doorway, Maggie couldn't see the figure in the bed as anything other than a vague shuffling bulk under a pink duvet cover.

'Louise?'

A white rabbit appeared around the corner of the wall. The fingers holding it were fat and pumped but the nails looked clean and neatly manicured. The rabbit shook in the air, white cloth ears flapping hysterically until suddenly the hand drew it back out of sight. Then came a voice that Maggie recognized.

'Tell me, Lucy... Is it Raymond? Or is it that nasty man who puts you in the washing machine? Alright, I'll listen carefully...'

'Louise?' Maggie walked softly over to the bed. 'Louise? What are you doing in bed at this time of day? Oh Lord!'

Louise sat up in the bed. Beneath the tangled grey of her hair, her face was a pink and white blob marked out with lipstick and mascara the way a child would fist a crayon.

Maggie stopped and looked around for a stool to sit on. There was one pushed under the dresser. It would do unless her legs gave way before she could reach it. She dragged it a foot then sat down. There was a book on it. She turned it in her hands, studying the cover briefly. Raymond Carver. She'd never taken the time to read him.

The white rabbit appeared again from under the duvet. It hovered over the edge of the bed and the blackness of its button eyes penetrated deep into Maggie's growing sense of shame.

'Louise... I'm so sorry. I should have insisted but you know what Ben's like. Couldn't get past him.'

She put the book down on her lap, remembering the interminable shopping lists that Louise used to give her... the repetitive conversations.

'I'm sorry, Louise. I should've seen this coming.'

Louise pushed away the duvet and waggled the ears of the rabbit. 'See... you were wrong, Lucy. It is Raymond... look!'

Maggie returned her attention to the book. 'Oh... I see...'

'Oh, Raymond...' Louise ran her hands over her own body in a way that made Maggie look away. '...where are you calling from today?'

Maggie thumbed the book open at the first story. 'Say, Louise. Do you remember the time when nobody said anything?'

'No...No... when was that, Raymond?'

Maggie bore deep into the text so she didn't have to watch Louise and the rabbit.

'Keep your hands still, Louise, and I'll tell you.' She was still telling when Ben walked in.

#

Ben took a moment to look around Maggie's sitting room. His chair was tight up to the table and he spread his long legs out beneath it, shuffling aside a pile of old newspapers and discarded slippers. His eye counted the familiar diminishing patterns of life around him... the places where Maggie no longer even looked... things perched where their lives had become their own, undisturbed by necessity.

'I apologize, Maggie. I shouldn't have torn you off like that.'

'Ben, you're a firecracker. What else should I expect.'

'All the same. I remember how close you and Louise were.'

'The half of it, Ben... You only got the half of it.'

'That was all you allowed me to have.'

Maggie turned silently away from his comment, poured tea into cups and offered him the vodka.

'Times are changing, Maggie. You never used to ask.' Ben pulled his legs back under the chair and leaned against the cushion. 'Glad to see you're not sore at me anymore, but why did you ask me over.'

'Who said I'm not sore at you? Of course I am. But what good will that do Louise? Why didn't you ask me for help?'

'Maggie... you have a way of helping that...'

'That what?'

'It's kind of hard to describe...' Ben leaned away from her anger. Maggie's face bore the hallmarks of a question he didn't want to answer, leastways as he was, tucked tight to her table.

'You've always been at sort of... ninety degrees to the rest of us, Maggie.'

Maggie sat up, memory clouding her eyes. 'Where'd you hear that, Ben?'

'I guess it must have been Louise.'

'And that's a problem? You saying I'm not safe around Louise?'

'I'm not saying that, Maggie. I'm wondering if...'

'You been here twenty-four years, Ben... if it's a day.'

'Thirty, Maggie, and she doesn't remember a one of them now.' Thread veins stood out in the whites of his eyes.

'You alright, Ben?'

'Yeah, Maggie. I'm just 'shamed, that's all.'

'What you done to be 'shamed of, Ben?'

'I let it happen.'

'What could you have done?'

'I don't know. Perhaps I could've talked to her more instead of diving head-first into that computer the minute it happened.'

'It's called surviving, Ben, and there's no shame in that. And there's no glory in dying alongside her either. You did all you could on your own.'

'Then why are you still sore at me?'

'Because you did it on your own. I could've helped if you'd let me in.'

'Maggie... you've seen her... and that damned rabbit... how could I...'

'Who you 'shamed of Ben? Yourself or Louise?'

Ben thought about that for a moment. 'Me... I guess.'

'And the rabbit's just stuffing... right?'

'Maggie, you haven't seen the way it looks at me with those evil black eyes.'

'They're buttons, Ben... buttons.'

'Louise won't listen to me anymore unless the rabbit says it's okay... and even then she waits until it whispers what I said right into her ear. I'd burn the damn thing if it wasn't the only way to communicate with her.'

'Don't burn it, Ben. Use it.' Maggie stoppered the empty bottle and threw it into the log basket by the fire. 'I think I know someone who can talk to it.'

Bill Allerton

Ersatz Cats

'Hi Pav... Shirley?'

'Evening, Doc... can I get you boys one?'

'There's one in the tap.'

'For both of us?'

'I guess so, Shirley. Put it on my tab.'

'Thanks, Doc. I'll just have a medicinal.'

'Pav? Sit down a minute. Let Shirley get the drinks.'

'So what is it you don't want Shirley to hear?'

'Lots of things. My thoughts when I look at her for one.'

Gradzynski studied her at the bar. Without the stab vest he had to agree she did look something, but then Doc didn't have to spend all day with her.

'Doc? You're drooling.'

'Oh. Right. I have something to tell you that I can't say here. You know how gung-ho Shirley is.'

Gradzynski kicked out a chair but Shirley slid into the booth beside Doc.

'What are you girls whispering about over here?'

'Nothing. Just boy stuff.'

'Football, then.'

'Give us a break, Shirley. Let me out of the seat. I need

to take a leak.'

Gradzynski stood up to follow Doc. 'Think I'll take one too.'

Shirley slid back into the booth. 'You girls don't forget to fix your lipstick.'

'This needs to be good, Doc.'

'You're not taking a leak, Pav.'

'I'm waiting for the Greek Chorus. This is getting a bit theatrical even for you.'

'You have to, Pav. That's part of the deal.'

'What deal?'

#

Maggie fumbled the phone against her right ear. 'Yes, Maybelline?'

'Is that you, Maggie?'

'Maybelline, who else would say, 'Yes, Maybelline'?'

'Anybody knows me, I suppose...'

'Anybody knows you but me would've let it ring.'

'Well then I'm glad it's you, Maggie, or I might have thought you were out again.'

'Of course I'm out, May.'

'I thought you were in, Maggie. You mean I can't come around?'

'Maybelline, I'm out of the shower, out of sorts and out of fresh underwear. You got anything fits, bring it around. Second thoughts. You can't come over.'

'Oh, Maggie...'

'Don't 'Oh Maggie' me. I know you've only run out of biscuits.'

'Well... yes, I have... but that's not what I'm ringing about.'

'Spit it out, May.'

'Alright, alright. I was passing and I thought I heard a child crying and I hoped it wasn't you.'

'Seventy-some years ago Maybelline, it might have been. Your ears go back that far?'

'Not even my teeth go back as far as you, Maggie Gray.'

'Maybelline Watson…'

'So if it wasn't you, Maggie, who was it?'

'It's the cat, May. There's a new kitty on the block and you know how they are. Makes 'em skittish.'

'Maggie… are you alright?'

'Sound, Maybelline. Why?'

'Well… Maggie. You don't have a cat.'

'You mean… it's been stolen?'

'No, Maggie. You never had one. You don't even like them.'

'Well, Maybelline, it's the one I would've had… if I'd liked them.'

'I hope it's a tabby, Maggie. I do so like a tabby. Is it a tabby, Maggie?'

'Nope, May. It's a ginger tom.'

'I hope you've had him… you know… 'seen to'.'

'I do that to all the men. Now will you go away. My ear and my legs are giving me pain.'

'Is that connected, Maggie?'

'Only by telephone. Now go, May. I'm hanging up.'

'Maggie… would you mind if I pretended to have a cat too?'

'Maybelline… go away and pretend to be a biscuit.'

'Now that was your Aunt May…'

Maggie chucked Eugenie under the chin. She gurgled then broke into a new fit of coughing. Æppel patted her back until it subsided into a deep sob. Maggie picked her up

Bill Allerton

and draped her over her shoulder so she could see all the sitting room as she turned.

Eugenie took in the sight of old newspapers and the empty bottles in the wood-basket by the fire and quietened down some.

'Maggie? Will you be in trouble having us here?'

'Trouble? You never seen trouble, Æppel. Why... I've lost count of the times the police have been around here. Only last week...'

'The police, Maggie?'

'Don't worry child, they were only looking for you.'

'Maggie... we have to leave.'

'Set down again right there. Here...' She slid Eugenie from her shoulder into Æppel's waiting arms. 'Get this child warm by the fire. And there'll be no more talk of leaving.'

'But the police...'

'Didn't find you. Why would they come back?'

'Maggie. We cain't...'

'Hush now. Just you trust in your old Aunt Maggie. I've got 'looking out for' muscles I haven't used in decades.'

Maggie stumped through into the kitchen and dropped the breakfast pots into warm soapy water and stood there, wrist deep, mind a complete blank canvas on which tendrils of thought began to grow again, searching the shadows of the past and remembering old lessons. Something tricked in her head and her vision clicked back on.

Watching her through the kitchen window was Gradzynski. He had on a yellow-checked lumber jacket. There was dirt on his boots from Maggie's yard and he kicked them against the sill before entering. Maggie used the time to close the door through to the sitting room.

'Hi, Maggie.'

'Officer Gradzynski...' She peered around him. 'Where's hard-ass?'

'I'm on my own today. You got any tea going, Maggie?'

'With or without?'

Gradzynski frowned at her.

'Ok. I don't have any rocket fuel left anyway.' She kicked out a chair and almost fell over with the effort. She grabbed the table edge and steadied herself. Gradzynski watched her curiously and sat himself down. 'Can we sit by the fire and talk, Maggie?'

Maggie threw a quick, cautionary glance at the separating door. 'I haven't lit the fire yet.'

'Your chimney is smoking, Maggie.'

'It's old enough. And you're not dressed for arresting it if it wasn't.'

Gradzynski undid the bottom two buttons on his jacket as he sat down.

'Szarlotka?'

'And Bigos, Maggie. It's a wonder the pants fit. D'you give her the recipe?'

'Nope. Just some perfume to help persuade you to work it off.'

Maggie sat down and pushed her lazy leg under the table where the way it lay would be less noticeable. The foot had taken to leaning over at an angle the last week and mostly she just shrugged it off. 'Pawel?'

'Yep?'

'Grab the kettle…'

Gradzynski levered himself up and made tea by the sink.

'It's in the cupboard. The one by the stove.'

Pawel reached down the lemon slices and set them on the table. He returned with the teapot and three cups.

Maggie slid out the drawer beside her and took out a spoon. 'You expecting hard-ass to show up?'

'No, Maggie. Wait here.' He passed by Maggie as he walked around the table. For a second she thought to grab the back of his pants but her arm wouldn't lift in time. He opened the door into the sitting room and looked around.

'Where are they, Maggie?'

'Where's who?'

'Æppel and the kid.'

'What's an Æppel?'

'Don't get cute, Maggie…'

'I ain't been cute for seventy years. It's the nose, you see…'

Gradzynski walked across the sitting room and opened the door to the stairs.

'Æppel? Come on down. I know you're up there. I'd have heard the door go if you'd gone out. I stayed up half one night listening to the wind creaking it. I'm not going to hurt you, I'm a friend.'

From upstairs, where the sound of Eugenie's coughing had given her away, Æppel came down slowly, her back to the wall and clutching Eugenie tightly to her.

'I'm not going back you cain't make me I have a child she's mine they cain't have her I won't let anyone touch her how did they find me was it Maggie…'

'Hey, now. I'm Pawel Gradzynski. And I'm a friend. Like Maggie…'

Maggie's voice carried in from the kitchen. 'Only bigger…'

'Here…' Gradzynski held his hand out low, like he knew from childhood when a horse was shying around him. Æppel took his fingers and he led her over the bottom step. 'Come through to the kitchen with me and Maggie.'

Æppel hesitated, wild-eyed and breathing through her nose, Eugenie holding her breath and turning blue at the lips.

'Give me that child.' Pawel snatched Eugenie from Æppel and began pounding gently on her back with the heel of one hand. Eugenie coughed up a sticky smear of phlegm across his jacket sleeve and began to breathe normally. He carried her into the kitchen and sat her on Maggie's lap.

'How do you take tea, Æppel?'

'How come you know my name?'

'I wouldn't be much of a police officer if I didn't at least know that.'

'Police?' Æppel backed away to the door.

This time, Maggie managed to catch a pocket of her jeans. 'Sit down, Æppel.'

'But he's… police.'

'Some kind of… yeah. But he's harmless. I have him under my spell.'

'Thanks for the vote of confidence, Maggie.'

'You're welcome, Pawel. Æppel? Talk to the guy.'

'I want to know how he knows my name. And why you told him where I was, Maggie.'

'I never told him. But I know a man who took a Hypocritical Oath…'

Pawel poured the tea and fished among the lemon slices with a spoon. He held up the sugar and Æppel shook her head. Maggie pushed her cup across. Pawel teemed sugar onto the lemon.

'I was in the bar Friday night and talking to a doctor friend of mine and he was telling me about the times when he goes out to visit a client and ends up with two for the price of one. Says how sometimes that compromises him when it comes to patient confidentiality.'

Maggie stirred in the sugar then tossed the spoon onto the table. 'I can see where he might have a problem with that. He's too young to be patient.'

'So I asked him some more about it and, you'll never believe this, Maggie, but we're stood there in the john and he starts telling me how this elderly lady with a weird twist in humor had put him on a spot and how his first priority was to make sure this kid she was in charge of was being properly treated.'

'Too damn right.'

'But the darnedest thing, he said, was how she was studying the way he drove his car. Never seen anyone so interested, he said, they usually sit there with their eyes closed or holding the handle ready to jump clear.'

'You been in that car, Pawel?'

'Yep. I'm the eyes closed variety. What I don't see I can't arrest him for. So I said, why are we having this conversation in the john? And he said that was part of the deal.'

'And what did you say?'

'I said 'Maggie Gray'. And he said… "Æppel". That's all I can say about it. She's the only one not my patient.' So here I am. And I'm waiting to find out what this is all about.'

'This is dangerous ground, Pawel.'

'I can always send hard-ass around to get a statement.'

'No need for that. I'm sure we can sort this out like adults.'

'Some of us could, Maggie. Let's take this tea by the fire… you three go first.' As they made their way through, Maggie lifted her leg out from under the table and limped after them. Pawel held the door for her. 'You got a problem, Maggie?'

'Ingrowing hobnail. Been wearing those jackboots you left last time you were here.'

A Rabbit Thing

Around 7p.m., Leroy arrived back at Maggie's with the truck. He backed it up the driveway until it was level with the porch. Æppel picked up Eugenie and rushed out to meet him. He took the child and swung her onto his shoulders in one fluid movement. Æppel hugged him as if he'd been gone a year.

'Hi Maggie.' Æppel was still holding on to him. He began to disengage her arms from around his waist, passing a quizzical look at Maggie.

'Police been here today. Spooked her a little, that's all.'

'What did they want, Maggie?'

'Oh, nothing much. Just you, me, her and anyone else who dares to be different.'

He pushed Æppel away from him so he could see her eyes. 'What did you tell them?'

Æppel buried her face in his tee shirt and held him again.

Maggie took a deep breath. 'She told them nothing but the truth... and that can't hurt you. Leastways not too often.'

Leroy watched Maggie limp from the doorway to the porch frame. 'You need to sit down, Maggie. I got just the thing...'

'I can see it. Not sure I want that old thing back.'

'But it's better now than it was. Look. I cleaned it again. You can see the stripes now.'

'What makes you think I want to look at stripes?'

Leroy wrestled the old glider onto the porch. He hung the chains and set the swing seat and canopy then kicked it into motion. He picked up Eugenie and laid her on it, swinging gently.

Æppel threw a scrap of blanket over her and she closed her eyes. 'She's been fed. What about you?'

'Not a thing since ten.'

'Maggie has some stew on…'

'What's in it?'

'This and that…'

'Okay, but then I got to call back to the shack for some more of our stuff. I should bring back your cycle too, I guess, Maggie.'

Maggie came back to the porch. 'My guess is you should drop it in the lake…' She held on to the glider frame and swung the seat slowly for Eugenie. 'Not so fast, Leroy… what else you got there?'

'Only the rabbit, Maggie. I'll drop that off later when everyone's in bed.'

'You'll do no such thing. Drag that cage to the corner of the yard and bring him to me. I got a use for him.'

Maggie sat beside Eugenie on the glider and Leroy placed the rabbit gently into her lap. She stroked its ears and smiled absently. 'Had a few of these over the years.' She lifted the rabbit so she could see straight into the red of its eyes. 'Albino, hey? You're a dandy rabbit. Now… are you one of the good guys or one of the ones that bit Aunt Maggie and ended up in the pot?' She laid it back in her lap and the rabbit shuffled down and was quiet.

#

'Ben?'

Maggie leaned against the door while she kicked at the bottom panel. The door opened and Ben caught her as she fell in.

'Maggie... why didn't you just ring the... Oh... Whose is the rabbit? That's not the one that went...'

'You're running off again, Ben. You use this treatment on Louise? No wonder...'

'I think you'd better come in, Maggie.'

'Hi Louise.'

Louise shuffled herself upright in the bed. 'Is that you, Maggie?'

'No, Louise... it's Attila the... Yes, Louise, of course it's me.'

Very slowly, a white stuffed rabbit began to appear from under the covers. Its black button eyes gleamed in the soft light from the lamp.

'Say hello to Lucy, Maggie.'

'Hi Lucy. I brought you a friend.' Maggie held the rabbit into the light. 'This here's Dandy Rabbit. He's come to make sure that Louise is looking after you properly.' Dandy Rabbit shuffled around on Maggie's lap and sat staring at Lucy.

'What's he doing, Maggie?'

'He's communicating, Louise. It's a rabbit thing.'

'Will they be long? Raymond is coming again today and he might be here soon.'

'They won't be long, Louise. Rabbits never are. They just do it more often to make up for it.'

'Make up for what, Maggie?'

'Shush Louise, they're communicating.'

Louise leaned toward Maggie and whispered, words

hissing from a crudely painted mouth. 'Maggie? Are you my best friend?'

'Sure am, Louise. Wouldn't have it any other way.'

'Will you still be my friend when we go up to High School?'

'What does the Lucy say, Louise?'

Louise held Lucy to her ear and waited a while, smiling crookedly.

'So?'

'Lucy says Dandy is a fine rabbit and can they communicate again?'

'What did she say about me, Louise?'

'She says that you're a friend of the nasty man who puts me in the water and gets soap in my eyes.'

'Did she also say that the nasty man is really helping you and if he didn't, they'd smell you clean across the State?'

'Where is Raymond?'

'Raymond won't come to see you if you smell, honey. He likes really clean women so you got to remember to shout when you need to go.'

'When I shout, that nasty man comes.'

'He's not really nasty, Louise. He just don't know any better. You'll have to teach him what you want.'

'What do I want, Maggie?'

'Same as the rest of us, Louise, a little dignity I guess. It's kind of hard in your case, you let go too early. It's a long way back now.'

'Are we on the bus again, Maggie?'

'Suppose so, Louise, seeing as there's only ever been one bus, but tickets seemed so much cheaper back then…'

On the Bus

**Chicago
Illinois**

1974

The man took a seat in the row in front of them and turned around. His clean-shaven face carried a wide smile over even, white teeth.

'Miss Collins?'

Maggie hadn't been called by that name in an age. Louise looked around to see who he meant. Maggie nudged her.

The man touched the brim of a fedora and nodded.

'Ladies…'

Maggie felt a sudden desire to reach out and stroke the nap of the light grey felt, the way she remembered Ma Collins doing each night Anton Kowalski came home. She also noticed the way his suit jacket took an unusual twist as he leaned into the seat.

'You carrying more than that smile, Mister?'

The man shuffled slightly in the seat until the jacket seams aligned again.

'Something wrong with the smile?'

Louise turned a slight shade of pink. 'Not that I can see, Mister.'

'Miss Burdon. I thank you for the compliment.'

Maggie took a hold of Louise's arm, shaking the willing smile away. 'Sit on it, Louise. This is no social call. Not since last time I went to a dance anyway.'

The man turned a little more so he could address Louise directly.

'Are you a good dancer, Miss Burdon? No, no, don't answer that. I've seen you. You are very good.'

Louise opened her mouth to reply but Maggie clamped her down. 'You been watching us, Mister…?'

Louise tugged her arm free. 'And it ain't no 'Miss' neither. It's Mrs Burdon to you.'

'I know that, Mrs Burdon. I just thought that maybe you didn't want to think that way right now.'

'I'll thank you to let me think whichever way I want to think, even right now.' Louise edged up her seat, one gloved hand gripping the chrome rail along the back of the row in front. 'Especially right now.'

Maggie drew her back into the seat. 'Down girl. Can't you see what he's trying to do? Getting you all wound up like you don't know what?' She sat back against the seat squab. 'Take a hike, Mister.'

Although the smile had never left the man's face, it seemed to Maggie to intensify a little as he spoke.

'No questions before I go?'

'Only one.'

'And what might that be, Miss Collins?'

Maggie pointed in the direction of his hat. 'Is that a Knox?'

'No, Miss Collins. It's a Swann Pastel.'

'Snow Grey, but that's the wrong ribbon. They never did a green.'

The man took off the hat and passed it over.

Maggie rubbed the nap between finger and thumb, turned it upside down then studied the label before passing it back. 'Like I said. Wrong ribbon.'

'And you are something of an expert on fedora hats, Miss Collins.'

Maggie sat back in the seat. 'I wouldn't say that, exactly.'

'No, you didn't say that, Miss Collins. I did.'

'Then why bring an adulterated hat to the expert. What's that make you?'

'It makes me a husband, Miss Collins. This ribbon was in my wife's hair the day we were married.'

'Then why are you coming on to my friend Louise? Especially as it seems you know her problems.'

'I am not 'coming on' to Mrs Burdon, as you so quaintly phrase it. Nor to you, either.'

'Do you no good. No good at all.'

'I am aware of that, Miss Collins. By the way, your stop is coming up.'

Louise began to button her jacket. Maggie grabbed at her briefcase and stood up before the man could. 'You getting off here, too?'

'No, Miss Collins. I'm sorry to disappoint you, but I shall be staying on the bus. I was merely being polite.'

Maggie stood in the aisle and stared him down. 'Does this look like a face that's so easily disappointed?'

'No, Miss Collins. It looks like a face that both has cares and does care.'

'About what?'

'I think we can safely leave that discussion until another time, Miss Collins. Have a good day, Mrs Burdon. You too… Maggie.'

'Who do you think that was, Maggie?'

'Not sure, Louise. What's more important is who he thinks he is… and my fifty cents is on Bogart.'

'I know. Calling you Maggie in that way.'

'And what way was that, Louise?'

'Like he knew you. Like he knew who you was…'

'Oh, he knew me okay, Louise. Who I was… is… and probably will be. Gets under your skin, knowledge like that, especially when you think your tracks are well skeetered over…'

'But he was kind of good-looking…'

'Louise! How long you been a widow-woman?'

'Not long, Maggie, but maybe long enough.'

'What about the guy in the lunch queue?'

'Maybe not long enough for him yet.'

'What's wrong with him?'

'Lilian likes him.'

'Your mother, huh? That's a killer.'

'Yup.'

'Same bus tonight?'

'Don't forget to wait, Maggie.'

'Louise, when I come out of work I can't wait to forget.'

\#

'Miss Kowalski?'

Maggie looked up from her desk, the scrawl she'd been trying to decipher playing havoc with the floaters in her eyes until it settled out and refocused into the squat, iron-haired, barrel-shape that was Szymon Kaminski.

'Yes, Kaminski?'

'There's a gentleman here to see you.'

'Didn't you ask him to wait until lunch? The way you did when my mother was dying and the nurse turned up to find me?'

'Miss Kowalski… do we have to continually reprise my imperfections? I can assure you that yours are of Shakespearean proportion.'

'A Plague on Both Our Houses then, Kaminski. What does he want?'

'I assume he wants you, Miss Kowalski. Though quite why I cannot imagine.'

'Tell me a thing, Kaminski. Is he wearing a hat?'

'Don't most gentlemen these days?'

'When you get home, Kaminski, get the boyfriend to put yours in the fire.'

'Perhaps you could wear it when you spend your Eternity in there, Miss Kowalski.'

'Okay, Kaminski. I'll let you chalk that one on the board. Where are we this week?'

'About even today, I should think.'

'That is my constant, fervent wish, Kaminski.'

'What's that?'

'That one day you should think. Does this guy have a green hatband by any small chance?'

'What if he did, Miss Kowalski? Would that make him Irish?'

'Only by descent, and once you get this far out of New York that's one hell of a drop without a silk.'

Every screen around Maggie was made of glass and if she could have reached through she could have touched another three or four 'secretaries' easily, but they all had their shoulders hunched and were head down into their transcriptions. Once Kaminski left they might ease up a little, but not while he was in full view.

'You have an empty office I can use, Kaminski? One where I don't feel like a force-fed goose?'

'There's only mine, as you know.'

'Guess that'll do, then.'

'Miss Kowalski, if I allowed myself, I would be aghast at your presumption.'

'Would that be a first?'

'Hell no, Miss Kowalski. But I could make it a last.'

'Then give me the key and show him in.'

'The key?'

'You never know. Might want some privacy.'

'That would be novel.'

'Go chalk it up, Kaminsky. But give me the key first.'

'Okay, feller. Go for it.'

The man took off his hat and smiled as he passed it across the desk to Maggie.

She slid it straight back. 'You knew Ma Collins.'

The man smiled and nodded in assent. 'Anton Kowalski first, but yes... later on I met your mother. Beautiful woman, despite all...'

'Well... I ain't her, Mister. I ain't so easily charmed, even if Anton wasn't worth every last bead of sweat she ever possessed and that smile's no weapon... leastways not against me. You ever look at anybody without that smile? You some kind of a walking cliché?'

'If I was, Maggie, you'd soon pull the rug out. That about right?'

'Damn right, Mister. What do you want from me?'

'Access, Maggie.'

'And damn you, stop calling me 'Maggie'. We ain't been introduced.'

'Alright, Miss Collins.'

'And damn you for that too. You know I changed it.'

'Correct, Miss Kowalski. And I know why you changed it. And I also know why you left Pennsylvania in a hurry.'

'You do, huh? Okay. Access to what? You know what I can do so why are you asking. You guys usually take whatever you want and threaten to lock me away.'

'You guys?'

'Yeah. You guys. The ones with the lumpy jackets. You

forget where I've been.'

'It's not like that, Mag... Miss Kowalski.'

'Maggie... damn you. Sounds like we got to get acquainted anyway.'

The man opened the button of his single-breasted jacket and peeled back the wide lapel. The only thing beneath it were suspenders over a shirt with a blue feint stripe and a white stud collar. His waist was so slender the shirt and waistband seemed shy of one another where they tucked, giving him a sort of rushed appearance.

'Your wife still around?'

'I'm afraid not... Maggie.'

'You looking for a new one?'

'Are you offering?'

'Hell no.'

'That's alright then.'

Maggie leaned way back in Kaminski's office chair. 'So if it's not my body you want, what's this access you got set on?'

'I want access to your mind, Maggie.'

'What's so special about that you can't get at the corner store?'

'It has a way of seeing that's... well... there is no scale, but maybe it's at ninety degrees to the rest of us. You see things we don't. All you got to do is learn how to handle that better.'

'And you can teach me?'

'I can try.'

'Is that all? I swap one Kaminski for another? Only with better taste in headgear?'

'I need access to something else, too, Maggie.'

'So what's the other? My spare underwear? You want to dress better?'

'This one might not be as easy as that, Maggie.'

'What can be harder than getting into my underwear?'

'I need access to Louise.'

#

'Oh, Maggie. There you are. I thought we were going to miss it.'

'And you'd have been right, Louise. We are going to miss it.'

'No we're not, Maggie. The bus has just come around the corner.'

'Louise. Do you still drink coffee?'

'Not after two o'clock, Maggie. Keeps me awake all night.'

'Then I hope you got a good book to read.'

'I got the latest Raymond Carver from the Library only yesterday when…'

Maggie took Louise by the arm and dragged her firmly through the traffic to the other side of the way. 'I'm sure he'll do you fine, Louise.'

She looked up and down the block for a coffee shop and drew a blank. 'You hungry?'

'Don't know for sure, Maggie. What is this?'

'Just answer the question, Louise.'

'Well… I suppose so.'

'Have you got a man to go home and feed?'

'You know fine well I haven't, Maggie. What's this all about?'

'One more, Louise. Do you like Chop Suey?'

'Who doesn't, but…'

Louise found herself dragged up the stairs behind the Chinese Deli. Maggie pushed her into a booth by the window and sat down opposite. The bulbs from the sign outside flicked on and off periodically, casting a sometime glow in Louise's eyes as she stared widely at Maggie.

'Maggie Kowalski! What's occurring here? I've never known you eat Chinese food. You always said it was dirty.'

'Maybe that's just another of today's lessons.'

'Don't tell me Kaminski's fired you... again.'

'Huh. He'd call around for me again tomorrow in that new car of his. Hey, you remember the old one he had with the gearshift that was always right by your knee?'

'You been in that car, Maggie?'

'The once. We went over the line to fetch some papers they didn't trust the mailman with. He got out of the car and trashed his ankle in a grid. I had to bring it back.'

'How did you get it back?'

'I drove it, Louise. What do you think I did?'

'Without a license? I know you don't have one.'

'It needed a new gearbox too by the time we got back. I can make a new license anytime.'

'Did you make one?'

'Sure I did. Not that we got stopped or anything... but I saved it just in case...you know... and Kaminski traded the car in for an automatic. That stopped his excuse in its tracks too.'

The waiter came and took their order and Louise turned in her seat so the bulbs on the sign outside the window were a little less direct.

'What are we doing here, Maggie?'

'Reflecting a little, Louise. That's all.'

'You got a problem, Maggie?'

'I never been short of those in my life, Mój skarbie.'

'What's that you called me? You dredge up these sayings from your past and I never know wha...'

'I just been given a lesson in misplaced patriotism, Louise. Or maybe it was about friendship... or both. And I called you 'my treasure' in Polish, for your satisfaction and reassurance.'

'Does this have something to do with the man on the bus this morning?'

'No, Louise. It has everything to do with the man on the bus this morning.'

Maggie's Chop Suey was cooling rapidly on the plate. Louise watched her twirl the chopsticks again and again amongst the noodles to little effect.

'If you ask them, Maggie, they'll get you a fork.'

'It's not a fork I need, Louise. It's an appetite.'

'You got the acid again, Maggie?'

'Only when I speak, it seems, these days.'

'So talk to me then. I'm kind of immune to it. I hate it when you're quiet like this and thinking... you know... inside. I never know what's coming out next.'

'You think I do? You want to see this mess from inside? You want to know what life looks like only when you see it happen to other people?'

'I love you, Maggie, and don't...' Louise put out a hand to touch Maggie's where it swirled noodles around the plate.

Maggie looked up into Louise's eyes, seeing the light-flicker from the sign intensified now the room itself was turning dark. 'I know you do, my...'

Louise removed her hand abruptly. '...and don't call me anything Polish. It's not appropriate and it's too much like being at work.'

'Work is something we need to talk about, Louise.'

'You know we're not supposed to do that, Maggie. That's why we're in different buildings.'

'What would you think if we could work together?'

'How could we do that, Maggie, without... you know... compromising?'

'Seems it's easier than you think, Louise. You see... I just been made an offer that you can't refuse.'

The Oppenheimer Option

Homeland Security
Chicago
Illinois

1980

'How is it that I can see where these things fit, Maggie?'

'It's about mind, Louise. Mind. Hang on tight to yours and push these things around in it until it fits with what we're doing.'

'But I'm tired, Maggie. I go home and I…'

'There'll be plenty of time to relax once this here war is over, Louise. Until then, take the stress and ride the adrenalin for all it's worth. It's what makes sure you still got a home to go to.'

'This is some kind of a war, Maggie. I can't handle the responsibility for it. How can I hold up that much weight when I'm this tired? Can't I go back to being just another secretary?'

'Sure you can, Louise. But you never were 'just another secretary' and just imagine what would happen if we gave Ivan time to get his act together.'

'I tell myself that all the time, Maggie but I… I think it's the… the not being able to tell anyone. Not being able to share it all with someone close, I can feel the… I don't know… maybe the dishonesty of it all.

'In the immortal words of Sonny Bono… 'I Got You

Babe'.'

'I know that, Maggie. But who's got me?'

'Look out that window, Louise... no... don't you glance out there at the sky like you were wishing for snow... look down there... on the street... see all those people? Do you think they'd be any happier if they knew what we know?'

'I... I guess not.'

'Count the people in that bus queue, Louise. Go on. Count them.'

'Looks like there's twenty-three or so...

'Now multiply the way you feel by twenty-three. Can you imagine the weight of that? No, you can't. Now multiply that by a Nation and you can't do that either. So who's right here, Louise? Is it better that you and me hurt and do what we can, or watch a Nation sink under all that weight? If you want to know what you're worth, get out a pencil and start calculating.'

'Is that supposed to make me feel better?'

'Hell, no, Louise. I'm only supplying bandages. Wrap 'em around your soul wherever you think fit.'

'Where do you wrap yours, Maggie?'

'What makes you think I'm wearing any? I have to expose my soul to a transcription before I can decipher intent. Yours is the easy job so why the hell you need the bandage I don't know.'

'I have to get inside of these people, Maggie. I have to wade deep into their thoughts and personalities in order to recognize them from your scraps of radio and phone calls and tell you who said what to who and where to find the links between them.'

'Yours is a gift, Louise. God-given to save us from the bad men.'

'Where did Oppenheimer fit into that?'

'He fitted into a world that left him no option but to

make what he did.'

'How do you think he coped with that?'

Maggie lifted a clear bottle out of the bag by her feet and put it on the table between them.

'Probably the same way I do.'

Louise picked up the bottle, trying to decipher the Cyrillic script on the label.

'What is it?'

'One hundred percent Imported Rocket Fuel, Louise. You let it down with a shot of Earl Grey. It's how Anton Kowalski got to sleep nights.'

'Do you think Oppenheimer used it?'

'Had to, Louise. It's the only thing clears the shit out of your brain. Every morning's a brand new day. Even if it hurts.'

'But what if he hadn't?'

'You'd be speaking German, Louise. Just like me. Or Japanese, even.'

'And Polish, Russian, Hebrew…?'

'That's my trick, Louise. You just keep making sense of joining up my scraps and when it hurts, I'll look after you.'

'But it hurts so much, Maggie.'

'It'll all stop one day. It'll feel like leaving Pennsylvania in a rush…'

'With or without the threat of Probation?'

'I never wrote checks, Louise. You know that. I never made that kind of money.'

'But Food Stamps, Maggie. I mean…'

'Yeah. Food Stamps. It was the paper supply let me down. Only way they could tell. Should've stopped right there.'

'Why didn't you?'

'I was surrounded, Louise.'

'Is that how they caught you?'

'Hell no. Well yes. I was surrounded by the legitimately hungry, except they were non-registered… and you know the government won't call them citizens. Guess you were pretty much protected from it, having a government job an' all. The rest of us had Nixon slave to everything that Keynes ever wrote, an economy tanking fast and the rich sitting on a pile of dollars riding up the interest rates to wait for better times, and though it never is, that wasn't any good time to be an illegal. They had nothing. So I gave the stamps away. I was working. They couldn't. Even when they wanted to. It seemed more than fair.'

'Seems more like a gift, Maggie.'

'I have another gift too, Louise, I'm an anarchist, and between your insight and my hand we can bend these bozos into any shape we want, so long as it's a harmless one. And not just the other side… we can bend our side too. Stick around and watch. When we really get going they won't know their asshole from breakfast time.'

'Don't be so crude, Maggie. Tiredness aside, I know all these things … but there are other things I need to share… things you don't seem to need so much. Instead of feeling some spook's personality crawling over my skin I want to feel the touch of a hand that I know wants to touch me… one that I want to touch me… that cares about me all the time.'

'I care about you all the time, Louise. You know that.'

'But you're not there when I get home. Your car isn't in the drive with the hood still warm from dashing just to see me. I need another hand to wash away all these bad thoughts. I need to be cleansed, Maggie, in ways the shower can't reach.'

'Don't go getting religious on me, Louise. I can do many things most times, but I can't do that. And you know there are some things you can never share, don't you?'

Louise nodded uncertainly. 'That's where it hurts most, Maggie. I know what I can do but I can never tell anyone else about it. I can never see that look of appreciation lit up in their eyes.'

'You want to be famous, Louise?'

'No. I want to be ordinary… and appreciated for that.'

'Then get what you can while you can, girl. That guy in the lunch queue. He still around?'

'I don't know, Maggie. I haven't been back in that old building for a couple of years now. Somebody will have snapped him up.'

'What if their mother liked him, too? He might still be around. What was his name?'

'Ben.'

'You still got your lunch pass?'

Louise rummaged through her purse. 'I guess I have. Don't remember throwing it.'

Maggie sifted through the growing pile on the desk and picked it out. She waved it in the air in front of Louise.

'Then guess where we're eating today…'

Bill Allerton

Chopsticks

1985

'I need a favor.'

The fedora in the new style was narrower at the brim, mid-brown, and although Maggie had a problem with the shape... which she felt somehow less comfortable, less enticing to the fingers because now the nap was shorter, stiffer and brush-like... the same green ribbon with the pressed bow still held the base of the crown. Before he sat down, he took off the hat and placed it on the desk between them.

'That the same ribbon?'

'Of course it is, Maggie. Why would I change it?'

'Then it's no good me asking you about moving on anytime soon.'

'How do you want to move, Maggie?'

Maggie hesitated a moment, then buried her face in her hands. 'Pawn to King 3, I think.'

'That's Checkmate, Maggie. Means you're going nowhere. Not just yet, anyways.'

'Why's that?'

'Because you still need to untangle some of the knots you got me in.'

'I only practice on you, Johnson. Just imagine the knots

the other guy's in already.'

'Your saving grace, Maggie. It's what's keeping you out of the chokey.'

'When was that?'

'Most days. So what's the favor?'

'It's one you need to repay, and not before time too. This time I want access to Louise.'

'You know I can't…'

'You know you can. You just don't want to.'

'How honest do you want me to be here, Maggie?'

'Would you know if it bit you?'

'After working with you since I moved Louise on, I guess not. That's when you really left the rails.'

'Then why am I still here?'

'Because by the time I filter out the crap and your wilder flights of imagination, there's still value in there if I take the time to find it. Only recompense is that Ivan must wonder what the hell is going on with his own communications.'

'Louise.'

'I can't.'

'The Hell you can't.'

'What I can do is ask.'

'Then be like the rest of us, Johnson. Do what you can.'

He stood up and brushed the desk dust from the underside of the fedora brim before adjusting it on his head. He glanced once at the mirror on the wall and nodded to himself.

'Maggie…?'

'What?'

'Think you done enough yet?'

'Is there anybody left we haven't damaged already?'

'The Chinese are coming up on the rails.'

'That's somebody else's life you can ruin. I don't have the language for that one. Give me a couple more years then I'll go.'

'That's too soon for your pension, Maggie.'

'That's my second favor. Get on it unless you want I should write my own.'

#

Louise had shuffled a few pans out of the cupboard onto the stove ready for an evening meal when there came a loud knock at the door. She answered it and stepped back sharply.

'Maggie Kowalski! How'd you find me here?'

'You're looking good too, Louise. And as healthy as you forgot to ask me if I was.'

'I'm sorry, Maggie. It's such a shock. I got a letter last week but I was thinking how to reply.'

'What would you have said?'

'Well... now you're here... I don't know how I should answer that.'

'Carefully, Louise. Carefully.'

'Maggie. I'm not sure...'

'Do you still like Chop Suey?'

'I guess...'

'Then get your hat and coat. It's my treat. The bus is due back any time now.'

'We don't need the bus, Maggie.'

'What? You cook noodles yourself now? That's a new one. How long did it take to progress from egg-boiling?'

'Maggie... I have a car... it's around back. Ben bought me my own car. I can't see how we can afford it, but he did.'

'And your next question is... what do I think about that?'

'Why should you... what I mean is... what difference...'

'Has it got gas?'

'Yes, plenty.'

'Is it good to go?'

'Well, yes, but I have to leave a note for Ben.' Louise flipped a pad beside the telephone and began to write.

Maggie shuffled her feet on the doormat in impatience.

'While you're telling him the dinner's in the dog, tell him you just ran off with the Ghost of Occupation Past.'

'That what you've become, Maggie? A Ghost?'

'Not yet. But it's what I intend to be as soon as I can figure some things out.'

'Like what?'

'Like how to use chopsticks.'

'You haven't managed that yet after all this time?'

'I just graduated in shoelaces. I'm working on buttons right now.'

'I think you're up there on that one, Maggie. You always knew how to push mine.'

#

'What are we waiting for, Maggie?'

'That there booth.'

'Which one? The place is empty.'

'You know damn fine which one, Louise. Just wait here a minute.'

Maggie walked over to the couple in the booth by the window.

The woman was young, preening a little, fingers filtering her hair, watching the man's lips and hoping to hear a little truth to hang the day on. He was older, a little more rigid, under control in the way he fitted neatly into the arc of shade that side of the table.

Married, at a guess, Maggie thought. But not to her. For certain.

The woman flicked a glance at Maggie standing there then looked away to the man. He stared at Maggie for a short time, taking in the lack of style and co-ordination, so unlike the younger woman she had walked in with. He looked up and across at Louise. He could see a thing in there, right in back of her eyes. She was dressed, blonde-haired and handsome, older and less impressionable yet less confident somehow than his date. Worth a smile, maybe. On another day.

Maggie leaned over to whisper to the young woman then walked back to Louise.

The young woman signaled the waiter for the check. She paid in cash straight out of her purse and stood to leave. She hid her expression from Maggie as they walked past.

'There you go, Louise. Set down right there. Does this bring back a memory?'

Louise slid into the warm booth seat and settled back. The light bulbs outside the window shook as a bus passed on the street beneath. The floor seemed to tremble slightly, but Louise couldn't make out if that was just herself.

'I guess so, Maggie. What on earth did you say to her?'

'I just asked if she knew that shade of makeup turned bright green in this light. And I told her it happens to his wife, too, whenever he brings her in here.'

'Am I green now?'

'Only by inclination, Louise. Some things never change.'

'What is it you want, Maggie? I thought you sucked everything right out of me before I left.'

'You didn't leave, Louise. You were moved on. If it hadn't been making you ill you would've still been in there with me, bending the world. I know, I know… it was the weight. You think it's been any easier on my own?'

'They not give you anybody?'

'For sure they did. I wore out three or four. None of

them had your stamina, Louise. Kids today. They thrive on misinformation, psychedelic drugs and fake news so much they don't ever see it for what it is. If their friends say it's the truth they think it's beyond manipulation.'

'I lost sight of it myself, Maggie. Still don't know if I got all the truths back in my life.'

'You got Ben.'

Louise leaned up and placed both elbows on the table.

'That's true…'

'Maybe that's all the truth you need.'

'If only I could shake off this conscience, Maggie.'

'You tried for kids? They shake the shit out of anybody.'

'Doctor said I was too old.'

'You are not too old, Louise. What kind of a doctor was that?'

'The kind that says all my eggs dried up, like I was an old woman.'

'Do you feel like an old woman?'

'Only when I stop to think about it, then the weight starts to come down.'

'And I guess me turning up is not helping.'

Louise lowered her hands across the table towards Maggie.

'I wouldn't say that, Maggie.'

Maggie turned to stare out the window at the traffic below and the bird deflectors on the sill right outside the glass.

'What would you say, Louise?'

'I would say that when you're around I feel sort of complete… and… and it feels like that weight gets more… shared out between us. Only you carry your share more easily than I do.'

'Appearances, Louise. It may only appear that way.' She turned away from the movement outside to stare into the empty well of Louise's eyes. 'Isn't Ben doing it for you?'

Louise withdrew her hands and hid them in her lap. 'Ben is wonderful.'

'Oh yeah? What did he do about the infertility problem?'

'He bought me a stuffed rabbit. She's real cute.'

'Some response. Sure you did the right thing with him?'

'Ben would kiss the ground I walk on and I make fine and sure that he never thinks I feel anyway different from the way he does. But does that make me complete? I don't know. Maybe I can never be complete after the things we did. Maybe life is such an anti-climax that I can't ride all the way back. I don't know, Maggie, and I think that's where the real weight is. The not knowing. Especially when you're not around.'

'And when I'm here it helps you to know? Is that it?'

Louise raised a slow smile. 'Heck no, Maggie. It just reminds me that there's someone around who's more complex, compromised and cussed than I am. And someone who hurts more and never complains about it the way I do.'

'What do you know about my pain, Louise?'

'I know that you know about pain, Magdalena Kowalski Collins.'

'Did I ever tell you what my real name was, Louise?'

'Do you know yourself? For real, I mean? Long as I known you, you was either Collins or Kowalski.'

'Before either of those, Louise.'

'There was a before?'

'What you think I came out of, Louise? An egg?'

'Only if it was scrambled, Maggie.'

Maggie was silent for a moment.

'What's the matter, Maggie? I offended you?'

'Hell no. I never contradict anyone who's right.'

'So what was it?'

Maggie took the bottle of Vodka from her bag, placed it

on the table between them, signaled the waiter for two glasses and sat back into the shade of the booth seat.

'Listen, Louise. I've been many things in many places. Some of them felt right and some of them felt so wrong it didn't make sense. I keep running them back like I'm looking for a memory of I don't know what and never finding it.'

'What did you find?'

'It's all a bit grey out there, Louise. I can chase my own paperwork back through Adoption, Schools and such... then I hit a dead end.'

'Maybe you're looking for something that doesn't exist?'

'Then that makes me the Ghost you accused me of being.'

Louise pushed back the glass that Maggie handed her. 'I'm driving. And it was you that said...'

Maggie downed the glass in one shot and poured herself another.

'Louise... you ever visit your own grave?'

Terms of Endearment

1987

'Johnson…'

'You call me that after all these years?'

'It's the nearest to a term of endearment you're likely to get.'

'You ever hear from Louise?'

'Went back to see her again and she'd moved away. When I asked around, seems no-one noticed them go and I can smell you all over this.'

'Was your observation did it, Maggie.'

'I don't believe that… and take that hat off. You're in the presence of a lady and if you look around to see who that is I'll steal your wallet.'

The new fedora floated like pale ash against the dark wood of Maggie's desk as if a misplaced breath could sweep it over the edge.

'When you going to give up on that ribbon?'

'Sometime, Maggie. Sometime.'

'That's some lonely ribbon.'

'And you would know, Maggie?'

'No shit, Sherlock. Least you could do is tell me where Louise went.'

'Didn't want you to know, Maggie. Said she needed more time to work her way back to reality. Seems you were too much of a distraction to let that happen.'

'I only went to see her the once.'

'That was enough.'

'So where is she, Johnson?'

He stood up and fitted the hat to the shape it had recently pressed in his dark grey hair.

'Piece at a time, Maggie. Piece at a time.'

'Know what you are, Johnson?'

'No, but I guess you do, Maggie.'

'You're an Advent Calendar that someone has stolen the treats out of.'

'One day, Maggie Kowalski, you too will be glad of a little empty space.'

The door closed softly behind him.

#

The phone on the board outside Maggie's apartment was ringing as she hurried along the corridor towards the warmth inside her own four walls. She kicked the remaining snow off her boots and walked past at first, tired of wrong numbers and her neighbor using her as a dating agency, then returned to pick up the call.

'What you want?'

'Maggie?'

'Yeah. Who is this?'

'Louise…'

'Louise? That really you? How'd you get this number?'

'You gave it me, Maggie. When you were over last.'

Maggie mulled that over for a second. 'Nah, I didn't. But I know a man who could convince you that I did. So… how are things out there in the sticks?'

'I need some help, Maggie, and I couldn't think of anyone else to...'

Maggie reacted instantly to the growing panic in Louise's voice. 'Louise? You need money? Something happen to Ben?'

'No... I think something's happening to me. Can you come over?'

'Right away. But you better tell me where 'over' is, first.'

'You don't know? I thought you knew and just didn't want...'

'I had nothing, Louise. No number. No address. Guess now you know why I call him 'Johnson'.'

Maggie dropped her shopping to the floor and rummaged in her purse for a pencil. 'Here, let me write this on the wall, hold on... okay, fire away... What? Is that in Illinois? Okay. Maybe the place is not so strange, just the folks.'

'When can you come over, Maggie?'

'What's the problem, Louise?'

'I wake up some days and know what the problem is, then next day I can't remember at all what I was thinking.'

'Have you told Ben this?'

'I'm not sure, Maggie. Maybe I have but he hasn't listened. He hasn't said anything I can recall.'

'You seen anybody about this?'

'I'm too scared, Maggie.'

'So am I when the vodka wears off.'

'When can you come over?'

'Soon as I can, Louise, soon as I can... but I have a score to settle first.'

#

Maggie stormed through the door and planted two

hands on the bare desktop. The hat stand in the corner shook under the stomp of her boots. The hat twitched but hung on.

'There any bones in your soul, Johnson?'

'Not from the look on your face, Maggie. But I do got soul in my very bones.'

'Then why did you keep me and Louise apart like that, lying to us both.'

'I thought it best. It was my decision so don't bother flying over my head with this.'

'What gives you the right...'

'Do you always second-guess the doctor?'

'You bet I do.'

'Set down, Maggie.'

Maggie drew up the chair from the corner with one foot and sat heavily on the carved wood seat.

'I'm not buyin'.'

'What aren't you buyin', Maggie?'

'Look here, Johnson, you already got everything except my ass... and you ain't getting that in a hurry.'

'Sorry to disillusion you, Miss Kowalski, but your ass has been mine since that day on the bus.'

'Then it's time you paid for it.'

'What's that going to cost me, Maggie? An Eternity in Purgatory?'

'You're there already. Been locked in since I met you. Just look here...'

Maggie pointed to the hat on the stand. Around the crown was a new red ribbon.

'I...I...'

'Yes, Maggie?'

'She good for you?'

'Absolutely.'

'She know about me?'

'Only what she needs to.'

'What'd she say to that?'

'She now calls me 'Johnson'.'

'Hope for her, then. Now what about my pension. I have two years to go before…'

'It's sorted, Maggie. You ready to disappear? Go when you want and I'll make it work. There's a house coming up later this year next door to Louise. You like the sound of that?'

'Louise is the only family I got but… Chain O'Lakes? This one of your safe houses?'

'Quiet area stock. We take a few off plan so we can manage our assets.'

'So who's the asset being managed?'

'Field guy. Spent two years monitoring Ivan's nuclear generation.'

'Where you moving him to?'

'The cemetery. Leukemia.'

'Sounds like dead man's shoes to me.'

'Talk to Louise about it.'

'I will, thanks… Jacob.'

#

'Where's the car, Louise?'

'I gave it up. Couldn't make the exit from the Mall one day and Ben had to come get me.'

'What did he make of that? Didn't he say anything? Ring the Doctor maybe?'

'I think he smiled and held my hand for a minute. Then I followed his car all the way home.'

'That was it?'

'What do you think he should have done?'

'Hellfire Louise, I don't know. Except I would have had

the Surgeon General around to take a look at you.'

'Someone did come... once.'

'What did they say? Don't hold back on me now.'

'I think they were from work, Maggie. Ben just listened and smiled but I can't recall what it was they said. Anyway... life got a bit easier after that. Ben went to the Mall and cooked. I got to put my feet up for a while.'

'When was the last time you went out anywhere, Louise?'

'I'm not sure, Maggie. Maybe it was to the Mall. Ben took me to the theater one time but I don't know if that was before or after. Don't need to go out so much and we spend a lot of time looking at old photos. Wish you were in some of them, Maggie.'

'Do you ever think about work, Louise?'

'I only remember you were always right. Were you ever wrong, Maggie?'

'How would I know? Ivan never rang to correct me.'

'What if they had?'

'Well, Louise, I guess that's what put the final cherry on my cake. Those wisps of information dried up like fresh rain on a sunny street.'

'What did you put that down to?'

'Easy. They got their own Maggie. Wonder what her name was?'

'Couldn't you have disguised yourself better?'

'The old telegraph operators didn't need to be told who was sending. They knew. Sometimes it was no more than an empty space between certain letters, or a repeatedly mis-spelt word, a period forever in the wrong place. It didn't take them long to figure it out.'

'Do you think their Maggie was as weird as ours?'

'Sure I do, Louise. Besides... I sort of got to like her. We had something of a competition going.'

'Did you move that up the line?'

'What? To that Johnson?'

'Do you have to call him that, Maggie? You know I know what it means and he's been very kind to us. He got Ben that job at the University when the others in line were better qualified.'

'Does Ben know that?'

'Don't you tell him, Maggie. It would destroy him.'

'I wouldn't do that, Louise.'

'I'm not sure about that.'

'I am, Mój skarbie. It would destroy you, too.'

Crusaders

**Spring Grove
Chain O'Lakes
Illinois**

2018

'Okay, Maybelline, I'm coming.' Maggie went to open the porch door, then stopped. She could see through the broken screen that this wasn't Maybelline. 'What do you want?'

The man on the porch remained silent but knocked again.

Maggie pushed the bolt home. 'Go away. We don't want any.'

The fold he held up to the screen looked to Maggie like some kind of ID but it was impossible to read through the mesh. She took a step towards the wall phone.

'You better leave. I'm calling Officer Gradzynski… right now.'

When she looked again, the man was still there.

#

Shirley's room above the station house was only temporary, she kept telling herself, although where else she could afford to live she really had no clue. She dragged out a box from under the bed and sorted clumsily through her shoes. The red ones would do. Just enough scuff to say 'shabby chic' and their once expensive profile still showing through. The jeans over the chair back were newer and thankfully tight enough not to need ironing. Two tee shirts, one long, one short with the hole in, and the faded denim over the top. In front of the mirror she let go her hair from the rubber band and allowed it to fall where it would.

Her old Toyota creaked into life at the third try. If she could ever get together enough cash that was the first thing she'd ditch. Then head for the shoe shop. She rarely took days off but Pawel had insisted. Had things to do today on his own, he said. He should know she'd keep a secret, but he seemed to have had more than a few of those these last few weeks. She shifted the gears without thinking, then her autopilot kicked in and took her away from the station down a familiar beat. Doing this kept her sane, and if they didn't want to pay her... well. Right now it was all the purpose she had.

Huron was quiet, as was most of the estate... suicidal old women only seemed to come out at weekends and evenings... so she cruised the houses, eyes searching the dead-ends for abandoned vehicles. She spotted a blue light in a bedroom and slowed to a crawl... no sign of anything else. She stopped and got out, walked around the back of the house to where two rattan chairs sat in the grass, one new and one faded old thing long past its best. What was that name now? The insurance scammer... Watson... Maybelline... like something from an old movie. She tried the door. Fast. Same as the windows. The blue light above her flickered brightly then went out. Then she heard a kettle being filled. She walked back to her car. Folks are not in trouble when they're making tea. That ricocheted her thoughts back to Pawel's 'friend', the drunk-driver. She drove a little way up the street to park behind a blacked-out SUV. The moment she opened the car she heard the commotion.

The neighbor was out in his yard peering over the fence.

'Anything I can do?'

'Ring 911 for backup.'

Ben disappeared inside. Shirley skirted around the porch, trying to see in the windows. From inside came a high-pitched scream. Who the hell had Maggie got in there? She heard a man's voice, then furniture being thrown. Someone cried out in pain and Shirley couldn't wait for backup. She shouldered the screen door and fell through into the sitting room.

Maggie was in her chair by the fire with a man bent over her, violence in his raised hands. Shirley's foot caught him in the crotch from behind, collapsing him into the hearth. Another was holding tight to a young girl and a small child who were screaming. A third came in from the kitchen and launched himself at her. Half-turning, she spun on one foot and lifted her leg high, taking him cleanly in the throat. The shoe stayed there. His full weight dropped across her legs, pinning her down. She turned her head in time to see a man burst out through the door with the girl and child. She scrambled up and kicked off her other shoe. Barefoot, she leapt out the door and set off after him.

Down by the road he threw the girl and child into the SUV, pushing them hard along the seat. Shirley could see the girl struggling with the door handle at the other side but it was locked. The SUV crashed into gear and lurched away from the curb.

Shirley threw herself at the open side window. Her fingers reached in and grabbed the man's ear, trying to make their way around to his eyes. One finger caught the side of an orbit as she was dragged into the roadway. She dug her nail in hard until his eyeball crushed. The man screamed in pain and accelerated, dragging Shirley along the road, her arm trapped in the window he was closing. It locked above her elbow and kept on grinding up the pressure. Shirley bounced the blacktop once with her feet and swung her legs up to grip the roof rail. Her arm twisted out of socket as her heel hooked on but wherever they went, she was going too.

She didn't see the street light he steered her into.

The man in the hearth dragged himself out of the glowing ashes and grabbed at the man on the floor. 'Ephraim? Ephraim?' He turned him over and could see that Ephraim was going nowhere. A red stiletto shoe penetrated his throat. There was blood soaking his shirt and pooling underneath him. His eyes looked kind of surprised. Maybe he was seeing angels. It would be a kindness to leave him be. Jacket burned through and smoking, he staggered back to the door holding his crotch... straight into the muzzle of Gradzynski's .45.

#

'So what we got here, Doc?

'Get enough customers through here, Pav, without our own caped crusader.'

'She wasn't caped though, Doc. If she had been it wouldn't be so much of a problem.'

'Off duty?'

'Off her head, more like.'

'Still...' Doc turned Shirley's face with a gentle hand. 'Was a good-looking head...'

'Doc... don't...' Gradzynski turned away, then stopped,

took out his cell phone and took a picture.

Doc ushered him into a room over the corridor and drew back a shroud. 'How old would you say this guy was? Forty-five or so?' The man's skin was marbled faintly blue-white in a way that Gradzynski had seen all too often. 'I guess. Big man, though. Take a look at that jaw.'

Doc held up a clear plastic bag with Shirley's shoe in it. 'And she managed to take him out with one kick of this...'

'Good job she did, Doc. Would've snapped her like a twig otherwise. Anything more than that?'

'Only this...' Across the man's shoulder was a tattoo, little more than a poorly drawn scrawl of a sun, with rays tracking raggedly down towards his heart. 'What about the guy you have banged up? He saying anything?'

'Not a thing, Doc. Just groans when we move him. Refuses to talk.'

'Maybe I should take a look at him. Give him a local or something.'

'Shirley already gave him something. And if you take away the pain after what they did to her, I might just do something to you.'

'It's my job...'

'Doc, go take a leak. Where's Maggie?'

'Pav, there's some things you need to know about Maggie.'

'There's a million things I need to know about Maggie.' Gradzynski took a picture of the man's tattoo with his phone. 'But maybe she can shed some light on this.'

'Pav. She's had a stroke. She may not remember things the way...'

'Listen, Doc. If Maggie has half a brain left it's still sharper than yours and mine together. Never met a woman with so much edge.'

'Okay. Wait here, I'll see if she's awake.'

Gradzynski took the time to go back across the way to where Shirley lay covered on the bed.

A nurse followed him in and closed the door behind them. 'Got to keep it warm in here.'

Gradzynski spun around. He'd been too absorbed by the injuries to Shirley's face to notice he was no longer alone. 'What you say?'

'Heat. A great healer. A body doesn't have to work so hard when it's warm. Blood flow...'

'I thought...'

'You thought what?' She took his hand and placed his fingers against Shirley's throat. 'That what you thought?'

'No.'

'It's an induced coma. Stops her worrying about the mess she's in.'

'The mess...?'

'You don't want to know.'

The door behind them swung open slowly. 'Pav? Maggie's awake and wants to see you.'

The nurse let his hand slide out from under hers. 'Don't worry. I'm here until she's readied for surgery.'

'Gradzynski! Never thought I'd be glad to see you after you let me down.'

'Is this you, Maggie, or the stroke I'm talking to?'

The doctor took the chair over the other side of the bed. 'Maggie's stroke was a few weeks ago, Pav. It happened when she was in my car. I've been treating her off the record ever since.'

'Is that ethical?'

'It's the only way she'll let me near her.'

Maggie hitched herself up in the bed. 'Look at you two. One spends all night with me alone and never lays a finger... Can you hear that Doc? Is it me needs the meds or him?

Look at me. How irresistible am I? And the other one drives a car fit to give me a stroke! What kind of men we got around here? Don't talk to me about ethical.'

Gradzynski fumbled in his pocket for his phone. 'I think this is where I came in… but while I'm here anyway… take a look at this, Maggie. Make any sense to you?'

Maggie's face paled and she slid down into the sheets. 'Oh Jesus. Not them, please. Where's Æppel?'

Gradzynski shook his head. 'Who is it, Maggie?'

'Find Leroy. Find the yellow truck. He'll be out working with his Pa. What time is it?' Maggie began to slide out of the bed.

The doctor pushed her legs back under the sheets. 'You're going nowhere, Maggie.'

'And you two? Look at you…'

Gradzynski put away the phone. 'Give us a chance to show you what kind of men we got around here, Maggie.'

Maggie sank back, exhausted. 'Okay. Give me a pen.' She took Gradzynski's pen while he held tight to the notebook. 'Here… this is where you'll find him. Go easy on him, Pawel. He's a good boy. A good boy. Know what I mean?'

'Could be he's one of a kind around here then, Maggie.'

'No. You're all good old boys. Doc? Can you get me some tea?'

'I'll ask the nurse.'

'No… don't bother the nurse. While you're doin' nothing look up Maybelline Watson and ask her to bring some. She'll know what you mean.'

Gradzynski tapped the address into his phone. 'Maggie? This farm… it's out of state… round by Twin Lakes, Wisconsin.'

'Gradzynski. Go fetch the boy.'

On the way out, Doc grabbed his sleeve. 'While we're sharing photographs Pav, tell me what you make of this one.' He thumbed the screen and held it up to Gradzynski.

'What is it?'

'It's Maggie. Well... her arm anyway. Took it while she was out of it for a while.'

'Yeah. But what is it?'

'It's a tattoo.'

'I can see that, Doc. What's it for?'

'It's her camp registration. Faded now. Must have been a child when it was done.'

'Who would do that to a child?'

Doc just stared at him.

In the bottom of Maggie's old biscuit barrel was Sam's battered hip flask. 'What's it doin' under there, Maybee?'

'I had to smuggle it through Security.'

'Where you think this is? O'Hare?'

'Well, Maggie... I thought perhaps...'

'You thought what? They might frisk you?'

'Well...'

'Don't let go that thought, Maybelline. The body search is on the way out...'

#

Gradzynski picked his way amongst the broken concrete slabs of West Main until he reached the drive that led into the farmyard. The flatbed was tucked behind a long, low shed. He parked alongside and got out the car. The heat was different here. There was a moisture in the air from the nearby lakes that belied the dust under his feet. Parallel rows of brown, tilled earth stretched out into the short distance.

'Hello!' He cupped his hands to shout again as a black man came out of the shed door.

'Hi, Sheriff.'

'I'm not the Sheriff.'

'Sho' look like one under that badge.'

Gradzynski held out his sleeve. 'Take another look…'

'Chain O'Lakes? That's Illinois. A bit stretched out here, ain't you?'

The old man was studying the grip of Gradzynski's gun where it showed from his holster.

On a whim, Gradzynski took out the gun and slid it into the glove-box through the car window. 'That feel better?'

'Suppose so. Who ya looking for?'

'Name of Leroy.'

'Leroy, hmm. Not sure 'bout that one. Not round here leastways.'

'Okay… let's say we try… Æppel.'

The old man looked around sharply. 'Never did grow any of them. But if I had, what sort of trouble would that get me into?'

'She's been kidnapped. Along with your granddaughter.'

'My granddaughter? Leroy never… Well… I'll be… Leroy? Get your black ass out here! Now!'

The door to the shed creaked open and Leroy slid into the sunlight. 'You're Maggie's cop, ain't you?'

'That's right. And now I'm yours. Get what you need. The One Light got Æppel.'

'Eugenie?'

'Her too.'

'Now hold on a minute, here.' The older man caught Gradzynski's sleeve. 'What's a 'Eugenie'?'

Leroy pulled him loose. 'Long story, Pa. When we get back, I'll tell you how it ends.'

Gradzynski caught the truck door as it was closing. 'How far is this place of theirs?'

'Some way… maybe three hours in the truck.'

'Then get out and come with me.' He spun the car

around in the driveway. The cloud of dust followed them all the way onto I12 where Leroy said to take a left and head on down towards Rockford. 'So where we going?'

Leroy settled back from the edge of his seat. 'About two and a half, maybe three hours. On the edge of Maryville, few miles out of Strawberry Point.'

'Get that belt on. Let's see if we can't shave that to two.' Gradzynski keyed the car radio. 'This is Officer Gradzynski out of Chain O' Lakes, Illinois. Anyone copy? Come back?'

He keyed off and the radio immediately cracked back.

'Would that be Pawel Gradzynski?'

'Yeah. Who's this?'

'Station Officer Reynolds. Jack to you.'

'Always knew you'd wedge your ass behind a desk. Just where is that desk?'

'In Rockford. Where are you headed?'

'Strawberry Point, just by Maryville. We're in pursuit of a kidnapping and they got more'n a few hours start.'

'That's Federal. How come…?'

'Not had time for the Feds. You could have them meet me in Strawberry Point.'

'Sure. Patch me your cell phone and I'll have them call.'

'Okay.'

'Take the first sign for I20 and head for Freeport. I'll switch off the cameras and get the boys to clear the junctions.'

Gradzynski settled down to watch the miles tick by on the odometer. 'Okay, Leroy. The One Light. Tell me what you know…'

Leroy shuffled his back into the seat and braced his feet against the bulkhead of the Interceptor. 'They're a cult. Somewhere along the way they got sex, pain and religion mixed up. But Æppel says it's more about retribution…'

The Teeth of Beasts

Strawberry Point
Iowa

2015

The harvest over, Æppel leaned back against a hay bale, then remembered to stand up straight. There were others here who watched for anyone who weakened in the service of the Lord's labor. The women stood at their stations across the field, casting rigid shadows over their bales. The Elders walked around, inspecting the length of the stubble and the fixing of the sheaves.

At the far edge of the field a short black man was in conversation with one of the Elders. Beside him was a youth, hands in jeans pockets, wearing a white tee-shirt that hugged him so tight it seemed the rest of him just flowed out of it to become arms, neck and head. Cornrows of hair bound in colored beads brought light against his natural darkness.

The older man was digging at the soil with the toe of his boot. The youth passed him a spade and he turned the earth once, lifting it into the air and winnowing it the way the girls would do with the grain now the harvest was in. He picked something up from the ground, probably a small rock like the ones that littered the surface by Æppel's feet, and threw it away in disgust. He dragged a wire riddle from the flatbed of a yellow truck and shoveled earth into it. As he lifted it the dust drifted like smoke. He slid a white bag from the truck and broke it open with the shovel. White powder slashed the field in quick strokes as he dug it in. He wiped his forehead with his shirt flap and leaned on the shovel.

The boy threw the riddle onto the truck. One of the Elders pointed him at Æppel and he set off walking towards her. By Æppel's feet was the broken scythe they'd made her use to finish off the harvest, all the while scolding her progress compared to the other girls. Now she lifted it like a barrier as the boy approached. He held out his hand. A whistle sounded from up the field. He turned and the Elder flagged down his arm, fingers outspread.

The boy dropped his hand. 'I forgot.' He reached out and picked up the scythe from where Æppel had dropped it in the earth, turning it to examine the broken blade. 'I can fix this…?'

'I… I cain't… not allowed… to talk to you.'

'Neither am I.' The boy dropped to his knees in the earth, turning the scythe pointlessly in his hands. 'I'm Leroy. What's your name?'

'If I tell you, Satan will hear. Then he'll know who I am, and when he comes callin' I'll hear him shout my name.'

'How old are you?'

'Sixteen.'

'I'm nineteen and my name's been shouted back at me so many times that, by God, Satan and all his Dark Angels should've come callin' by now.'

'Ain't you afraid of Hell?'

'Hell no. Eternity can take care of itself. I'm only put on this earth to live and that's what I'm gonna do.'

A whistle sounded loud along the field. He smiled at her. His teeth shone like none she had seen anywhere in the Family. 'I gotta go now. Be around when I get back with this.

I'll need you to test it…?'

'Æppel…'

'Oh, Dear Sweet Jesus… Now we're all damned and going to Hell on a handcart.'

As he passed by, Æppel dared to brush the skin of his arm with the backs of her fingers. It was silk with oil in the weft… the way they made their looms run easier on dark, candle-lit winter days… and a bright sensation ran the length of her arm and from there spread out fresh over her like a caul. 'Do you know how to play a game?'

Leroy ignored the warning whistle that echoed the field. 'I guess so.'

'Do you know Hide and Seek?'

'Yeah, I can do that.'

'When you come back… will you teach me?'

'Who was that you was talking to today?'

'Bramble Passion, you know we ain't allowed to talk to anyone outside the Family.'

'Then what else are you doin' when I see your lips moving'?'

'Chewin' old bones. Like you are now.'

'An' how dare you say my name out loud!'

'Cos I want Satan to get you… not that he ain't a'ready. I hear you in bed of a night, all that rustling and squeaking and breathing like you run off up the stairs.'

Bramble Passion's hair was blonde, unlike Æppel's dark glass sheen. She wore it in braids and plaits and woven around her head like a crown of flax.

Æppel watched the men of the Family when Bramble was around, moving about her with a purpose and design, weaving themselves in and out of her affections with a glance, waiting to see which one the Elders would give her to.

'Æppel Passion! I do believe you are jealous.' Bramble stroked into the curve of her stomach with one hand, arching her back like a cat. 'When's he comin' back again?'

Æppel backed away from the pantry. Bramble clung to the edge of the door frame with one hand, taunting her with rolling eyes and open lips, her other hand moving extravagantly between her thighs. Æppel slammed the door.

Jennings the Elder poked her with his stick and motioned her into his study room. He poked her again until she reached the Bible from the desk to pass to him. He opened it and flicked through until he found the well-thumbed page he wanted, then passed it back and directed Æppel to the lectern. He lifted a cane from the library shelf. It bent and flashed in the light from his meagre fire.

'Æppel Passion. Take off your tunic.'

Æppel slipped the black tunic over her head, leaving only an underskirt and a white cloth binding her breasts.

'Please, Elder. I have not yet healed.'

Jennings poked at the binding with his cane. 'Remove it. Now.'

Æppel unwound it slowly with one hand.

'Turn away.' Jennings stepped forward to examine her. 'It looks healed enough.'

'Elder... please... last night it bled. I had to wash my sheet again today.'

'Read!'

Æppel gripped tightly to the sides of the lectern and bent her face to the pages.

'The Lord found Jacob in a desert land and kept him as the apple of his eye, but the children of Jacob moved Him to jealousy with their vanities, and a fire was kindled in His anger that burned unto the lowest Hell.

And the Lord said: I will heap mischiefs upon them; I

will spend mine arrows upon them. They shall burn with hunger and be devoured by burning heat and with bitter destruction: I will send the teeth of beasts upon them. For vengeance is mine and the day of their calamity is at hand.'

Jennings braced his feet on the bare boards and swung the cane. 'Louder.'

'But Elder, she moved me to jealousy, as the children of Jacob did our Lord. And a fire was kindled in mine anger...'

'How dare you manipulate the Scriptures? Remember that the Lord also said 'I kill, and I make alive; I wound, and I heal; neither is there any that can deliver thee out of my hand.' He swung again. 'I want to hear The Song of Solomon sung with all conviction. Do you hear me?'

Æppel braced her knees backwards until they locked. She would not faint this time. 'I hear you, Elder.'

'Then sing.'

#

Two days later, the yellow flatbed pulled into the farm driveway. Leroy got out of the cab and lifted a scythe over the truck side. He called out but got no reply. He squinted through the sunlight over to the Chapel at the end of the field. The door was closed. Leroy had a vision of them in there, sweltering their souls up to heaven on a day such as this. He swung the scythe at a clump of low weeds and watched the tops shred and blow across the dirt. He picked it up blade first and checked the weld with his thumb. Satisfied, he carried it over to the workshop where he and his Pa kept a few things and where the Family locked away anything they considered dangerous or immoral. He opened the door and stopped at the threshold. There was a girl with her back to him, hands deep in rusty water, scrubbing at a sickle in the old stone sink. She'd jumped at the sound of the door opening, but hadn't turned around. As his eyes became accustomed to the light, he could see that her hands were shaking.

'Ma'am?'

At the sound of his voice she turned so she could see him from the corner of her eye. He was little more than a presence to her, a shape against the sunlit door.

He held out the scythe. 'I brought this. I'll just hang it with the others and be on my way. Sorry to disturb you.'

'Leroy?'

'Æppel?'

'Leroy... please go away. If they find you in here with me I don't know what they will do to you.'

'They cain't do nothin' to me. There ain't none of 'em I cain't take on a good day.' He peered back out the door and across to the Chapel. 'They're all still praying. How come you ain't in there?'

'Because of last time you was here.'

'How'd that come around?'

'We was seen talking... by Bramble. And I...' Through the window she saw the Chapel door open wide. The Family poured out, blinking in the sunlight. Some of them were walking, but some... the men... were running. She grabbed tightly to Leroy's arm. 'You remember what you promised last time you was here?'

'What promise? I never make...'

'To teach me Hide and Seek.' She glanced back out of the window. The men were a good third of the way across the field and still running. 'Hide me!'

Leroy glanced quickly around the shed. 'Where? There ain't nowhere here they won't find you.'

'Then take me with you.'

'You crazy? They'll hunt you down.'

'Do you know the game or don't you?'

'Since I was a kid. Sure'

'Leroy, I ain't never been a kid. So help me be one now.' She took a quick glance through the window. 'They're almost here.' Leroy tried to back away but Æppel followed him, chained by the grip of her fingers to his arm. 'Don't leave me here again.'

'They're your family. They won't hurt you.'

'No?' Æppel lifted her tunic, showing him the livid weals across her lower back. 'Would your family do this?'

Everything inside Leroy pivoted on his childhood and all the times he'd deserved a good switching and all the times they never did, and it all seemed to be for the same single reason. 'Any love in this family of yours?'

'None, 'cept Love of God.'

He grabbed her hand. 'Then come with me…'

Æppel turned to look out of the window. The first of the men were almost at the rear of the shed. 'They're coming!'

Leroy picked up the scythe and pushed Æppel through the door. 'Run for the truck. Get in and lock the door.'

He stepped out behind her and a body hit him from the side, bowling him over into the dust. He rolled back upright, scythe ready to swing.

The man who had hit him was twice his age and size, heavy-jawed and plain shaven. 'Now you put that down, boy.'

Leroy braced his feet in the dirt. 'Or what?'

'Look behind you, boy.'

Leroy glanced behind to see Æppel struggling in the arms of a younger man who had come from the other side. He lowered the scythe to the floor. 'Never did need it anyway.' He leaned back to see around the corner of the shed. The other men had stopped running and were now walking steadily towards them, surrounding the one they called Jennings. He kicked the scythe towards the man.

The man bent to pick it up. 'That's the first good sense you've shown so far, boy.'

Leroy spun on one foot. The other lashed out and took the man high in the chest, smashing him to the ground where he writhed around, face turning blue at the lips. Leroy turned to the young man holding Æppel. 'Now you let her go, y'hear?'

Fear shone plain in the young man's eyes. 'What you done to him?'

'Why? You want some?'

'Will he be alright?'

'Not unless you help him.' Leroy took a step forward. 'Made up your mind yet?'

The young man pushed Æppel away from him. 'The Lord knows who you are. You'll burn in Hell for this.'

The truck kicked dirt across the drive before Leroy turned it east along the highway. Pretty soon the blacktop leveled out and he slowed up so as not to attract attention. 'Ok. You can come on out.'

Æppel struggled out of the foot well and laid herself along the seat.

'Sit up, they cain't see you now.'

'I cain't…'

'Cain't what?'

'Sit up.'

An Ancient Flame

Strawberry Point
Iowa

2018

Gradzynski slowed the Interceptor at the outskirts of town and took time to check the clock. 'Two hours ten. Not bad.'

'Long time for Æppel…'

'They been driving too. Maybe only been there a couple hours or so.'

'Like I said…' Leroy stretched his cramped legs into the footwell. He hadn't realized he'd been braced all the way but this was the fastest he'd ever travelled in his life.

'Keep your eyes open for the Deli. It's left off West Mission. Should be on it about now.'

Leroy pointed across the highway to a wide parking bay. 'It's there…'

'Good. I need a leak.' Two men in sharp suits got out of a grey sedan as Gradzynski pulled in. 'Can you guys wait a minute?'

'Yeah, okay. Who's the kid?'

'Interested party.'

'You only have clearance for…'

'He's the only one knows what they look like. I got to take a leak.'

'Okay. We'll wait out in the car.'

As soon as Gradzynski went into the Deli, Leroy leaned across the seat and checked the keys were in the ignition. He took a quick look around and slid over into the driving seat. The wheels spun as he headed out up West Mission.

Gradzynski burst out of the Deli belt in hand and jumped into the back of the sedan.

The driver spun around. 'Where's he going?'

Gradzynski buckled down. 'Don't lose him.'

'That's a big V8 in there, Gradzynski.'

'I don't think he wants to lose us. He's just tired of waiting, is all.'

'What's his problem?'

'They have his girl and his daughter. And they already beat up on one of my cops and an old lady so don't hold out any hope for a conscience in there.'

'Fine. Larry, get the light out the glove-box.'

'Oh shit…'

'What's the matter Gradzynski?'

'Hopefully nothing we need worry about. Why've you let him get so far in front?'

'Told you, Gradzynski. We don't go chasing hot-rodders. Haven't got the budget.'

The Fed in the passenger seat scrolled his phone screen then looked out of the window. 'Farm's coming up soon, Dolan, 'bout a mile on the left. Can't see anything else worth…'

'There… look…' Gradzynski pointed out the buildings squat on the close horizon.

'We got two minutes tops, Gradzynski. How're we going to play this?'

'By ear, I think. Don't know what we're heading into 'cept that it's unfriendly.'

The driver studied Gradzynski through the mirror. 'You

seen any service, Gradzynski?'

'Some.'

'It's always good to have a plan.'

'Can I show you boys something?' Gradzynski thumbed the screen of his phone and handed it to the guy in the passenger seat.

'Christ, Gradzynski? What happened to him?'

'That's my partner… and it ain't no him.'

Gradzynski took back the phone and watched quietly as the buildings seemed to creep their slow way towards him.

The driver caught his eye again. 'You loaded up, Gradzynski?'

Gradzynski closed his eyes for a moment in silent hope.

'I think that might be a problem.'

#

'Æppel Passion. You remember how to hold that Lectern?'

'You cain't make me. I don't care how many times you drag me back here. I know what's outside now and I know you ain't right. Where's my daughter? What have you done with her?'

'If you mean the child that Satan wrenched unbidden from your womb, then it will be taken care of. Just the way we took care of you before you became the ungrateful, foul-mouthed and blasphemous wretch you are today. Do you have any idea of the torment you will have to endure to become clean again?'

'What have you done with my daughter?'

'You dare to question me? Do you not remember who I am?'

'I know exactly who you are. You have the face of Jennings the Elder but inside you're a Demon. I can smell you from here. I'm gagging on the sulphur and brimstone of your foul-minded breath and I will never be clean while I am surrounded by your filth and lies.'

She stepped up until she was in his face, eyes bright and burning. 'I see you, Spawn of Satan. I call you from your lair to answer for your crime. The crime of lies and deceit and incest. The only weapon you have against us is ignorance. I will tell everyone what life is like beyond these fields. I will tell them what it feels like to be human. Is that what you really want? To walk God's good Earth like a man? You think that will stop us from seein' what you are?'

Jennings backed away from her insistent raised finger. 'If this 'seeing' is what has afforded thy lapse from the Sanctuary of The Lamb, then I shall find a way to bring thee peace.'

He put the switch back on its hooks and opened the door. 'Take her to the workshop and wait for me there.'

He knelt by the Lectern to pray for the Lord's strength and forgiveness for what he must do next. He could feel the weight of Æppel's accusations on his shoulder like a burden, but he knew his duty. All he needed was to gather the strength.

#

Gradzynski's cruiser stood broadside-on to the drive with the door swung wide. The sedan pulled quietly up to it. They dropped a window to listen. The main house was silent but Gradzynski could see the faces of women behind the lace curtains, watching them. From the workshop further up came the sound of a pistol shot. Gradzynski leapt from the car with the Feds following him. They tucked for cover behind the cruiser but Gradzynski slid along the side of it until he could reach in and open the glovebox. The gun was gone. He crouched across the gap between the cruiser and the buildings. There were voices from behind the workshop door, raised in anger. He could hear Leroy shouting.

'Shut up! Get away from her!'

Another voice shouted back at him. 'Thy Hell awaits thee, boy. Put down that gun and face thy Lord. He will make thee kill this blasphemer before He allows harm to me.'

'Then I guess Satan will have to steady my arm...'

Then Gradzynski heard Æppel.

'No, Leroy. This is what he wants. Don't give them an excuse to kill us both.'

Gradzynski glanced back to the drive. Larry was beside him as he turned. Dolan was down beside the wheel of an old rusted van, taking a call. Larry signaled him to stay put but without further thought Gradzynski ran up and shouldered the door. He rolled and came upright inside the workshop, snatching the gun from Leroy's hand as he turned in surprise.

Æppel was trapped in the corner by a man with a red-hot bar held above her eyes. Leroy spun around, catching the heft of a falling scythe in one hand and dragging the man behind it out into the light from the door.

Æppel screamed. 'Leroy!'

Leroy turned and caught the tines of a pitchfork with the scythe. He swung the handle around and took the man behind the knee with the blade. The joint parted as the steel slid through tendons and his leg bent the wrong way. He went down like a sack, face contorted in a silent scream of agony.

Gradzynski stepped in behind and covered him with his gun. 'Any more?'

Leroy took a quick look around the workshop. 'Not since I came in. There will be others in the house, guarding the women.'

'Guarding the women?'

'They're a resource.'

Æppel was shivering in the firm grip of Jennings, the heat of the poker biting into her skin. Gradzynski leveled his gun at the man's eye so he could see what was coming. 'Let her go.'

The man tightened his grip on Æppel, sliding his body further in behind her for cover.

Leroy came to stand beside Gradzynski. 'Don't. You might hit Æppel.'

Jennings shouted at Gradzynski, fear bright in his voice. 'The Lord will stay thy hand, Devil. Thou art only Satan and I have thy Wit and Weft and I know thee by the tapestry of lies that thou weaveth.'

Gradzynski cocked the hammer of the pistol. Leroy knocked his arm aside and the gun fired from an involuntary squeeze of trigger. The bullet pierced a can of gasoline under the bench beside Æppel, showering her and Jennings with fuel and filling the workshop with an abrasive scent. Jennings wiped frantically at his eyes with one hand while the other brought the poker closer to Æppel's skin.

Gradzynski was taking aim again. Æppel was screaming. The Feds were shouting at Jennings to get down and let her go. The man by the hearth was writhing and trying to hold his leg together, blood pooling across the workshop floor.

The man under Leroy's foot had been pierced by the pitchfork as it fell and was groaning loudly as his lungs filled. Leroy shut down the noise and from memory mapped the workshop layout. Nothing had changed that he could see. Beside the hearth plate was a large box of matches. It was a chance he had to take. One he might have to spend a long time reconsidering…

He struck a match and held it against the floor of the

workshop. The blue flame outlined his feet, then flashed over the man with the pitchfork in his chest, spreading out across the workshop floor.

Gradzynski turned, shaking his feet clear as it travelled on towards Æppel and Jennings where it caught around Æppel's feet and leapt to envelop her dress. It took Jennings where the fuel had splashed his face and he punched her away from him, screaming as the flame took his hair.

Leroy leapt through and grabbed Æppel before she could fall. The flames caught him, taking in his hair, eyebrows and lashes as he held tight to her. He carried her across the workshop and threw her into the big annealing tank by the hearth. His hands plunged her deep into it as flames spread the surface, clinging to his arms and spilling onto the floor. She erupted from the tank, showering him with water, rubbing along his arms and hair with wet hands until the flames were extinguished.

He pulled her clear. 'Where's Eugenie? Have they still got Eugenie?'

Æppel tried to smooth the water from his hair but her fingers caught in the melted plastic beads. 'She's in the house. My mother has her.'

Jennings had stopped screaming. On fire from head to foot he staggered past Gradzynski and ran towards the house. The door opened to let him in. Then locked shut behind him.

Æppel rushed at Gradzynski, his gun arm frozen in shock as flames roared around them, devouring the dry old timbers of the workshop. She tried to pull him outside towards the house.

'Eugenie is in there!'

Gradzynski shook himself back to awareness. The noise of the flames was deafening and the nylon of his windcheater was melting. There was a strong scent of scorch and he realized it was his own hair. He pushed Æppel out of the workshop door into the waiting arms of the Feds.

Leroy was standing over the man with the broken knee as though he couldn't decide what he should do. Gradzynski grabbed him by the back of the tee shirt and together they fell out into the yard as flame took the roof and the old timbers sagged sideways into collapse.

Behind the windows of the house, fire was taking the curtains. Within the flames were faces peering out, distorted by the heat.

Æppel ran to the windows, leaping across from one to the other, searching the burning faces, seeing their skin curl and peel while Gradzynski and the Feds tried to batter down the door. 'You won't do it. There's too many bars and locks on there.'

Gradzynski picked a stone from the yard and threw it at a window. The glass exploded outwards in a shower of shards as new air fed the flames inside. He threw his jacket over his head and prepared to make the jump over the sill and found himself looking down the muzzle of a shotgun. He stopped... transfixed by the insanity of the situation.

Æppel pushed him aside. 'They don't want to be rescued. They want to die!'

Gradzynski drew her out of the line of fire. 'What about Eugenie?'

'It's too late.'

'It's never too late. I'm going in there.'

Gradzynski rushed the gun barrel from the side and wrenched it from the shooter's hands. Skin clung to the butt as he dragged it clear. He threw it across the yard in disgust. Leroy picked it up and swung it right way around. Dolan snatched it from him and threw it behind the car out of reach.

Gradzynski reached the window but the shooter was

barring his way, skin peeling rapidly from his face. Gradzynski pushed him aside and the man fell backwards to the floor. He buried his face inside his jacket and swung one leg over the sill. An inner door burst open into the room and fresh flame blasted him back into the yard. Hands grabbed him from behind and pulled him away. The cobble stones raked the flesh off his back as he was dragged from the heat. He tried to shake off whoever was pulling but his hands burned as though they were still in the flames and he couldn't get a grip. Across the yard came the sound of bolts being withdrawn. The pulling stopped and Gradzynski felt himself lifted up to sit braced against Larry's legs. The door opened.

'Mother!'

Æppel rushed across the yard as her mother appeared in the doorway in an aura of dense smoke. In front of her she carried Eugenie. The child looked fine, but strange, then Æppel realized that she had been drenched in water. Eugenie was crying and holding up her hands to Æppel. She took her quickly and wrapped her in her arms.

'Thank you, Mother.'

Her mother turned and walked away into the house, the back of her simple dress and hair a growing mass of flame. She neither turned nor looked back before the bolts were refastened.

Enigma

Chain O'Lakes
Illinois

2018

'Hello? Is that the Holocaust Museum? … Can I speak to the Curator please? My name is Franklin … Doctor Franklin. I need to research a concentration camp number. Is this still possible? … Yes, I understand that your records may not be complete … Okay.' He read the number from his phone, hoping he'd interpreted the slight blurring correctly.

'Yes… I'll hold…'

'Doctor Franklin? I am sorry for your wait, Doctor.'

'I'm hoping it will be worth it.'

'Time spent remembering the past always has worth, Doctor. Whatever you find there will illuminate your present.'

'I hope so, sir. What we have here is an enigma wrapped in a problem topped off by an alarming sense of humor.'

'Can you not get a straight answer, Doctor?'

'Nary a one, sir.'

'This is of course very familiar to me.'

'You know Maggie Gray?'

'No, Doctor Franklin, it is a coping strategy. It means

you don't have to look an uncomfortable world in the eye.'

'You see this often?'

'Not so much today. Most have gone now, but always the same way of seeing.'

'Surely they're not all like Maggie?'

'Same theme, Doctor, many symptoms, many variations. How many virus to make human cold?'

'Not sure we've found them all yet, sir.'

'But a cold all the same, yes? Anxiety is a fierce and lonely virus, Doctor, and for some, humor is the only symptomatic relief. I will send these papers for you, but only copies, you understand?'

'Copies will be fine, sir. Even email.'

'Email then will be fine. I shall get my assistant to... wait a moment, there is a thing I should mention. I find a familiar hand over all these papers. He seems to be everywhere.'

'He?'

'You will recognize him, Doctor. Always a different name but, like all great artists, he leaves his mark. Always the signatures have a little characteristic and even still today I see these things. A tiny flourish no more than might be a slip of pen. Nothing that anyone seeing individual papers would recognize, but I am a curator. I have no idea of what he looked like, but in my life he is most ubiquitous. Everywhere I look I find him, but particularly so in your case and for this time he signs as himself. I don't know why he would do this. If you find out please let me know.'

'Who is he?'

'Simply the best forger I have ever seen, Doctor. Probably best we ever had. And the man I would most like to have met.'

'But your records are then...'

'Doctor, to the victor belong not only the spoils but also the truth. This man chose to write a history that set many feet along successful paths. Who am I to deny him that privilege?'

Bill Allerton

A Kindness Today

Jersey Shore
Pennsylvania

1951

Ellie peered through the mesh screen. There was a man outside scuffing his feet against the plain boards without looking up. His grey fedora tilted against the noon sun and a leather bag swung by a strap from his shoulder.

'Mrs Butler?'

'Yes? Can I help you?'

'May we speak inside, Mrs Butler? It is hot out here.'

'Ain't much cooler inside... but first tell me who you are.'

'I'm from the school, Mrs Butler. I'm here about Maggie.'

'Then I guess you better come in.' Ellie sprung the screen catch and allowed him into the shade of the house. He turned around slowly, hat in hand, noting the obvious lack of excess.

Ellie waved a hand towards a bare couch. 'Set down there. Get you anything?'

'A glass of water would indeed be a kindness today.'

The man placed his hat beside him on the couch and watched her closely as she brought water from the kitchen. She sat opposite him in a stiff-backed chair, still a young woman, though the make-up failed to hide a toll around her eyes and life had left a sense of unease in the way her body folded.

Ellie handed him the glass. 'What's wrong with Maggie?'

'No… no, no. Let me put you at rest on that. Maggie is fine.'

Ellie turned away from the directness of his gaze. 'Then what's the problem? She misbehave?'

'Mrs Butler, I couldn't ask for a better-behaved child.'

'Then what? You going to tell me you have no place for her come next year?'

'No… not that either. Mrs Butler… I want you to look at me.' He turned his head sideways. 'Take a good look.'

Ellie studied him carefully, looking all the while for something that would really matter to her… but apart from the fact that he was a little older than her, that his hair at the temples was like smoky iron and he smelled like every other teacher she had encountered, that mix of chalk dust and deodorant that combines like soft, untreated leather… there was nothing.

He tapped the side of his nose. 'I am Jewish, Mrs Butler.'

'Do I have a problem with that?'

'No, Mrs Butler. But I do.'

'This some kind of inverted prejudice?'

The man laughed quietly. He held out his hand to her. Ellie watched it for a while but stayed put.

'Mrs Butler, my name is Anton Kowalski… and I'm Polish. And so is Maggie.'

Ellie sat bolt upright in the chair. 'Maggie is as American as you and me.'

'No, Mrs Butler. Maggie is as American as me. Not you.'

'Just because my daughter doesn't speak well…'

'On the contrary. Maggie speaks very well indeed. Her command of language is quite remarkable for a child her age.'

'Maggie hardly speaks at school. The other kids tease her because of it.'

'That's because they don't understand when she swears at them in Polish and German, Mrs Butler. But I do, and I can assure you…'

Ellie leaned toward him, hoping that her body language would convey some sort of threat that would safeguard herself and Maggie from any deeper questions this man might have. 'Where does this go from here?'

'From here? We will have to see.'

A tiredness she had held at bay for years softened Ellie's voice. 'What do you want from me?'

'Very little, Mrs Butler. I just want the story.'

'Who you going to give it to?'

Kowalski picked up the hat he had set down on the couch, snapped the brim and with the blade of his hand reaffirmed the crease along the crown, then set it down again and smiled up at her. 'We will have to see.'

'I have a child to fetch from school. But you know that.'

'I do, Mrs Butler.'

He flicked his sleeve to expose a wristwatch. 'That gives us say… two hours. We should have the gist of it by then.'

'Where do I begin?'

'Anywhere you please, Mrs Butler.'

'Okay. I'm not really Mrs Butler.'

'I think I know that, Mrs Collins.'

'Then why…? You made a study of me?'

'Good nurses are always on record.'

'I ain't no Mrs neither.'

'These are mere conventions, Mrs Collins. It is not for me to pass judgement.'

'No-one called me by that name in an age. Call me Ellie.'

'Mrs Collins, I want to know who you really are. That goes for Maggie too… but don't forget to give me a nod when we get to the truth.'

'What do you teach at school, Mr Kowalski?'

'Originally? I taught Philosophy.'

'To Kindergarten?'

'No, no. In the University in Krakow.'

'Then you are Polish.'

'Did I not say?'

'I guess you did. It's just kinda hard to…'

'I got out of Europe early in '38. The world was turning and I had to get off before it was too late.'

Ellie tucked her dress beneath her legs, smoothing it tight across her knees with an uncertain hand. 'Don't know where to begin.'

'Start with Mr Butler…'

Seeds

**Oswiecim
Poland**

1945

Magda climbed on the bench and slipped her hand into the jacket hanging on the wall. In her palm were several clusters of green seeds. She counted them out then put half of the clusters back into Auntie Graz's pocket. She slipped out of the silent building and made her way across the yard to the little patch of earth beside her own doorway. She separated the clusters the way Auntie Graz had shown her and with a sharp stick poked holes in the soil where it had backed up to the skirt of the hut, then pushed a wrinkled green seed into each one. She covered them with earth and went inside for water.

'Magda? What are you doing?' Her mother stood over her as she reached for the tin cup. 'And where have you been?' Magda shrank away from the sudden sting of her mother's knuckles. 'Don't lie to me, Magda.'

Magda thought for a moment, searching for the word. 'Flower.'

Her mother raised her hand again. 'Where? Show me... now.'

Magda clambered down the short steps to the dirt of the yard. She turned and pointed to the bank of earth beside the door.

'Magda? Why would you plant seeds? Tell me...'

'Flower.'

'Magda... do you know how long it takes to grow a flower from seed?' Her mother sat down on the step beside her, holding both her hands. 'It takes longer than we have.' Magda tried to shake her hands free but her mother held on tight. 'Soon we will move again... and... and your flowers will be left behind. Do you see? It's no good...'

Magda pulled away and stamped her feet. 'Flower good.'

Her mother's knuckles rapped the side of her head. 'There's nothing good here, Magda. How many times do I have to tell you? Nothing. Now tell me where you got the seeds.'

'Auntie Grazyna.'

'Where is... where did... did she give them to you?'

Magda shook her head and scrubbed her toe in the dust.

Her mother shook her violently. 'Did you steal them?'

Magda was whipped around to face her mother again. She shook her head one more time.

'Magda? Where did you get them?'

Magda hung her head, swiveling a foot in the dirt. 'Pocket.'

'What did she say when you asked her for them?'

Magda looked up and met her mother's eyes. 'I borrow.' She pulled herself away and began to tear at the earth with her tiny fingers.

'Magda. Magda...' Her mother lifted her away from the pile of earth. Magda's fingers were black. Flying earth congealed with tears streamed her cheeks as she struggled in the firm grip of her mother's hands. 'Magda... Magda... Where did you find her jacket?'

Magda reached out a mud-spattered arm and pointed to a long, low building across the yard.

'Oh God, Magda. How many times must I tell you that no matter what happens, you must never, ever, go in there.'

'Not Auntie Graz. Only clothes. She have new?'

'Yes, Magda. She will now have new.' Her mother stared anxiously across the open yard, then pushed Magda roughly away. 'Go and get the water now or your flowers won't be ready. There's a puddle over there... use your hands. Don't come back until you have them both full.'

'I'm frightened.'

'Go and get your water.'

Magda walked carefully over to the puddle that seemed to move closer to the tower with each step she took. She knelt down beside it and scooped water into her hands. The water disappeared immediately through her fingers. She looked up to the tower. The gun barrel watched her through a blackened eye. When it swung away to the far side of the platform, Magda tried again. It took some time to scoop enough together in her hands. When she returned, the hut was empty.

#

'Butler...'

The marine moved out of the line. 'Sarge?'

'Take Donetski and make for the corner of the first hut. Watch out for wires and mines. Stay on the tracks.'

'Sarge.'

The marines moved slowly into the compound where fresh tire tracks criss-crossed the ash-coated mud. Butler made his way over to the railroad, dropped to his knees on a tie and checked the area for ground-level trip wires. 'Looks clean, Sarge.'

'Okay. Fan out amongst the huts. Miller... Lopez... you're with me. Let's check out the exploded building at the far end.'

The huts were single story, some eighty feet long by thirty wide, raised up from the earth on short brick piles. There were maybe a hundred of them. Donetski stopped beside a deserted sentry tower. Beyond that a wire fence ringed another field with at least another hundred huts.

He heard the sound of a door being kicked through behind him, then silence.

'Hey, Yankee. What you got?'

'Jeezus, Donut. Come and look at this.'

The smell hit Donetski before his eyes accustomed to the gloom inside the hut.

'Dear God!'

'What you reckon, Donut? Must've been a hundred or more in here. Wonder if they're all the same. What's a hundred hundreds, Donut?'

'Too many...'

'What you got, boys?'

'Take a look for yourself, Sarge.'

'Don't have to. I can smell it from here. The other huts are empty. Hell, I expect most of 'em are. See that embankment over there?'

Beyond the railroad junction a rampart of raised earth shielded a section of the yard.

'There's a pit over there. You never seen such a mess of arms and legs. Pull back into the yard by the switch. We need to think about this.'

Grouped on the hard ground by the rail terminal, they chowed down on K-Rations that no longer held any taste.

The Sergeant stared blindly at the cattle trucks collected against the buffers.

'Radio. Find out when the brass are coming. Don't want to disturb anything 'less I have to. Need a camera crew here. Butler... get up off your ass and see what you can find. Take

Donetski. Make another sweep along the wire but don't touch a thing.'

'Donut, come here. Somebody's been burying something. Wonder what they had left worth keeping.'

Butler reached into the disturbed soil at the edge of a hut. His hand came away with a couple of green seeds. He turned them in his palm. They were beginning to germinate, pale tendrils wrapping around them. A small hand shot out of the darkness and snatched them away.

'Hey!'

'What you doin', Yankee?'

'We got ourselves a live one.'

Donetski reached across and scattered the earth with his rifle barrel but it was too dark to see. He backed off a little and worked the bolt. 'Kommen sie aus. Raus! Schnell!' The gap under the hut was silent. 'Okay, you asked for it... Aus, oder ich schiessen!'

Butler nudged him aside and sifted out another seed. He pushed his hand through the earth into the space beyond and waited. Beneath the hut, he felt fingers close around the seed. He gripped hard and dragged out a tiny, emaciated child.

Donetski sat down hard. 'What is it?'

'Cain't say. I seen more flesh on a pipe-cleaner.'

The child was shaven headed, around two feet tall, looked to be two years old but the eyes said older, and dressed in a faded black and white pajama suit. Butler retained his grip on the tiny hand, almost afraid that he would pull it off.

Donetski pulled down the front of the pants, peered in and pulled them up again quickly. 'What's your na... Wait a minute... Ihre name?'

Butler loosened his grip on the tiny hand only to find

that it was gripping his. 'What makes you think she's German? If she was German she wouldn't be in here, would she?'

Donetski tapped his forehead. 'Donut... see... Do... nut.' He tapped Butler and drawled slowly. 'Yan... kee... Boy.'

The child tapped her own head. 'Nazywam sie Magda.'

'What was that?'

'Polish, at a guess.'

'With a name like Donetski you should do more than guess.'

Magda pointed to the uprooted seeds. Butler handed them to her. She gave them straight back to him. He shook the loose soil from them and nodded in thanks. Donetski pulled out a Hershey and held it up. Magda remained unmoved. He went to put it back in the pack.

Butler stopped him with a nod.

'She don't know what it is.' Slowly, he released his grip on her fingers but Magda had a good hold of him. 'You stop her if she goes thataway.'

'Okay. But what kind of a kid don't know what a chocolate bar is?'

Butler glared at him, then bit a piece off the end of the Hershey and chewed it slowly, a huge grin on his face, before holding it out to Magda. Without warning, she pushed the whole bar into her tiny mouth. Donetski reached in with a finger and hooked it out before she choked. He gave it back to her slowly... warm, sticky chocolate covering his fingers. She bit off a piece and chewed, grinning the way Butler had. She ate the whole bar then suddenly vomited melted chocolate onto Donetski's combats.

Butler reached out and stroked her face. 'Too much at once, and too much sugar. Who knows when she last ate?' Magda grasped at his hand and clung on tight.

Donetski picked up the pack and rifle. 'Well... let's see what the Sarge has to say about her.'

'Wait a minute... You still got that drawstring bag in your pack?'

'Yeah. Why? Oh Hell no, Butler. You cain't...'

'You seen the way they treated the survivors at the last camp.'

Butler grabbed a hold of Magda's pajama suit. Magda twitched and the threads came away in his fingers. 'An' look at these! I ain't having none of that for our little magpie here.'

'Magda. She said Magda.'

Butler took off the child's jacket and pants and pushed them out of sight under the hut. 'I'm leaving these behind. You bet they'll be full of seam squirrels. Get that drawstring open before she catches her death.'

Between them they slid her, unprotesting, into the warmth of the bag.

'Donut... you got any idea what...'

'Shut up, Yank. There's always an angle.'

Donetski opened the top of his pack a little wider. Magda's face loomed up at him like a full moon... her eyes a question he didn't know how to answer.

'What about when she needs to take a leak? Or worse?'

'Yank... stop building bridges we ain't got to cross yet. We gotta kick around here a few days. You heard what they said about the people from the town.'

'You think they'll do that? Make 'em walk through here, I mean?'

'I hope so, Yank.' Donetski slid his hand into the top of the pack. Between his fingers was a hardtack. Magda slipped it from him without a whisper. 'Say what you like, Yank, this is one quiet kid.'

'Prob'ly how she made it.'

'Think a body can learn that? Learn how to be quiet?'

'Must'a had to… and quick.'

'I was thinking… when the people come up from the town, maybe we could slip her in amongst them as they leave.'

'And what they gonna do with her? Make her Mayor? You think they want her reminding 'em of what they done up here? You think she won't just disappear somewhere dark o' the night?'

'Yank, she's just a kid. Who would harm…?'

'Donetski… go take a look over there by the crater then come back and tell me.'

'Tell you what, Sarge?'

'You girls were so busy philosophizing you'da let Rommel sneak up on you with a tank. Thought you were finding me somethin'.' The pack by Sarge's feet shifted a little. 'Perhaps you did. What you got in there, Donetski?'

Donetski reached over and pulled the drawstring tight. 'Not a thing as didn't oughta be, Sarge.'

The sergeant tapped the chevrons on his sleeve. 'They're what says what oughta be.'

'You want I should salute, Sarge?'

'No, Donetski, I want you should open the bag.'

'I'd be 'bliged if you didn't ask me that, Sarge.'

'And I'd be 'bliged if for once you took me at my word.'

'Sarge, what was you before the war? Back home I mean… Stateside.'

'About as mean as I am now… that answer your question?'

'You ain't mean, Sarge. Had myself a dog like you once. All bark an' whiskers. You don't really want me to open this bag.'

'Believe me, Donetski, there's nothing more important in my life right this moment than for you to open that bag.'

'Sarge… you need to get out more…'

The sergeant lifted out his pistol and slipped off the safety. He pressed the muzzle to the side of the bag. 'Ok, Donetski. Let's see what kind of a dog you have in there, though how one survived here without being eaten I'll never know. I'll give you five… One…'

Donetski pushed away the gun. 'You don't want to do that, Sarge. It ain't no dog.'

'Cat, then… fox… whatever…' Sarge pushed the gun back against the bag. '…Two…'

Donetski caught his hand to stop him but Butler reached across and shook the drawstring loose. 'Can it, Donut. Know when you're beat.'

He rolled down the top of the pack. Magda blinked in the sunlight that lit the stubble burr across her shaven head. The sergeant sat back in the dirt. Magda stared at him… eyes burning deep into his… then handed him a seed. She leaned out of the bag and touched his chest with a finger.

'Jak masz na imię?'

He lifted her finger until it touched the center of his forehead. He let go and it stayed there, pressing urgently.

'Nazywam się Mieczyslaw.'

'What was that, Sarge?'

'Shut up, Butler.'

Magda touched her own forehead. 'Nazywam sie Magda. Gdzie jest Ciocia Grazyna.'

'What she say, Sarge?'

'She's looking for her Aunt Grazyna.'

'Under the hut? Think there might be more of them under there? We never thought to look.'

'Co robiłeś?'

Magda looked around carefully before replying. 'Ukrywanie od mamusi.' Three dark weals stood out against the pale skin of Magda's back. She held still while the sergeant touched them gently. 'Momma to zrobił?' Magda nodded. The sergeant smiled, hoping to dispel the fear in her face. 'Momma nie jest tutaj.'

'Sarge?'

'Kid says her Ma did this to her. She's been hiding from her ever since. Never know but what it saved her life. Find any more, Butler?'

'Nary a one, Sarge.'

'Good. I didn't want you to find the one that did this.'

'Sarge? When the people come up from the town, do we give her to them to look after?'

'You mean the way they looked after the rest of them?'

'Maybe they didn't know.'

'You lost your sense of smell?'

'No, Sarge.'

'Well they ain't lost theirs either. Every time the wind turned around they knew what was goin' off here.'

Donetski rolled back the top of the bag so Magda could get her shoulders free. Her arms reached out and her fingers touched his face, exploring the stubble. 'We got to get her some clothes, Sarge. Cain't keep her in here much longer.'

Sarge pulled Magda's head towards him and examined the new growth of hair. It was no more than a fraction long but was already beginning to soften some of the scars. He looked for lice in the stubble, but she was clean. 'Don't get too attached, Donetski. There's a medical unit five miles behind us. They'll take care of her.'

'They got nurses with 'em, Sarge?'

'So I hear.'

'How do I get a transfer?'

'Donetski, you're the healthiest gyrene I know. Give it up. Wait 'til they pitch up here and I'll sort it.'

'Will they let me stay with her?'

'Are you sick?'

'No…'

'Then what do you think?'

After they had gone, the sergeant lifted his hand to smell the seed. He knew what it was. It had the finest beginning of root. The Geranium flower when it came would be full and red with an orange throat like the ones he'd left behind in his garden. He clawed at the soil by the side of a rail then gently folded it in.

A crowd of Marines gathered by the gate as the townspeople were ushered in.

'What you thinking, Butler?'

'Was thinkin' I ain't never seen so many folks glad to be alive but wantin' to be anywhere 'cept here.'

'How'd you live with this on your conscience?'

'Donut. There's a guy there about your size…' A man in scholarly spectacles and a dark tweed overcoat walked slowly through the gate. He stopped to rub dirt from a corner of his eye, then stared down at the mud clumping his feet and stumped on up the yard. 'Go walk a mile in his shoes, Donut. See how the world looks from in there.'

'In there… out here… What's the difference.'

'It depends which end of a gun you're at.'

'Makes no difference to me, Butler. I been at both ends.'

The arrival of the first truck drew the Marines away from the gate. Two nurses in combats in the front seat… a young blonde and a brunette around thirty or so… and four more under canvas on the back.

Donetski helped them down from the truck and set them on a tie by the railroad where they could stand out of the mud.

'Where's the Nurse uniform? I wanna see some leg here… Cut your hair, turn you 'round, you look just like me.'

The brunette beckoned him forward. 'Listen, Joe. See this mud? You been up to your nuts in it for years, right?' Her face was so close to Donetski's he could smell fresh gum on her breath. 'And sometimes it's only your nuts stopped you sinkin' right under?'

Donetski swallowed hard. Her lips were so close to his he couldn't take his eyes off them. He wanted to attach himself like a limpet, steal in there and make off with the gum. 'I... I guess...'

'Well, marine... we ain't got no nuts. So the only thing we Ladies got to stop ourselves sinkin' is effort. So we have to swim twice as hard as you just to stay afloat in this war. Got that?'

Butler pulled him away. 'Leave him alone. Where he's been this last year you might as well be from Mars.'

'Venus.'

'Wherever. You're goin' to get him in trouble with the Sarge.' The Sarge was striding up the ties towards them.

Butler reached out for her arm. 'Wait... I got a question...' The brunette pushed him away. 'I got more answers than you ever thought of asking. But not right now. We got mud to stay upright in.'

'Hey Ladies...'

The brunette half-turned, giving the Sergeant scant attention. 'What can we do for you?'

'You can leave my boys alone. Where they've been for the last year you might as well be...'

'We done that already. Catch up.'

The sergeant tapped the chevrons on his sleeve. The brunette rolled down her own. The sergeant took a step back. 'Yes Sir, Ma'am. How can we help?'

'I want two boys. This one and that one.'

'Butler, Donetski. You heard the officer. Jump.'

'Sarge? About the bag...'

'I'll get it. Sorry Ma'am. Butler here has a personal problem. He needs his bag to sort it out.'

'Will it stop him working?'

'You wouldn't think so.'

#

Donetski and Butler offloaded a pile of timber decking onto a dry area, laid it out in a big square then pitched a tent on the top of it. The Sarge arrived with the bag and placed it carefully in the back of the tent. Donetski loosened the drawstring and shushed Magda with a finger to his lips. He pushed a Hershey in with her and went back to work.

'You Joes want a coffee?'

Donetski took the mugs from a nurse's hand and passed one to Butler. 'Is this real coffee?'

The nurse looked him up and down and smiled. 'You mean… is this real coffee… thank you, Janice?'

'Are you for real?' Donetski leaned against a fresh pile of decking as she turned to walk away. 'Last time I saw something sway like that we was on the English Channel.'

Janice glanced back over her shoulder. 'Yeah, and it made you sick to your stomach then.'

Butler took a sip of his coffee and took it in back of the tent. The canvas was dark camouflage green with a double fly to keep out the dust and water and it was in here that they would set up the generator lights and the surgery after the next trucks arrived. He stumbled around equipment until he found the bag.

Magda was asleep with chocolate smeared around her lips. He dipped his finger in the warm coffee and wiped it off. Magda opened her eyes and whatever small light there was caught in them. He offered her the mug and she took it with both hands. She drank it to the dregs and passed it back.

'What you got there, Joe?'

The blonde nurse rolled off a camp bed at the other side of the tent.

Butler hadn't noticed her when he'd arrived. 'Oh shit. Ain't nothing but a dog.'

The nurse knelt beside him on the floor. 'Never did see a coffee-drinking dog. Mind if I take a look?'

Butler brushed her hand away and tightened the drawstring on the bag. 'Might bite you. It's not sure about strangers. Took me a while to coax it out.'

'Move over, soldier. I ain't afraid of dogs. We even got penicillin here, and some of you boys been itching like you could do with a shot.'

She pushed Butler out of the way and rolled back the top of the bag. Magda stared out at her, huge-eyed in the gloom of the tent.

The nurse rocked back against her heels. 'You goin' to introduce us, Butler?'

Butler put out his hand to reassure Magda. 'This is Magda… Magda… this is…'

'Ellie…'

Ellie held out her arms. Magda struggled free of the bag and fell into them.

'Butler! She's naked!'

'Well… I was… we was… sort of working towards that when you girls arrived.'

'Who's we?'

'Me, Donetski and the Sarge.'

'Anybody else know?'

'No.'

'Keep it that way. She clean? I cain't tell in the dark.'

'Yeah, she's clean. Used all my powder on her. Ain't

nothin' left alive on there.'

Ellie took her across to the camp bed. 'You need a toilet, honey? Go pee-pee?' Magda stared blankly until Butler attracted her attention. 'The john?'

Magda shook her head, no. Ellie wrapped her in her own blanket and laid her down on the camp bed. 'You want anything little one?'

Magda rolled herself back out of the blanket. 'Hershey.'

'Butler? I see you been teaching her American.'

#

'Sarge?'

'You boys got the do-all of assignments I ever heard. The lieutenant here put in a special request.'

'My ladies can't carry guns so I guess you get the job of looking after us.'

Donetski and Butler exchanged glances. 'The bag...'

'With special dispensation for the bag.'

'When do we start?'

'Right now. Start by taking down the tent. We're shipping out.'

The guy ropes and poles came down more quickly than they had gone up. The bunks were dragged out and loaded onto the truck. For a moment they all stood around staring at the bag, before the Chief Nurse swung it carefully over her shoulder.

Donetski put a hand under the bag to support the weight. 'Do you know where we're going, Ma'am?'

'Berlin went down, so my guess is Okinawa.'

'No shit!'

'That's right, Donetski. No shit... Ma'am.'

'Hey Butler, what you think about this? How come we

get drafted to Okinawa? What shit kind of a job is this?'

'Look on the plus side, Donut. At least we get to go with the nurses.'

'Yeah, I know. But I want to end up in the Pacific? Never been that far west.'

'We all have to end up somewhere.'

'That's fine but I've had enough of being shot at.'

'Shot at. Shit on. Shut up. Just enjoy the ride through France.'

'Like you enjoy riding through Ellie?'

'Donut… It ain't my fault you got Janice pissed at you.'

'She pulled rank…'

'Not often a woman can do that…'

'You ever been ordered to do a thing you'd want to do anyway? And suddenly you cain't… because you're supposed to?'

'How on God's earth did you ever get your shit together long enough to join this man's army?'

'I was drafted.'

#

They drove the truck over slings, tires jolting on the harsh cords, then got off and watched it disappear into the hold of the cargo ship. Butler, Donetski and the nurses followed the lieutenant up the gangplank. A rating held out his hand for their side-arms.

'You won't need those on board, soldier. We're all friends here. What you got in the bag?'

The lieutenant took the bag from Butler and swung it over her shoulder. 'It's mine. What you think we're doing here? Smuggling out Nazis?'

'Sorry, Ma'am. I have to ask.'

'And I done told you. It's personal. Can you swim,

sailor?'

'No, Ma'am.'

'Does it get dark at night out on the ocean?'

'Reg'lar as clockwork, Ma'am.'

'Then you and I might put both those things together one evening. Now… what's in my bag?'

'Don't know, Ma'am. But if it's personal then it's fine by me.'

The cabins were cramped and stank of oil and old sweat, the bunks stained and dusty. The floor paint peeled back to reveal rust it would take a jackhammer to shift.

'Think the girls have a better set up than this?'

'Butler… it floats… and tomorrow it heads off for America. What more can I get you?'

'Room service?'

'You been having it on a plate since before we left the camp. How you pulled that one I don't know.'

'She looked into my softer side… and liked what she saw. Cain't say I'd blame her much.'

'Thought it was something a little stiffer than that.'

'Cain't say I'd blame her for that either.'

'Ok. Let's go find where they got put.'

#

'Butler… you got anything to add to this?'

'No Sir, Ma'am. About what, Ma'am?'

'About we're a week out, the sea's like a millpond and Ellie is hung over the side seven o'clock of a morning retching up her toenails.'

'Don't know Ma'am. Perhaps she had something she shouldn't.'

'That's my opinion too. Except the thing she shouldn't

have had is still attached to you, Butler.'

'For how long, Ma'am?'

'At least as long as you make me two promises.'

Butler sat down on the bunk to listen.

'One. When we get state-side you take Ellie to meet your folks.'

'Maybe she'd be better off with hers.'

'She don't have any, Butler.'

'And two?'

'You take her and the bag and make sure they're safe and that no more harm comes of it.'

'That all, Ma'am? I can sure do that much.'

'And three.'

'Three?'

'Officer's privilege. You come back from the Pacific in one piece, y'hear? And then you find them again and you make it right.'

'That's a lot of promising, Ma'am.'

'Butler. Can you swim?'

Ghosts

**Jersey Shore
Pennsylvania**

1951

'I never did meet Clay's folks. He was shipped straight out to Okinawa and never made it back, but then neither did the lieutenant and the other nurses... I should've been there.'

'Survivor Syndrome.' Kowalski picked up his hat and dropped it again from a measured height.

As Ellie watched, it settled slowly and without sound. 'What?'

'"Why me?"... It's called Survivor Syndrome.'

'Guess you have to be alive to feel that?'

'I guess there's no other way.'

'Then who's the lucky one?'

'I'm not immune to it myself.'

'You, Mr Kowalski?'

'Mrs Collins... there is a parade of ghosts through my bedroom each night. All of whom could have done what I did had they had the time, money and foresight.'

'Then that wasn't your fault.'

'Perhaps I had enough of each for all of them.'

'Maybe that wouldn't have been enough.'

'What do you mean, Mrs Collins?'

'Folks have to have belief too. If you'd asked me what I thought before I got to Europe, I would'a told you I couldn't believe no man could do those things to no other man. Whatever he was.'

'And now you know?'

'Makes me ashamed and I don't know how to move on from that.'

Kowalski sat up to the edge of the couch and smiled at her. 'Same way as I do. You wake up in the morning and brush off the footmarks they left on your soul and set about telling the world that it doesn't have to be that way. Makes you kind of lonely at times, though.'

'You lonely, Mr Kowalski?'

'I have my ghosts, Mrs Collins.'

'What about Maggie?'

'You have done your part, Mrs Collins. You gave her a life.'

'And now?'

'And now I have to help her to use that gift.'

Ellie stood up straight from the chair and watched him for a moment, looking deep into his eyes, searching for the soul behind his reassurances.

'Can I get you something? A tea maybe?'

Kowalski glanced briefly at the window. The shabby timbers were closed up tight and their glass soft-edged by the hot dust from the yard outside. 'That would indeed be a kindness today, Mrs Collins.'

'I only have Earl Grey. How do you take it?'

'Black, Mrs Collins. With two slices of lemon.'

'I guess I don't have lemon. Anything else do?'

Kowalski shook his head. While Ellie busied herself in the kitchen, he reached into his leather bag and lifted out a small bound folio. He placed it beside his hat and sat back as Ellie returned with cups and a pot.

'Papers… Mrs Collins.'

Ellie held her breath a moment, taking stock of a situation that had been spiraling around since his first knock at the door, finding a curious comfort in the soft presence of the hat beside him and the way his fingers twitched out occasionally to caress the brim.

'I haven't given the school any papers. They let it go for a while but now they are asking again. Is that why you're here?'

Kowalski watched her eyes as she studied his hat. A smile momentarily graced his lips. 'I'm afraid it is, Mrs Collins.'

'And what are you going to do about it?'

'The school has asked me to verify that her papers are in order.'

'Like I said, what you going to do about it?'

'Can you verify her papers are in order, Mrs Collins?'

Ellie sat back into the chair, eyes set loose in her head. Kowalski's hand reached out for the hat. She leaned forward and moved it along the sofa.

'Now look at me, Mr Kowalski, when I ask you again… What do you aim to do about it?'

'Why, Mrs Collins. I intend to present the school with Maggie's papers. All correct and in order.'

'You know I cain't do that. What are you saying to me? I have no money…'

'I do not need money, Mrs Collins.'

'That's kind'a peculiar around this neighborhood.'

'There are things more valuable than money, Mrs Collins, salvation being only one of them. Another is never allowing anything to go to waste. Especially a life.'

'Then I guess we have to move again. Is it alright for me to tell you that? You won't tell on me? It might take a few days this time.'

Kowalski leaned over the sofa and retrieved his hat. He snapped the brim and re-creased the crown with the blade of his hand.

Ellie offered him a smile. 'Sorry… It was kind of distracting.'

Kowalski settled the hat down again beside him. 'It was meant to be. The more things there are to distract you the more easily the truth slips out between them.'

'Are you one of them…'

'Not at all, Mrs Collins. I learned when it was used on me. I'm what you might call a quick study.'

'Like Maggie.'

'Brightest button in my box.'

'And you're happy to see us moved on again?'

'Not unless you want to move on again.'

Ellie leaned back in the chair. The back was hard and the pressure of the bars somehow restrained the worst of her imagination, keeping her in a moment where nothing had yet happened and finding she needed all her focus to make sure that was how it stayed.

'Can I say I'm too tired right now to move on?'

'Mrs Collins. Can I say right now that Maggie is one lucky little girl?'

'I suppose one from two ain't the worst odds ever.'

Kowalski pushed the hat towards the edge of the sofa where Ellie could reach it without stretching. 'I know about your own daughter, Mrs Collins.'

Ellie stroked the brim of the hat. 'So do I… every minute… every day.'

'But you know that continuing to pass Maggie off as your daughter, God rest her soul, is never going to work. Not without help.'

'Only thing I have for salve is that Clay never knew. He must've died thinking he had a child comin' whose chance at life he paid for.'

'He saved two out of three, Mrs Collins. Not the worst odds ever.'

Ellie managed a smile then, and reached to stroke out the finger marks she had left in the felt. Kowalski lifted it from the sofa, three fingers pressing into the front of the crown. He leaned forward and placed the hat on Ellie's lap. Without thought she folded her hands around it, thumbs stroking the stitched edge for comfort, her scars stretching to allow the movement.

'Papers, you see, Mrs Collins… are something of a speciality for me. Since nineteen thirty-eight I have been making the most convincing papers you have ever seen.'

'That how you got out of Europe?'

'Exactly. They even fooled the Nazis.'

'The school board ain't the Nazis.'

'Don't believe everything you hear, Mrs Collins.'

He picked up the bag from where he'd set it on the floor beside his legs. 'Can we take this conversation to the table?'

'Can I get you something?'

'A chair would indeed be a kindness today, Mrs Collins.'

'How many of these papers you made, Mr Kowalski?'

'I am afraid to count, Mrs Collins.'

'Why?'

'Because it reminds me of all the ones I did not have the time to make. And when I start to question my judgement it slows me down.'

'But you did right. Right?'

'But if you can be right, does that mean you can't be more right? Should I have chosen only to save the ones who seemed to have more capacity for life?'

Ellie drew up a chair beside him and sat down. 'There ain't no such thing. Life comes in screaming and it either takes or it don't.'

'But some souls catch fire, Mrs Collins. What do you think about that?'

'You think you're Solomon, Mr Kowalski? Closing your mouth on that subject right now would indeed be a kindness today.'

Kowalski pulled a sheaf of papers out of his bag. Ellie watched as he unfolded several of them across the bare wood. 'These are maps, Mr Kowalski.'

'Indeed, Mrs Collins.'

'What of?'

'Graveyards, Mrs Collins. Death used to be the end of hope in this life. But since the war we're all just so much salvage.' He unfolded a map and pinned it down with a finger. 'Here…'

Ellie leaned across him to see. The writing was small and consisted of what looked like a grid reference. She looked up at him to read his face. He tapped the map again.

'Magdalena Grau. Born June 1st. 1942.'

'How does that help?'

'Look. Deceased September 28 1946.'

'You want me to name Maggie after some stranger's dead child?'

'If you could have salvaged something from your own daughter's death that might have made a difference to someone else, would you have at least considered that?'

'I might've.'

'Well, you couldn't… but these people can. And perhaps a degree of familiarity by name will bring a comfort to all. Would you deny them that?'

Ellie looked over to the sofa, wishing the hat was closer now. 'I guess not. What do I have to do? Do I have to meet them?'

'Only if you wish to, Mrs Collins.'

'I might take some while to think on that.'

'That's your prerogative. Meanwhile, I've got to get to work on this.' He folded up the maps and returned them to the bag. 'Do I have your permission?'

Ellie nodded, stood up and passed him his hat. He made to put it on then remembered he was still inside the house. As he was going out the door, she reached out to catch the brim for one last time, but missed. He placed the hat on his head and tipped it ready for the sun's scorch just beyond the shade. 'One week. Give me one week.'

While she remembered it clearly, Ellie went into the kitchen and wrote down the grid reference for Lewisburg Cemetery.

Bill Allerton

232

Touchstones

Lewisburg Cemetery
Pennsylvania

1951

Faded flowers in a pewter vase sat just below the small black stone. Ellie hadn't been expecting that, and the sight of them sprung loose her insides until the tears streaked her cheeks and brought salt to her lips. She licked them clear. The taste was bitter and sharp but now, nearly two years on, they at last felt right.

'Can I help you?'

Ellie stepped back alarmed. She had been so deep for a moment that she hadn't heard the footsteps approaching. The woman's head was wrapped in a peasant scarf that tied under the chin and draped black lace across her shoulders. The face inside it was still young but, like her own, scarred with sadness. The flowers in her hand were fresh and vibrant.

'I...'

'What you want by my daughter's grave?'

'You are Mrs Grau?'

'Yes... you must be woman who rescue child from camps. Collins, he said.'

'Ellie...'

Mrs Grau took the old flowers from the vase and passed

them behind her without looking. Ellie took them in silence, feeling the petals crumble in her hands. Mrs Grau took a small perfume bottle from her pocket and placed it in front of the grave beside others already there. She took a pebble from the path at her feet and balanced it on top of the headstone. The top of the stone was crowded and the woman chose a flat one for Ellie and showed her where to put it.

'I am here every time. I am sorry. I miss Magdalena so much I leave space for no-one.'

'Don't be sorry. You make me ashamed.'

'Of what you should be ashamed?'

'Of all the times I don't visit my daughter. I want to but...'

'Think only then of special times. You see perfume? It is her birthday. I say she have one each year for so long as I live, but now you are here, all this is change.'

'I am sorry. I don't mean to bring change. I don't know what to do now... I don't know...'

Mrs Grau put out her hand and touched Ellie's sleeve. 'All you will ever do is in the past and is in the future and is in the now. How you think we survive, knowing this is happening around us? Only knowing it is written keep us sane.'

'Is it enough to survive?'

'You must have think so, to bring the girl home with you.'

'We wanted to give her a life. At least I think that's what we wanted. Out there we were never sure that even our own thoughts were the truth. We saw so many things...'

'I too see many things, but Kowalski give my daughter chance for life.'

'But... your daughter...'

'Kowalski he say... not all souls catch fire. God made me

234

not strong for to blow spark, but you are strong woman, you take her name and you take her life and you make it good one.'

She touched the gravestone with a fingertip, caressing dust from the edge of it.

'This is now a nothing. Only place to come and weep. But perhaps I weep not now so much as before. Do you love our little girl, Mrs Collins?'

'With all my heart, Mrs Grau.'

'Then give address please so I can send things.' She reached down and gathered the perfume bottles in one hand. 'Make these hers now.' She held them out to Ellie. 'And when you hold her, blow spark with breath from both mothers.'

Ellie placed the bottles together in her pocket. They rattled her with every jolt of the bus on the way home.

#

'Mrs Collins. A good day to you.'

'Mr Kowalski. A week passes so quickly.'

'So quickly in fact, Mrs Collins, that it has taken two of them to make my return. You must have been concerned.'

'I'm not sure what I've been. Part of me was afraid of you coming back. We always thought there'd be four of us to work this out.'

'Great wars, Mrs Collins, are followed by greater uncertainties as we look around and try to recognize this new land.'

'But I always lived here, Mr Kowalski.'

'But no you did not, Mrs Collins. It may look the same but peace has an intangible quality. It is filled with an odorless, translucent substance I call Potential.'

'Do you still take lemon with your tea, Mr Kowalski?'

'Yes, I do, Mrs Collins. Why do you ask?'

'Because I bought some. It's in sugar syrup. It was all I could find.'

'There is no better kind, Mrs Collins.'

'Would you try a cup, Mr Kowalski?'

'That would indeed be a kindness today, Mrs Collins.'

'So this is all I need?' Ellie shuffled the papers into a neat pile and returned them to the folder.

'I have filed all other necessary papers, Mrs Collins. The school, the local Health Board, and with our Mr Truman's proposed new hospitals for lower income areas, we may soon be able to get you back to work.'

'I need that, Mr Kowalski.' She studied the backs of her hands. The sense of failure the sight of the skin grafts left her with remained sharp in her eye as she looked up into the kindness of his smile. 'I need that more than ever. I thank you, Mr Kowalski.'

'Gratitude is neither warranted nor deserved, Mrs Collins.'

'Mr Kowalski…'

'Yes, Mrs Collins?'

'I don't know… I don't know what I wanted to say.' She stared straight into his eyes. 'Mr Kowalski? May I touch your hat?'

He placed it in her lap and watched her fingers stroke away the marks he had just made in the nap and reassert the dimples in the crown exactly the way they'd been the day he'd first arrived at her door.

'Mrs Collins?'

Ellie was staring past him, through him.

'Mrs Collins?'

'…yes?'

'May I touch your hands?'

Slowly, she held them out to where he could reach. 'That would indeed be a kindness today… Mr Kowalski.'

Bill Allerton

Stroking the Cat

Spring Grove
Chain O'Lakes
Illinois

2018

'Maggie?' The doctor held Maggie's hand and twisted it gently so the inside of her forearm showed clear in the bright hospital light.

'Scratches, Doc. Strange what you get up to when you're a kid. Trick is not to let it ruin your life.'

'More than scratches, Maggie. These are numbers.'

'I can see that, Doc. We shared phones you know… at school.'

'No cell phones back then, Maggie. But maybe they were lucky numbers. You ever run them in the Lottery?'

'They never got me anything special before. Even my mother used to beat up on me. I had to learn to hide…'

'Guess that's how you stayed alive.'

'Not sure about that, Doc. Just seems to have taken me another seventy-five years to get to the same place.'

'It's not the arriving, Maggie, it's the journey.'

'Well yeah, I suppose that's been kind'a fun at times. Had its problems too… maybe it still has. You hear from Gradzynski yet?'

'Not yet.'

'How's Shirley. Hear they smashed her up pretty bad.'

'Who told you that, Maggie?'

'Doc? Can I confirm a medical fact with you?'

'Sure. Fire away.'

Maggie smiled and closed her eyes. 'When my eyes are closed, do my ears stay open?'

Doc shook her gently by the shoulder.

Maggie's eyes opened again. 'What'ya got? Another new machine you want to try out?'

'What's the point, Maggie?'

'Yeah, you're right. What's the point at my age?'

'No, Maggie. I mean you're as right as you're ever going to be.'

'What about the arm, Doc?' Maggie tried to lift her left arm and managed about an inch or so before she let it flop back to the bed. 'Can't even pour vodka with his useless piece of…'

'Give it time. You'll adapt.'

'To what? Tea with no rocket fuel? You any idea what Earl Grey tastes like on its own?'

'To using one arm, I meant.'

'Don't you worry about that, Doc. I got a plan…'

'Now you be careful, Maggie. You might still have a way to go before you meet the saints.'

'Ma Collins said there's only three saints I should ever concern myself with.'

'Which ones are they?'

'Saint Donetski, Saint Butler… and a real special one.' She turned away as her eyes filled. 'Don't pay me no mind, Doc. I'm just an old woman. Have you been through my papers yet?'

'Yes Maggie, I have.'

'Have you read them all?'

'Yes, Maggie. Every one. Took most the night.'

'And?'

The doctor choked on his reply. He turned away and took off his glasses, polishing the lenses on his tie. He put them on and walked away from the bed without looking back. Maybe the local Rabbi could see a way to get Saint Kowalski confirmed as Hasid.

#

'Hey Joseph?'

'Gradzynski? Where've you been? You haven't been taking your calls. Mariel's been in twice already this morning. If you don't get back soon I'll put on ten pounds.'

'It's a long one, Jo. Meanwhile, there's something I need you to do. Some twenty-four hours ago, I deputized a young man by the name of Leroy.'

'Leroy what, Pav?'

Gradzynski looked across to Leroy behind the wheel of the Interceptor, then down at his own bandaged hands. 'Hang on...' He looked at Leroy for an answer. Leroy just shrugged his shoulders and stared back at the highway flashing under the hood.

Gradzynski glanced out the side window as they streaked past a sign into a small town. 'Dubuque, Joseph. Leroy Dubuque.'

'He on the register, Pav?'

'Nope. I reckon not. But get him on the insurance for my car.'

He ended the call and half-turned in his seat, wincing as the leather grabbed his clothes and dragged them across the live graze under his shirt. Æppel was asleep in back. Eugenie sat up under the same seat belt, eyes wide, staring at him. He reached over and passed his bandaged hand gently down across her face. Her eyes closed and she snuggled back into the curve of Æppel. He logged the phone on again.

'Hi. This is the police. Can you put me through to Doc Franklin... Yeah, I'll wait... What? Gradzyns... tell him it's Pav.'

Leroy leaned across the seat. 'Don't forget to ask him about Maggie.'

'You just watch where we're going... Deputy. You know how much shit that Fed got you out of with that suggestion?'

Leroy nodded quietly, eyes watching the lines flicker on the blacktop. Gradzynski glanced at the plastic beads melted against his scalp as he nodded. Fixing that was going to hurt.

Thoughts of yesterday began to prey on his mind. So many questions barbed his conscience. He should be used to this... but what do you when folks don't want to be saved? The phone jerked him away from the grey depression that was descending.

'Pav?'

'Yeah, Doc. Four customers on their way in.'

'Who is it?'

'Well... me for one and I'll tell you about the others when we get there.'

'Anything I need special?'

'Got anything that stops burns from stinging?'

'Pav? You okay?'

'Well... three of us got kind of a scorching here and there and the other's a case of smoke inhalation. But other than that we're fine. I think...'

'Where've you been? Have you been treated?'

'Yeah, Regional Family Hospital in Manchester.'

'In Iowa? What... you...? Never mind, I'll ring them now and get your case notes sent through. Have something ready for when you get here. How far away are you?'

'Way my new Deputy drives, make that two and a half

hours.'

'New Deputy? By the way, Mariel has been calling.'

'She didn't bring you food yet?' Leroy nudged him. 'By the way, Doc. How's everyone else?'

'Two and a half hours, you say?'

'Thereabouts…'

'Okay… It'll hold until then.'

The phone clicked off. Gradzynski threw it into the door pocket beside him and turned in his seat. 'What do you think he meant by that?'

Leroy hit the pedal to the floor by way of a reply. The acceleration pushed Gradzynski into the seat where the graze on his back hurt like hell.

#

Gradzynski was glad that the door was automatic. He couldn't have worked out which part of his anatomy would have been least painful to push it open with. He walked through Reception and along the corridor to the wards, Leroy and Æppel following close behind. He stopped at the room where he'd last seen Shirley. All the machines were still beside the bed but now the wires trailed the floor, their dials silent and immobile.

Doc Franklin caught up with him. 'Pav! Let me take a look at those hands.'

'Don't bother none with me, Doc. Us boys can wait. Check out Eugenie and Æppel.'

Æppel lowered Eugenie to the bed and held her still while the doc listened to her chest.

'Smoke inhalation like they said. Where you had this child, Pav?'

'No time for that now, Doc. What you going to give her?'

'Time, I think, Pav. Just time and a little oxygen. Otherwise she'll be fine. She's just finished a course of antibiotics. Now you, young lady…' He turned Æppel's face with his hand, examining the scalp where her hair had burned before Leroy could get her into the water. 'Anywhere else?'

'All my face is sore. My legs… and the back of my neck too.'

'Okay. Follow the nurse and get gowned up. I'll see you in a minute. Take the little one with you. Now then, young man… let's take a look at your head.'

Leroy bent his head so Doc could see the damage. 'Doctor at the hospital did a good job. Only hurt enough to keep me awake on the way back.'

'Well, I'm not going to poke around in there and make it any worse. Soon as new skin grows it'll push the plastic off. Meanwhile it's sterile from the fire and the hospital sprayed you with an antiseptic. I'll add a little anesthetic spray to that and for now you'll just have to wait it out. Maybe three weeks before we can tell what you're going to need.'

'Doc. I ain't got no money…'

'Deputy…' The doctor looked up at Gradzynski, who nodded slightly. '…you don't need money. Pav? Let's get those hands unwrapped.'

'Whoa, Doc. Before you do, I want to hear about Shirley.'

'Are you sure you're ready for this, Pav?'

'After yesterday, Doc, believe me I'm ready.'

'Then let's get some fresh air.'

Doc led him back along the corridor to a set of stairs going down. Gradzynski followed him closely, allowing the doctor to open doors for him. They went down one flight and along the corridor beneath the ward. A door they came to was propped open. The far wall of the room had closed drapes and Gradzynski hesitated as he saw through the gloom that in the center was a pathology table. The doctor ushered him along the corridor and through another doorway. The drapes in this room were drawn back and the green of the lawn behind the hospital showed bright outside.

'Doc? What are we doing here?'

Doc slid back a patio window, led Gradzynski out into the light and took a deep breath. To the right of the window was a wheelchair. Covered by a blanket up to her chest was Shirley.

Gradzynski turned away at the sight of her face. 'Oh… Doc…'

'Superficial now, mostly. We drained the brain bleed and limited the damage. Some of it may turn out to be permanent, but only time will tell us that story.'

'Is she… awake?'

Doc pulled up her blanket. 'Sometimes the sunlight seems to draw her out. Doesn't like being changed though…'

'And her mind?'

'Oh… it's in there, Pav. It may not be as sharp as it was and it's probably still in shock, but it'll come out when it's ready.'

'Can I have a minute with her?'

'Sure.'

Gradzynski waited until the doctor's footsteps were out of earshot. He leaned down to the side of Shirley's head and put out a bandaged hand but was afraid to touch her.

'We got them, Shirl.'

He waited for a smile… but it didn't arrive.

#

Maggie was sitting up in bed when Gradzynski called in. 'Ma Collins had hands like that once, Gradzynski. What you been up to?'

'Like... bright yellow, you mean?'

'Under that. The yellow's only temporary.'

'Hope the rest of it is too, Maggie.'

'Here... let me look.'

'You the doctor now, Maggie? I hear a lot of them have a drink problem too...'

'Stress of being right all along. Terrible cross to bear.'

Maggie held his hand in her own good one and turned it over in the light. 'It'll be fine.'

'Not like Ma Collins, then?'

'Ma's hands were fine. It's not always about how they look.'

'What did she do with hers?'

'She failed.'

'She did a fine job on you, Maggie.'

'Maybe. But most of her life she thought she was a failure.'

'Doc says she was a nurse. That right?'

'Well... she tried again, later... but couldn't see straight. No matter how many she helped, they all wore the face of the one she couldn't.'

'Spill it, Maggie...'

'Well... we were out in a car. Don't think it was hers... it was a way back... she wouldn't have had the money. Or the inclination. Always said she learnt in a truck in the war and nothing felt safe after that. Don't know where we were going or why except maybe somebody was asking questions about me.'

'What kind of questions, Maggie.'

'You know the sort of thing... the size of my honker... how come I didn't speak American like the other kids...

these stupid numbers on my arm...'

She allowed Gradzynski to pull up her sleeve and look at them.

'You ever entered these in the Lottery, Maggie?'

'That's what the doc said but I always had to work for whatever I got. You more Polish than me, Gradzynski?'

'Only by name, Maggie.'

'Well, names being what they are, 'Collins' didn't sort of fit with all those other things so before Anton Kowalski turned up we shifted around a bit from time to time, like I said.'

'The car, Maggie. What happened?'

'Like I was saying... the back seat was full of boxes... medical equipment... swabs, alcohol and stuff... she worked from home, you know... couldn't keep a regular job with all that moving... but anyone with no money, well... that was all the ticket they needed for Ma Collins... and there was plenty of them in those days... all these guys back from the war and wandering around looking for work they forgot how to do... so little Janice is in the back seat in some make-up kind of a cot in the middle of all this stuff and we get sideswiped by a truck. I'm on the front seat next to Ma and we get thrown out onto the grass and we rolled and rolled and the car slid on in front of us until it was stopped by a tree. Next thing I remember is blue flames coming out the back window. Then the whole car went up. That's when Ma Collins climbed in.'

'Thought you said it was just her hands?'

'That's the only part she ever let you see...'

'Kowalski?'

'Gave us the next twenty years of his life. Turns out that's all he had. Never saw a man so tender with anything... or anybody. Know how you stroke a cat? That way. Ma Collins nursed him the same way 'til he went. Fulfilled her somehow. Said she changed then… accepted her life and the way it all went. Just a shame, she said, that someone else has to die to make all the strings pull together. So here I am, Gradzynski. I'm all woman and I'm all yours. What you going to do with me? Room for three in your bed?'

'No… but I know where there is room for someone else while you're in here. If you don't mind?'

'I'm okay with that, but make me one promise.'

'Anything, Maggie.'

'Make sure they're still there when I get out'a here.'

Sub Routine

'Hi Mariel.' Gradzynski reached around to give her a hug. She pushed him away to take a look at his hands. 'Where have you been, Pav? What have you done? Does it hurt?'

'Hurts like Hell, Mariel, and by the way this is Leroy.'

'Hi Leroy. Does this need changing, Pav? There's yellow bleeding through. Oh! And his head!'

'Yeah, Mariel. We got anything to eat? I think Leroy could use some food right now.'

'I have some bigos left in a jar.'

'You mean Joseph didn't finish it off?'

'I didn't give him all of it. He's getting fat behind that desk. There's enough if I put a little something on the side.'

'Like what?'

'Like Szarlotka?'

#

'Gradzynski! Welcome back to the world of the underpaid.'

'Joseph… this is a long one… but get me Shirley's file.'

'Sure… what are you missing?'

'Answers.'

Joseph handed a slim file to Gradzynski. 'Pretty slim pickings in there, then.'

'How come it was on your desk?'

'Been trying to raise folks. Let them know she was injured.'

'And…'

'And no-one home so far.'

Gradzynski took the file into his office. He leaned back in the chair and winced in pain. The graze was taking some time to heal. Every time Mariel rubbed salve into it she found other things of his to attend to as well. He picked up his pen, then threw it back and shouted Joseph. 'Hey, Jo. Come in here and take a few notes, will you?'

#

'Are you sure this is right?' Leroy tapped the screen of the GPS. It showed their location right by the zip code he'd punched in. The house beside them was shuttered and boarded. The gates hung raggedly and the garden had grown right through the wrought iron. 'Nobody's been here for years.'

Gradzynski frowned, but kept back any thoughts he had. 'Try the next zip code…'

Leroy looked around for the house. 'There ain't one, Pav.'

'Go try the paint shop over there. See what they know.'

'Used to be houses here, but that was some time ago. We've been here what… say… fifteen years? That right, Sally? I been around here once when I was a kid. The houses ran thataway across our drive if I remember right. I could be wrong. It was a while back now. I think there's a picture in the store room. Sally... go find it for the man.'

Sally returned with a black and white aerial picture of where the paint shop now stood. The houses had run across the drive, just like the man said, but even back then there had been an air of severe dilapidation showing in the shingles and the way the yards had been left to riot. Leroy took it from her and turned it around to see if there was a date on the back. 'Can I borrow this?'

'Only if you bring it back...'

'Thanks Ma'am.'

'D'you hear that, John? He called me Ma'am.'

'Put it in the back seat, Leroy.'

'Look here on the back... it says 1996. That's what? 22 years ago? And the houses were a mess even back then.'

'You trying for detective grade already?'

'Just trying to help.'

'I know, son. But all this trying... you and me both... ain't helping any. Maybe the answer's locked up in Shirley's head.'

'You think she's in there, Pav?'

'Doc says she is... and that's all we got to hang on to. Two kinds of ways she could be, he says. Says some folks're like a tiger in a cage and can't get out through the bars of their injury. Drives 'em crazy with frustration... an' some folks're like a kitten curled up in a box, waiting to open their eyes once they're no longer afraid of what they might see. Never had Shirley figured for a kitten but it's the only way I'm hoping.'

'Try another address?'

'Leroy, I smell a rat. In fact, I smell so many I think it's time we went home and got out the traps.'

#

'Joseph…' Gradzynski pointed to the file Leroy had just dropped on the desk. 'There has to be more than this. What we got here ain't worth a damn.'

'I don't know what to say, Pav. That's all I can give you.'

'And what you got that you can't give me?'

'There's no answer to that, Pav.'

'Oh yes, there is. Shirl goes back two years… and the months she's been here. Before that? Zip.'

'There was her time at the Academy.'

'Right. Room and board at Arlington for what? Four years?'

'It says here she flew in two, Pav. 'A' stars all the way.'

'So how come we get her, Jo? How come the Feds didn't snatch her before we saw hide nor hair?'

'We got lucky, I guess.'

'You ever take patrol with her?'

'Nope.'

'Didn't think so…'

'Not much more I can give you on this, Pav. You have all that floats right there in that folder.'

'Then keep your sonar running, Joseph. I think we got a U Boat out there.'

#

Gradzynski ripped the police tape off the street light some yards below Maggie's house. The standard green was liberally smeared with dried blood and a gloss black paint residue where the driver had brushed Shirley off the van. There must have been severe damage all along the side of it but not enough to make it undriveable. He stood back to replay a few details over in his mind, then walked back along

Maggie's drive.

He propped himself against the open door frame and glanced around. Maggie's living room looked like a tornado had whipped through.

'Think you can do anything with this, Leroy?'

'I can do anything with anything, Pav.'

'Then set to. If you need anything from the store, tell 'em it's for me.'

'I'll call my Pa. Once I get my truck up here I got most of what I need in the cab.'

'Just one more thing, Leroy. Take a walk with me.'

'Where we going, Pav?'

'Not far. I want to see if your memory is better than mine.'

They walked down to the street light and stopped. Gradzynski ran his bandaged hand across the paint smear. 'Recognize this paint, Leroy?'

'Pretty standard, Pav. Why?'

'See anything this color up at the farm?'

'Hmmm… No. Mostly all they had was piles of rust. They don't like machines so I wouldn't expect there to be any out there that worked.'

'Thanks, Leroy. Oh, and a word to the wise, for Heaven's sake stay out of Maggie's bedroom.'

Leroy walked back to the house, shaking his head.

Gradzynski glanced once more at the street light, took a deep breath, then set off in the direction of the hospital.

#

'Hi Doc. How are my patients doing?'

'Well… depends on how you mean that.'

'Who's giving you the most trouble… don't answer that…'

'You'd be surprised.'

'You mean it's not Maggie?'

'Only problem with Maggie is getting Mrs Watson out of the ward. There's biscuit crumbs everywhere and I'm sure she's interfering with Maggie's drip. Never seen Maggie so cheerful.'

'I'd frisk that Maybelline when she comes to visit if I were you, Doc.'

'I would if she didn't always look as though she's waiting for me to do it.'

Gradzynski allowed himself a smile, first of that morning, a morning spent fruitlessly searching for evidence of Shirley's past. The fact that he came up with nothing but blind alleys was most illuminating of all. In fact, it had been the pivot on which his investigation had turned. He'd run the past few weeks through in his head in case there was something he'd missed, perhaps a loose word somewhere, but Shirley had the tightest rein on her mouth he'd ever come across... unless it related to Maggie, then it was open season. Then he'd thrown the ripple out wider...

'How is Shirley, Doc?'

'Well... that's sort of giving me a problem.'

'Has she spoken yet?'

'No, but she moved her head a couple of days ago so I've kept her where I can keep an eye on her.'

'Where is she?'

'Room next to my office.'

'Can I see her?'

'Yes, of course. Come on, but let me tell you... I saw her lips move so I bent down real close to listen.'

'What was she trying to say?'

'She didn't say anything. She kissed my ear.'

'Now I'm getting worried, Doc.'

'That's not all. She did it again yesterday.'

Gradzynski studied Doc's unusually pale cheeks. 'So today you had a shave? Right?'

'Yeah. Damn right.'

Shirley lay propped against several pillows with wires and tubes tucked around her. The swelling was receding but the wounds seemed more livid for all that. 'The best I can do, Pav. I'm no cosmetic surgeon but later maybe…'

Her eyes were closed and Gradzynski leaned across to inspect the stitches in her face. 'They'll fade, won't they? I only hope the memory does too.'

'Not since they invented the mirror. But she was a looker to start with and she still will be. As long as she believes that she is.'

'There was a kind of perfection about her that she might find hard to lose.'

'I hope not, Pav.'

'Why's that?'

'You've seen the way I look at her. I've been figuring her out since the first time she came to work with you and this has brought it into focus.'

'You're not looking any more.'

'Heck no, Pav. That kind of perfection leaves a man with nothing to forgive. And a man needs a layer of forgiveness in his soul.'

'Have you said this much to Shirley?'

'Not yet, Pav, but I will. Soon as I know she understands, I'm going to tell her to look at me whenever she needs a mirror… just so she can see she's my kind of perfect.'

'And no-one's ever going to tell her otherwise… that right?'

'Right… Officer.'

Eye of The Storm

'Gradzynski?'

'Yeah, Joseph. What's new?'

'Just got a call in for you. Feds.'

'What do they want?'

'They want you to go over to Strawberry Point.'

'For what?'

'They want see if your statement matches up with theirs.'

'What do they really want? I can email my statement anytime.'

'I think it's you they want, Pav. Perhaps they want you to join.'

'Fat chance of that. Anyway, I can't drive.'

'Then you'd better take Dubuque with you… and he's another one I can't find hide nor hair of in the records.'

'He's a gift horse, Joseph. Stop checking his teeth.'

'I got paperwork…'

'It'll wait.'

#

Leroy swung the cruiser in off the highway and dropped

into the parking lot beside a grey sedan. He got out of the car and a guy in the sedan motioned him to get back in.

Gradzynski climbed out the other side and walked around to where a rear door had been pushed open for him. He slid into the seat and allowed the door to close behind him. He didn't recognize either of the men in the front.

'Show me some ID.'

'What you going to do, Gradzynski? Arrest us?'

'It's a consideration…'

'Here…' The man behind the wheel leaned over and flashed his shield where Gradzynski could see it. Gradzynski nodded and settled into the seat. 'Where's Dolan?'

'I'm Bronski, his line manager. He didn't need to come along personally.'

'So how can I match up the statement with him?'

'You don't need to do that, Gradzynski. We'd been watching the squirrels up at the farm for some time. In a way you did us a favor turning up like that.'

Gradzynski held up his bandaged hands where the Fed could see them in the rear-view mirror. 'I don't have too many of those to give. Not for a while anyway.'

'You got your phone, Gradzynski?'

'Hell yes, why? You want to make a call?'

'No. I want to borrow it. Hand it over.'

Gradzynski carefully removed his phone and handed it over. The Fed handed it back. 'Unlock it…'

'This ain't police issue…'

'Just unlock it.'

Gradzynski passed it back over. Bronski sat quietly thumbing through the pictures, then leaned across and showed one to the other guy who winced visibly, before handing it back.

Gradzynski slid it into a pocket. 'So why drag me all the way out here?'

'We have a legitimate reason for being out here, Gradzynski. Tell us what you know about Shirley Hunter.'

'You mean I know something you don't already?'

'Like… are you involved with her?'

'Only when she's a pain in the ass and then I get kind of angry…'

'Let me rephrase that… are you sexually involved with her?'

'Hell no. I'm married.'

'Have you ever been…'

'I expect this kind of grilling from Mariel, not you…'

'Who's Mariel?'

The guy in the passenger seat nodded in Gradzynski's direction. 'That's his wife. Don't you read your own paperwork?'

Gradzynski peeled his back off the seat. 'What's my wife doing on his paperwork?'

'Everyone's on our paperwork somewhere, Gradzynski. Don't feel special.'

Gradzynski stared out the side window. From there he had an oblique view of the side of Leroy's head and the melted plastic still clinging to his scalp. Leroy had refused to protect it with a hat, satisfied to wait out the pain of recovery.

He shuddered at the thought of the chance that Leroy had taken. 'I'm not special. I'm just doing a job.'

Bronski turned in his seat and nodded at the bandages around Gradzynski's hands. 'And doing it well, too, we hear.'

'Up my pay, then.'

'I'm giving you the Irishman's rise. More work for the same money.'

'You better talk to Mariel about that. Seems I'm not home enough as it is.'

'This won't keep you away, Gradzynski. Fact is, it might

keep you closer.'

'Who do I have to kill?'

'No-one. You're just our first line of defense.'

'The Russians are coming?'

'Not the Russians this time, Gradzynski. Someone much closer to home.'

'So who am I defending?'

'Shirley Hunter.'

'What's so special about Shirley that I'm not already finding out for myself. Six blank addresses is telling me something and I'm only just warming up my ear to listen.'

'Stop now, Gradzynski. Your digging has flagged up an alarm.'

Gradzynski sat back into the seat, laughing, until his back reminded him of the still-livid graze. He sat back up abruptly. 'Is this Witness Protection?'

'Could be.'

'So you protect someone by sticking them up in the air and dressing them as a Police Officer?'

'You ever hear of hiding in plain sight, Gradzynski? Go find a reason to stop digging.'

'On one condition. You give me the details.'

Bronski shrugged. 'You know I can't do that.'

'Then we're done here...' Gradzynski pushed open the door with his elbow.

Bronski reached over and held him back. 'Get yourself killed by all means, Gradzynski, but don't spread it around like a disease.'

'Then you better vaccinate me with the truth.'

'This is not easy, Gradzynski. If this gets out it blows up an expensive project.'

'Then why did you station her with me?'

'Because nothing ever happened to you, Gradzynski. You were always the perfect eye of the perfect storm. So what changed?'

'Maggie Gray.'

'Who's Maggie Gray?'

Gradzynski shook Bronski's hand off his jacket. 'That says more about her than you'll ever know.'

The guy in the passenger seat turned around and studied Gradzynski's expression for a moment, then turned away.

'Bronski, for Christ's sake tell the man. He's all day long a cop.'

'Okay, Gradzynski. Tell me what you know about Shirley. Not what you suspect, but what you actually know.'

Gradzynski shuffled in the seat. 'She's a pain in the ass.'

Bronski straightened the mirror so he could study Gradzynski's reaction to the questions. Despite his natural cynicism, he couldn't help warming to the guy. There was a directness and honesty here that he was unaccustomed to. He was beginning to understand the 'why' when Gradzynski had come up as a choice.

'That's a given. What else?'

Gradzynski looked up and met the eyes reflected in the glass. 'What do you want me to say?'

'I don't want you to say anything you don't feel.'

'You already asked me that one. She feels more like a piece of work than anything else I could put a tag on.'

'And that's exactly what she is, Gradzynski. Your piece of work.'

'Where did you find her?'

'College.'

'There's a million bright kids in there.'

'They can't all defeat the system the way she did.'

'She a computer whiz?'

'Nope. Doesn't need one. That girl has the most intense sense of logic we ever came across.'

'And what exactly do you expect me to make of that?'

'You have to make her human, Gradzynski. That's all. Just make her human.'

'You telling me she's some kind of a robot? Hell! I could buy that in a heartbeat.'

Bronski laughed out loud. 'Along with the rest of us, but no, she's no robot. Just a touch special.'

'You're telling me? I work with her, remember?'

'She's special because she has the highest IQ of anyone ever recruited to the Bureau. As a matter of fact, one of the highest ever recorded. You give her a bunch of random data and she comes right back at you with an answer. Is that special enough for you?'

'I guess.'

'Precision is okay for scientists but the truth, as you and I know it, Gradzynski, can weave around a little. With Shirley, everything's a straight line. And a straight line is either right or wrong depending on your direction of travel.'

'So she's fifty-fifty. What do you want from me? A change to the Laws of Probability?'

'Nothing so easy. Shirley is always right, and straight lines get you killed in the kind of jobs we had lined up for her. We watched you. You know how to drift with a curve and she needed to learn that before she spun out, and while she was learning she needed some protection.'

Gradzynski stared into the eyes in the mirror. 'You realize you just posed a fundamental paradox of the Laws of Physics?'

'How so?'

'What happens when an irresistible force meets an immovable object.'

'Maggie Gray?'

'Damn right, Maggie Gray. I only have one argument with your explanation, Bronski. The arrows on each end of your straight line don't point outwards. They point in.'

'Where does that leave you?'

'In the crossfire.'

'Well… I'm sorry to say this, Gradzynski, but you're going to be in it a while longer.'

'How do you reckon that? Where she is right now isn't going to affect anybody. I even tried to let her folks know…'

'Hear me out… She has no folks. They got caught up on the wrong side of a bust. We've had our eye on her since twelfth grade. You're right, she can't affect anyone in her present condition, but that's not the problem. The problem is… there's someone looking to affect her.'

'So who do I have to protect her from?'

Bronski chuckled lightly, then glanced back up at the mirror. 'I could say from herself, mostly. She's a bit screwy in places but you already worked that one out. No, mainly from a man with revenge on his mind.'

'You have a file on him?'

'Yes, Gradzynski. We do have a file on him. Thick as you like but never enough to make anything stick. I'll send it over if you can't find the copy Shirley was working on.'

'Shirley was…? Who is he?'

'How many names you want? Different one every job. His code name's Magpie. Goes around stealing back anyone these cults think they misplaced. This guy's a real needle in the criminal haystack, Gradzynski. We got DNA from 'most everywhere he's operated but he's managed to stay off register and until we find a big toe to put the tag on we're blowin' in the wind. Nearest I can say right now is that he hired a van near Chain O'Lakes on a fake ID. We found it battered and torched in the shallows of Grass Lake. Tried to drown it but the mud held it back. Must have really pissed him but it was too burned to get prints off anyway. Plates probably cash from a local shop somewhere. The man's a professional, Gradzynski. Word on the street says his last job was for some religious nuts out by Strawberry Point. Sound familiar?'

'Yeah, but where does Shirley come into this. If he's who you think he is, he almost killed her anyways.'

'Word also has it, Gradzynski, that before he tangled with Shirley he had two eyeballs and both of them worked. Not any longer, and I wish we'd known that before the Doc got to work on her. Maybe we could have recovered some DNA from her fingernails or such. Could've tied this one to him as well.'

'You checked the Hospitals?'

'For sure. But a man who's been around as long as this one has access to private meds somewhere. There's plenty happens underground where the money ain't fresh and traceable.'

'Where is he now?'

'That we don't know, Gradzynski. He is an expert at getting lost and never hangs around after he's been paid, but perhaps this time he'd gone under somewhere local to get his face fixed. Street says he thought he'd killed her... until her picture popped up in the press along with the report.'

'I made no report.'

'We know you didn't, Gradzynski.'

'Then who did?'

'Gradzynski? Are you a cop? Work this one out for yourself.'

'Okay... I can see this. So tell me what else you know.'

'Not much, Gradzynski or I'd give it you. But what I do know is... he will be spiraling in one direction. Shirley's.'

'How come you haven't taken him out before?'

'We thought to could keep tabs on him, find out how he got his contacts. But he always knew when we were comin'. Don't ask me how, but he knew.'

'You presiding over a sieve, Bronski?'

'If we only knew how deep some things ran, then maybe they wouldn't.'

'That sounds like a Rumsfeld.'

'Don't tell me, Gradzynski, the only holes you have are in your socks? I need you back on the job, Officer. Only this time… do it right.'

#

'Phone call for you earlier, Pav. Feds. Asking about Shirley.'

'What did you tell them, Joseph?'

'Hey! You know me. I know nothing…'

'Good. Why didn't you keep it that way when you showed Shirley's picture from the file to your sister?'

'She said the Editor wouldn't run it unless you okayed it personally.'

'Well… looks like you made a bad day worse, Joseph. Forget about going home. You're on permanent shift until I sort out the mess you just made.'

'You can't do that, Pav. She gave me her word…'

'You can choose your friends, Joseph, but not your relatives. You tell me which you have to be most careful around. These people who rang. Did they say who they were?'

'No. But it wasn't the same guy rang last time.'

'Get the number?'

'Of course…'

#

'Gradzynski? You the guy whose ass got dragged out of the fire? How's it healing?'

'Some things might never. Who is this? Why did you call

me?'

'You know who I am.'

'Yeah, I guess I do. What do you want?'

'Just wanted to know about Shirley Hunter.'

'She's dead'

'That's bullshit, Gradzynski.'

'Dead to you, anyways.'

'I know that, Gradzynski, but what do you want me to say?'

'I want you to say you'll stay well clear. And never call again.'

'I can't promise that, Gradzynski.'

'You know how much damage you did already?'

'There's always collateral…'

'You doubt my ability to protect her?'

'You doubt my ability to get past you, Gradzynski?'

'The best thing you can do is hold out for the cuffs right now.'

'I know where she is, Gradzynski, but I'll pick the time and I'm in no rush. She must be in some real pain right now. I like that but, unlike mine, hers will only be temporary because you can't hide her where I can't find her. This is too small a burg and the Bureau won't let you take her off-state. After that, Gradzynski, I'm coming around for you.'

'You know where I am. Make this your first call.'

'Patience is a virtue, Gradzynski. Keep me posted on Shirley.'

'Not a chance. Now get off the phone.'

Gradzynski ended the call. The phone rang again immediately. He didn't know the number but recognized the voice that picked up.

'This is Bronski. Strawberry Point. Remember?'

'Yeah. How'd you get this number? This is a private phone.'

'How many secrets you think you have left, Gradzynski? What are you doing ringing our boy?'

'He rang the station.'

'So you rang him back on your cell phone? Thought you were better than that, Gradzynski. Now we both have your number.'

'That's okay with me. I just turned myself into a magnet.'

'What you gonna do with that?'

'If you use a magnet, Bronski, the needle in the haystack comes to you. Now leave me alone. I need time to think.'

Broken Biscuits

'Hi Pav. Got time for a beer later?'

'Maybe, Doc. Shirley still in the room next to your office?'

'Sure. Let's go see her.'

Livid scars webbed Shirley's face. Gradzynski studied her in silence for a while. Connected to pipes and wires she looked so vulnerable something almost broke inside him.

'The swelling's past its peak now, Pav. You'll soon see the old Shirley coming back. That'll be a comfort to her.'

'I wish that was a comfort to me right about now, Doc.'

'The hands troubling you?'

'The head. Trying to make it fit around a problem.'

'I don't recall you saying you'd hit your head?'

'I didn't, but for the job I just been given I'll let you do it right now.' Gradzynski pulled up a chair and sat by the bed. 'Mind if I watch her for a while?'

'Fine. But if she moves her lips don't be tempted to lean over and listen. It's just a ruse.'

'Professional opinion?'

'Nope. Jealousy.'

The machine by the bed ticked quietly to an overlapping rhythm. The monitor threw hypnotic sine waves across the screen until they disappeared off the other side and Gradzynski reflected that most his life had been that way... riding the troughs between little waves... and happy to do that most the time. But when had that come to be enough? He leaned close to Shirley's ear.

'Shirl? I don't know if you can hear me in there, but if there's anything you remember about the driver of the van, right now would be the time to give me a sign of what you got.'

The machine leapt into insistent bleeping. Waves flashed to the top of the screen then flattened off and began to throw themselves rapidly across. An alarm sounded out in the corridor. Shirley convulsed under the bedclothes, uncovering her arm from the top sheet. The arm was cradled in a wire cage with metal pins driven through the flesh to fix the bones beneath.

Gradzynski pulled back the chair in shock.

The doctor banged through the door, hitting him where he stood.

'Pawel. Move. You're in the way.' He leaned across the bed, checking the monitor, the drip, and all the while feeling for a pulse in her injured arm. The nurse dragged in a trolley and pointed for Gradzynski to leave.

He held the edge of the door. 'She okay, Doc? She going to be okay?'

'What did you do to her, Pav?'

'I didn't do a thing. You know I...'

'What did you say to her, then?'

'Well... nothing you'd notice... I just asked her a question and along came technical Armageddon.'

The doctor slid a needle from the trolley into the line below the cannula clamp.

'She'll be fine in a while but you can't be here, Pav. Whatever you said or did she doesn't need.'

'Her arm…'

'It'll be good. It's the circulation in it concerns me right now.'

'Knew it would be you, Gradzynski…'

'Why's that, Maggie?'

'All the bells and whistles. You been in there with your jackboots on?'

'Thought you were still wearing them?'

'Will be when I get out of here, and I'll kick your ass all the way home if you hurt that girl after what she tried to do for Æppel.'

'She killed a man, Maggie.'

'I was there, Gradzynski. Remember? What else was she supposed to do? Arrest them by sheer force of personality?'

'I was on my way…'

'So was Christmas… only that comes around faster these days. Have a biscuit.'

'No thanks, Maggie.'

'Last chance before Maybelline gets here.'

'Maggie… she killed a man.'

'Broken biscuits, Gradzynski… broken biscuits.'

Gradzynski remembered the stiletto heel wedged through the man's throat. 'It's how you break 'em, Maggie.'

'Get your ass out of here, Gradzynski, and stop chewing on it. The expert has just arrived. Hi, Maybelline…'

'You being arrested again, Maggie?'

'No, Maybelline. I'm just giving the Officer here a personality transplant.'

'It's amazing what they can do these days.'

'Yes, Maybelline. Now stop stroking his uniform and sit down.'

#

Maggie's house felt strangely undisturbed, if you ignored the odd wallboard leaning on the furniture and the screen door being laid out on the table for repair.

Gradzynski balled up the last of the police tape and threw it into the hearth, then moved on through the sitting room and into the kitchen. The drawer that Maggie couldn't ever close was now firmly shut and yet it slid it out willingly at a touch. He opened the top cupboard, the one that Maggie had to stand on a stool to reach, and sifted through the bottles there. He cleared them all out to the recycle bin.

The house would soon be ready. Leroy was good. He'd changed nothing much, just added a little 'happening' to it. He was beginning to like that boy. Really like that boy.

He went upstairs to the bedroom. It was untouched and he was glad of that. If they tidied it while Maggie was up to the hospital, she would never find anything ever again. He found himself searching in the closet for the wall cupboard Mariel had told him about. It was locked. His fingers drifted the top of it and found a key.

It was just as Mariel had said. So much perfume. He pulled a stopper on one and sniffed but perfumes all smelled the same to him. Like methylated spirit. Mariel complained he never bought her any. Truth was, he couldn't tell her that it made her smell like a drunk.

On the bottom shelf was a cardboard box. Gradzynski lifted the lid and found a few old photographs. Down below he could hear Leroy shifting things around. He heard the creak and pop of a paint can lid and knew he could take an undisturbed minute or two to satisfy his curiosity. He cleared a space on top of a small chest and sat down.

The first photograph was an old monochrome of a

grave. The headstone was covered by tiny pebbles and it was hard to make out the names and dates but 'Magdalena' seemed clearer than the rest. When he turned it over there was a set of numbers on the back. He set that aside.

The next one showed a good-looking woman in her twenties, obviously expecting another child but with one already holding her hand. The child's hair was dark as can be but the woman's was bright blonde and flowing. Could be it was from a bottle, he thought, Mariel does strange things like that occasionally.

The house behind them was white with a small porch, much like the house he was in right now. He turned the photograph over and on the back was a scrawl. He held it to the light from the door… 'Ellie and Magda Dec. '45 Penn.'

He set that to one side of him and picked another from the box. The next picture was in color. There were three people in this one. Different house… and the woman was now slender and graceful in the way she stood. The little girl seemed older than in the previous one. He picked that up again to check. Yes, maybe five… six years older. The woman wore heavy make-up and there was something a little more exact in the way her blonde hair now framed her face. The third figure stood between them, tall, dark but shading grey, holding the woman's hand in his and a pale fedora in the other. He wore black-rimmed spectacles… heavy… Gradzynski could tell from the way they expanded his eyes and made him look like Doc Franklin. The girl clung to the hem of the man's jacket, holding him inescapably close.

He searched their faces for a similarity but only their smiles were the same. How many times had he seen a hesitant smile? Enough to know that these were true. He held it into the light and studied the little girl. That particular smile he had seen before. And much more recently. He turned the photograph over and read the names on the back, then slipped it into his inside pocket.

'Forgive me, Maggie. I know I should ask first but...'

'Pav? Everything okay?' Leroy was standing quietly behind him.

'Everything wonderful, not just okay. When you have the door fixed?'

'Well... it took a beating but...'

'That was me...'

'And someone did a fool repair to it.'

'That was also me. You digging a hole here, Leroy?'

'Day after tomorrow.'

'What?'

'Is the answer to your next question. When will the house be ready for Maggie.'

Gradzynski struggled upright using his elbows on the doorframe, hands still unable to take the pressure of his weight. 'What you got left to do?'

'Just a little something with the furniture.'

'I'll get Doc to come around Saturday. See if there's anything else we need. Handrails and such.'

'We tried that one. Doc said the air turned blue.'

'Sneak one in on the stair, Leroy. She can't hold a screwdriver long enough to take it out.'

Gradzynski put the photographs away.

'A. Kowalski' was embossed in a dark script along the front edge of the chest he'd been sat on. It also had a clasp and a shiny lock attached. He searched with his fingertips along the ledges and architraves but came up empty. He opened the photograph box again and this time tipped it out. The key was in the bottom, bright and silver, impressed against another picture of the man in a dark suit.

Gradzynski lifted out a wooden tray fretted like an artist's selection box. Stacked in it were dozens of detachable nibs that slid into stained, silver holders. Below that was another tray of different colored inks arranged in a rainbow-like fashion. He lifted it out and set it aside on the floor. Under that was a large sheet of blotting paper in a leather binder. Beneath that were many packets of paper, some opened, others still bound in their original jackets. He picked up a few, recognizing an official seal on many of them as he shifted them around. Some of these went way back in time, before his time anyway… but some of them…

He re-stacked the chest, locked the lid and put the key back, then held his eyes tight closed for a moment… the way he did in Doc's car.

#

Leroy put a light to the kindling and waited patiently for it to catch.

Maggie settled back into her old chair by the fire. 'Hear that's kind of a speciality you got going there.'

'You got your underwear on, Maggie? We could do with the draught today.'

'Where's Æppel and Eugenie?'

'Down the store getting groceries.'

'I'd kind of hoped they'd be here when the ambulance dropped me off. I missed that kid after they got discharged.' She looked around the room for signs of their occupation, but it seemed as if she'd just walked out and back in again, except it was a little brighter for the paint job. 'Where've you been sleeping?'

'Down here, Maggie. Right by the fire.'

'Æppel and Eugenie?'

'Over to the Gradzynski's.'

'You didn't use the bedroom?'

Leroy shook his head and his scalp flashed pink with the scar tissue that was pushing away the molten plastic.

'More'n my job's worth, Ma'am.'

'Don't tell me... Uncle Jackboot.'

'Means well, though. You need anything, Maggie? Anything special? What about I fetch back your cycle?'

'What about you toss that in the lake? Everything I need is just arriving...'

The yellow flatbed lurched up the yard outside and stalled inches before it hit the shed. Eugenie scampered through the porch door on all fours, saw Maggie and stopped. She pulled herself up on the table leg and tottered across the rug to fall against Maggie's knees.

'Well... look at you? How long you been waiting to show off that trick?'

Æppel put down the bag of groceries on the table, picked Eugenie up and sat her in Maggie's lap. 'First time I seen it, Maggie.'

Eugenie began to bounce immediately and Leroy put out a hand to steady her from the fire. Maggie sat upright in the chair, limp left arm tucked into her apron pocket.

'What you got in there?'

Æppel opened the top of the bag so Maggie could see in.

'Biscuits? How am I going to eat that many biscuits?'

'I... well... I sort of asked Mrs Watson what you liked best.'

Maggie ran her fingers through the tousle of Eugenie's hair. 'What I like best I have right here.'

'I'm sorry, Maggie. I thought...'

'Don't worry about it. You kids these days are easily led. Especially by cantankerous, scheming old ladies.'

Leroy pushed Eugenie upright where Maggie could keep a hold of her. 'Like you, Maggie?'

'Yeah, spark. Like me. Æppel, pass the biscuits and make sure not to break any. That'll show her.'

Moving Pictures

'Who else we expecting?'

A third beer sat on the table between them. It was fresh and Gradzynski followed a clutch of bubbles to the surface while he waited for an answer.

'It's for Shirley.'

'That's one hell of a quick recovery, Doc.'

'We're going to drink it for her, and tomorrow I'm going to tell her what we did and how good it tasted.'

'She listening now?'

'I think so. Not that she's giving me any signs I can follow.'

'Except the kisses. They still coming?'

'Except the kisses. Yeah.'

'Do you think she hears you?'

'I think she hears everything, Pav. That's why she reacted so strongly to you. You never did tell me what you said.'

'I didn't say anything. I asked a question and off it all went.'

'What was the question?'

'I can't tell you that, Doc. Sorry.'

'Not even if we take a leak?'

'This one comes from higher up the food chain even than Maggie.'

'Everything ends in a question, Pav. Even the research I did on Maggie throws up a weird loop I wish I could resolve.'

'Try this…' Gradzynski took a photograph from his inside pocket and handed it over. 'Check out the smile on the little girl.'

The doctor held it under the table light. 'If you're this good, Pav, how come you're still in uniform?'

'It seems I'm where I need to be right now, Doc. You have a problem with that?'

Doc Franklin turned the photograph over and slipped on his glasses to figure out the scrawl on the back. 'Can I borrow this?'

'As long as you give it back.'

The doctor threw a bill on the table. 'Absolutely. But right now there's somewhere else I have to be.'

'What about the beer?'

'You drink it. You just earned it.'

'And Shirley?'

'I'll lie…'

'She'll know, Doc, but go ahead and close your loop.'

#

The answer machine at The Holocaust Museum played an out-of-hours tape. Doc was about to hang up when it gave an emergency number. He rang again then tapped the number into his cell phone. It rang for a while before a woman's voice snapped at him. 'Yes?'

'I… I'm trying to get hold of the Curator.'

'We are having our evening meal, young man.'

'I'm sorry to disturb you.'

'Please ring the Museum in the morning.'

'I will… it's just that I thought… this seemed important to him.'

The doctor heard another voice join in from a distance. 'Who is it at this time? What do they want?'

'Young man…'

'Listen. Please just tell him the name, Kowalski.'

'Kowalski?'

A man's voice cut in abruptly on another line. 'Kowalski, you say? What about Kowalski? Wait… I know your voice… the doctor from a strange place…'

'Chain O'Lakes Hospital.'

'Yes, yes. What about Kowalski?'

'I have him. And now… so do you.'

'You have him? He is still alive? But no… not even a Saint has lived that long.'

'I have sent you an email. Check your inbox in the morning. I'm sorry I disturbed your meal but I couldn't wait to tell you.'

'Do not be sorry, the meal can wait. It is a nothing. I am glad to hear from you.'

The woman's voice cut back in from the other line. 'I heard that. My cooking is now a nothing? After all these years?'

#

The voice on the line next morning was thick and heavily affected. 'Doctor Franklin? This is Doctor Schweitz from the Museum. I have just been given the image from your email last night.'

'Are you okay, doctor?'

'From one doctor to another, although mine is in Psychological not Medicinal, I have rarely been better.'

'Only you sound…'

'This is because I am crying, doctor. You cannot see this but tears are streaming my face and I can taste them like when I was a child.'

'I am sorry. I didn't mean…'

'Do not distress yourself, my friend. You know how many times in a life that prayers are answered? I will tell you that it isn't many at all. Maybe next time is when my wife employs a cook.'

'Kowalski looks a fine man. People must have really believed in him.'

'Kowalski was indeed such a fine man. Maybe such as yourself.'

'I'm only a humble doctor.'

'Doctor, be whatever you want to be in your life but never, ever, be humble.'

'Thank you, Doctor Schweitz.'

'You are welcome, doctor. Shall we say that our respective fees are now mutual?'

#

'Maggie's? Has it been cleaned?'

'Not in a decade, Doc. Though Leroy's doing a fine job out there.'

'If it's not sterile then…'

'I have no choice.'

'No, Pav. I'm not moving her.'

'Is she stable?'

'Well, yes, but that's not an indicator of…'

'Look, Doc. I'm not doing this for nothing. I want to give her the best chance…'

'Then the Hospital… stands to reason it's…'

'Not this time, Doc. This could turn out to be the worst

place in the world for her.'

#

The streetlights had been on for an hour before the panel truck reversed into Maggie's drive. The doctor and Gradzynski maneuvered the wheelchair out on the tail lift until it was level with the porch. Leroy took a hold and pulled it quickly through the doorway while Gradzynski and the doctor wheeled out clamps, pipes, drips and wires. A space had been cleared opposite Maggie's favorite chair by the fire and they set up there. The doctor connected Shirley to the monitor and drip.

Gradzynski shook out a fresh blanket. 'Don't say anything, Doc. And take that look off your face.'

'I hope you know what you're doing, Pav.'

'So do I. But do you know everybody comes through your hospital?'

'No... there are too many.'

Gradzynski looked around the room. 'I know everybody comes through here. I know which way they stand and what they're about. Couldn't ask for more.'

Bill Allerton

Pricking Out

'…and so I went all the way to the store without my mother's list and only my memory…'

'How can you say that? You're not Raymond. I know Raymond and he doesn't look like you at all. You're a girl.'

'That's right, Louise. I'm not Raymond. But he's a good friend of mine and he sent me here because he couldn't make it today.'

'I want Raymond.'

'Louise…. ask Lucy what she thinks.'

Louise picked up the rabbit from the pillow beside her and held its woolly nose to her ear for a moment. 'Lucy says what's that you got there?'

'Where Louise? Point it out.'

'There… on the little chair. Right where Raymond sits.'

Eugenie sat quite still on the dresser chair, fingers twisting around each other, fascinated by the staring black eyes of the white rabbit.

'This is Eugenie, Louise. Same as yesterday, same as the week before that too. Don't you remember?'

'Just a minute…' Louise held the rabbit to her ear again then held it out to Æppel. 'Lucy wants to talk to the

Eugenie.'

Æppel passed the rabbit over and sat it in Eugenie's lap. Eugenie's eyes opened wide and her hands made circles around Lucy's ears and paws, stroking the ruffled fur. Her fingers prodded the rabbit's stomach and were rewarded with a faint squeak.

'Lucy likes the Eugenie. What's your name?'

'I'm Æppel, Louise. Remember?'

'No. I'm not going to remember. Where's Raymond?'

'I'm just now telling you, Louise. Listen to the note he sent telling you all about his day.'

'Why isn't he here?'

'He's at the shops, Louise, and he's about to get in trouble for forgetting his mother's shopping list.'

'I hope she doesn't hurt him. Please tell her not to hurt him. I love Raymond.'

'Louise, if you stop squirming like that, I'll tell you what happened.'

Louise straightened up in the bed and pulled herself up the pillows. 'Where's Lucy?'

'Eugenie has her.'

'Give her back.' Louise's hands reached out for Lucy, fingers wriggling in the air.

Æppel took the rabbit from a surprised Eugenie and handed it back. 'Okay now, Louise?'

Louise listened to the rabbit for a moment. 'No. She wants to go back to the Eugenie.'

Æppel caught the rabbit mid-air and sat it back in Eugenie's lap. 'Raymond says… when he got to the shop, he remembered that his mother needed some really nice-smelling soap and some shampoo for her hair. The kind that would make it all soft and shiny the way it used to be.'

'He's a good boy.'

'Yes Louise, he is. He loves his mother so much.'

'Do you think he loves me too?'

'He loves you very much, Louise. He loves you so much that he sent that nice-smelling soap and the shiny shampoo right over here for you.'

'For me? What shall I do with it?'

'Well, Louise, in around five minutes we can try it out. Raymond says that when the bath is full and we have you all shiny and new he'll try and get along himself tomorrow.'

'Why didn't he come today?'

'He was out shopping for his mother, Louise. You wouldn't want to get between a boy and his mother, would you?'

'I never had a boy.'

'You remember that, Louise?'

'I never had a girl, neither.'

'No?'

'Never a one, Raymond.'

'I'm not…' Louise turned right over in the bed and began to sob like it was her soul escaping. Æppel closed the book and went to turn off the bath water.

#

'Doc? I have a problem.'

'Anything new, Maggie?'

'Yeah. I want to go deaf.'

'I think that usually happens on its own, Maggie.'

'I was alright until you encouraged her to talk.'

Shirley was sound asleep in the wheelchair by the fire. The bed had been temporarily pushed into a corner but the pipes and wires were a few days gone. The swelling was almost down and her features were beginning to achieve some of their old clarity, despite the scars around her left eye and cheek.

'You want her to stay in a coma, Maggie?'

'Guess not. But it was quieter that way.'

'What are you girls fighting about?'

'Shirley made some comment about Eugenie being born out of wedlock and I said, she should've been born out of earshot. Would've saved us all a problem.'

'Don't get your blood pressure up, Maggie. You're probably not far from another stroke if you get excited.'

'Excited? You know what excited is around here? It's when the mailman brings you a coupon for some trash you stopped eating forty years ago.'

'I realize retirement might seem kind of quiet after your career, Maggie. Let's see. Former racing cyclist, rally car driver, alcoholic...'

'That's kind of insulting, Doc. Don't assume it's all former. There's still a leg on the turkey.'

'But there's not much of the stuffing left, Maggie. Take care of what you got.'

'Can I have a prescription for a gag, then?'

'No. But you can have one for two.'

Shirley's eyes opened slowly. 'You'd better take a measure for hers, Doc.'

'Shirl? How are you feeling today?'

'Like I hit a street lamp. How do you expect...' Her eyes closed as she fell back into the arms of the sedative.

Eugenie banged open the screen door and tottered into the house carrying a white toy rabbit. Its eyes were black as jet and they seemed to stare into every corner of the room as Eugenie held it out to Maggie.

'Where'd you get that?'

Æppel followed her in and set down a bundle of nightclothes on the floor by the kitchen.

''s'alright, Maggie. We're on a mission.'

'Must be one hell of a mission. Never could prise that

old thing off of Louise.'

'She sent Lucy to find out if you're hiding Raymond over here. We have to take her back to report. If Louise bounces on her bed she can just see into your yard and all the comings and goings have got her wondering.'

'Is she recovering?'

'Not likely, Maggie. Why?'

'Because it has me wondering too.'

'Soon as we find a place of our own, we'll be out of your hair.'

'Don't take on like that, young lady. It's my fault you're here.'

'Didn't think it was anyone's fault.'

Maggie shuffled the cushion beside her. 'Go and put on the kettle. I want to relax a little here.'

'I have these to wash, Maggie.' Æppel picked up the clothes by the kitchen door and took them through.

Maggie heard her own washing machine door click open and shut. 'Ben not got a gizmo for doing that?'

'Sure. But it needs Leroy to take a look at it.'

'You brought the powder over? Right?'

'Right, Maggie.'

'Where's Ben?'

'He just got back from the store. Went straight on his computer.'

Æppel came back into the sitting room. 'Who used to give you all the gossip before we came, Maggie?'

'Gossip? Well... I suppose it was me. I used to go out there and see things. Maybe do things too...'

'Then get off your ass and go prick out some Geraniums.'

#

'Maggie's House.'

'Oh… Oh… is that the girl with…'

'With the strange name. Yes, Mrs Watson. What can we do for you today?'

'Well… can I speak to Maggie? It sounds strange to have to ask… but can I?'

'Why is that strange, Mrs Watson?'

'I don't know, really. Only you sound kind of… prickly today.'

'I'm sorry, Mrs Watson. It's kind of a prickly day. I just been arguing with Maggie. Well… more the other way around.'

'I guess that will do it every time. She can be so…'

'She's in the yard, Mrs Watson, taking it out on the Geraniums. If you call over, she'll be happy to see you.'

'Thank you, young lady…'

'Æppel.'

'Yes… indeed.'

'The kettle's on and I have biscuits.'

'I see…'

'You see what, Mrs Watson?'

'I see you can't be all bad.'

'Is it safe, Maggie?'

'Is what safe, Maybelline? Pricking out Geraniums with one hand? Pass me that tray. And the soil. And the trowel. And the seedlings.'

'How were you going to do this on your own, Maggie?'

'I wasn't. Leastways not until you arrived.'

'Then what were you doing?'

'Sulking, Maybelline. I was out here sulking like a spoiled brat. Nothing like young people to make you wish you'd grown up better.'

'Did we ever have that, Maggie? That eye for life?'

Maggie leaned heavily on the edge of the bench. 'Maybe we always had it, May. Then when we stop using it the little jiggers come up from behind and make us look as stupid as we probably were in the first place.'

'The world hasn't got any better for it, Maggie. It all just seems to get worse.'

'Cut me three examples, Maybelline.'

'Well... look at the size of biscuits for one. When I was a child, Maggie, they were...'

'Should still be about the same size then, Maybelline. Like your brain.'

'Maggie Gray! I come over here just to make sure...'

'... that I got biscuits in the tin and rocket fuel hidden somewhere Jackboot Harry can't find it. That about the size of it?'

Maybelline stood quietly for a while, studying Maggie's face.

'And what you looking at?'

'I'm waiting for the smile.'

'Short supply today, Maybelline. Will a pack of biscuits do?'

'With cream and jelly in?'

'Reckon so.'

'I need a sample... just to make sure they're the right ones.'

'What's a representative sample, Maybelline?'

'Oh... 'bout half a pack.'

'Then you're going to have to learn how to say that girl's name.'

'Hi Maggie, Mrs Watson.'

'Gradzynski! Where've you been this last week or two?'

'I've been around, Maggie. Just keeping a low profile, is all.'

Maggie stared him up and down. 'Getting harder to do these days, Pawel. Mariel still making bigos?'

'It's not the bigos, Maggie. I'm not getting any exercise.'

'The hands better?'

'Some. Luckily no grafts needed, but I'm sore in parts I never knew I had.'

'Still got your gun?'

'Yeah, why?'

'Mariel says it's an aphrodisiac.'

'Does she need one?'

'No. She says you do. Look after the woman, Pawel.'

'Know how hard it is to stay awake after szarlotka, Maggie?'

'Maybe I'll ask her over to make dinner for Shirley...'

Gradzynski sat in Maggie's chair and leaned up to take a closer look at Shirley.

'Hi Shirley.'

Her eyes flickered open at the sound of his voice. 'Pav?'

'How're you doing?'

'Like I was...'

Maggie leaned heavily against the table edge. 'For God's sake take that record off. Don't listen to her, Pawel. She's been nothing but self-pity since she woke. That and cussing me out just for being here.'

'She might take a while to come to terms...'

'I been taking all my life just to come to terms. It don't work. Don't whinge about the hand you're dealt. Get up to the table and play it.'

'That sounds kind of harsh, Maggie.'

'Harsh? I'll tell you what's harsh... you're born one minute screaming then you wake up next morning and you're seventy-eight and you can't remember what happened between. That's what's harsh.'

'Sit down, Maggie. You're out of breath.'

'Then get out of my chair, Gradzynski… and while you're about it, get her out of hers too.'

Winner takes All

'Maggie?'

'Yes, child?'

'I been thinkin' 'bout what Shirley said.'

'Shirley says lots of things. Mostly with hooks and barbs. What's so special?'

'About Eugenie being born out of wedlock.'

'A sight late to change that, Æppel.'

'I know. But maybe there's something we could change. It don't have to carry on being that way.'

'You ask Leroy about this?'

'I did.'

'And?'

'He says all he wants to do is make me happy.'

'I think he's doing that already. Got himself a steady job. Must be making some, Gradzynski makes sure we hardly catch a sight of him.'

'We got a lot of ground to make up, Maggie.'

'So what are you planning on doing?'

'I got an idea, Maggie. And I know just what dress I want to wear, too.'

'Given your capacity for being fashionable, this dress

must go back a way. I have an old Sears Roebuck in here somewhere...'

'Not that far back, Maggie. Maybe only ten, twelve years or so since I seen it.'

'Like yesterday then. Go talk to Mariel. I got toilet rolls older than that.'

#

A piece of cloth fluttered beside the soda machine. Æppel knew she should never go near that machine because Satan can reach out the dispenser and grab a hold of your hand and never let go and in the dark glass bottles were his messages... sent out like the shipwrecked Jonah that he is... to infect little children with his tales of greed and perversion, but Æppel had never seen such a pretty piece of cloth. It had tiny rosebuds embroidered in rows, stitched flowers in garlands and perfect pink bows. A hand, pink, clean, unlike her own, reached out and pulled the scrap of cloth back into the shade of the machine. Æppel followed it.

The girl put a finger to her lips. 'Shhh. Go away. If he sees you he'll know where I am.'

'Who will? Satan?'

'No. My brother. I'm hiding from him.'

'Why? Is he going to whup you?'

The girl's hair shone gold in the fluorescent light that escaped the broken seams of the machine. She shook her head and ringlets trembled into a shape that framed her face.

'No, silly. It's a game.'

Æppel stared at her. The girl's skin was smooth and untouched by the sun. She caught sight of her own reflection in the side of the machine... face burned dark already by helping with crops in the withering light. 'What's a game?'

The girl's eyes lit with a peculiar intensity. 'You know... like Hide and Seek.'

'Is that a game?'

'Of course it is.'

'What does it do?'

'It doesn't do anything. You have to play it.'

'Why would you do that?'

The girl tugged the front of Æppel's dungarees and dragged her back into the shadow. 'How old are you?''

Æppel stopped a moment to count on her fingers. 'I'm eight.'

'So am I! And you don't know how to play Hide and Seek?'

'No.'

'Well... it's easy. You got to get a head start on whoever is looking for you, then find a good place to hide. Somewhere they'd never think of looking, and then...'

Æppel's feet left the ground. She was swung around and dropped to the floor in front of her mother.

'What'd I say to you about talking to those kinda people? What will the Elders say if they find out what you been doing?' Her hand cuffed Æppel around the ear. Æppel stumbled and fell sideways to the ground. The blonde girl leapt out of the shadows to help her, only to be swatted away by Æppel's mother.

'Get away from my daughter. Who knows what damage you done already. Æppel? How long you been talking to this... this...'

A young boy jumped quickly between them. 'Her name is Charlotte... and she's my sister. Leave her alone.'

'Get away, boy. Leave my sight. You any idea how long my daughter will have to pray to rid herself of this? Take your devil-spawn sister and go.' She lifted her hand to cuff him the way she had Æppel, but the boy nipped in quickly and kicked her hard on the shin. Æppel's mother hopped around but he was more than a match for her speed.

The girl quickly squeezed Æppel's hand. 'Remember the game.'

She was snatched away by her brother and hand in hand they ran off down the street. The girl looked back twice, then they were gone behind a clapboard storefront.

'Æppel. What you looking at? What did she say to you?'

'Nothing, Mother.'

'Don't lie to me. I see the mark of Satan plain on your face. I shall have to scrub for a week to get that off.'

'No, Mother, please. Not that.'

'What did you say to her. What did you tell her about us?'

'Nothing, Mother. Nothing at all.'

'I heard you talking. Don't make this any worse than it is already. I don't want to have to ask the Elders for punishment for you...'

'I said... she had a pretty dress... and I wished I had one just like it.'

'What you want a dress like that for? Fit to burn in Hell, is all, fit to burn with her inside of it, curls all going up in flames until nothin's left but teeth an' bones an' hurts goin' on forever. That's what you get with a dress like that. That what you want, child? To die in the ignorance of God, with Demons breathing your smoke from the eternal pyre? That what you want? If that's what you want, here...'

She dragged Æppel in front of her, turned her away and gave her a push towards the center of town. 'In that direction lies Damnation Eternal. If that's what you want, go get it. I'm tired o' trying to protect your spirit. You always want somethin' different. You think you're better'n the rest us... so go. But don't you never come back, y'hear. Not once.'

Æppel turned and held on, her arms wrapped around her mother's waist as she clung tight to the only rock she knew could stand firm in the wrath of God's Storm.

#

Four major stores in along the Magnificent Mile, Mariel sat heavily on a plinth outside Bloomingdales. 'I'm sorry, Æppel. Fashion changes so fast these days.'

'Don't it come back around? Maggie says it does.'

'Depends what it's a fashion for… and when it does come back around there's no telling how much we've changed. Take hula hoops…'

'What's a hula hoop?'

'Okay. I give up. Let's try in here.'

They searched amongst the racks of roll ends, even venturing into the stuff that Gradzynski would wince at the price of. Some things came close, but…

'Can I help you, ladies?'

Mariel took a seat by the cash register and smiled up at the assistant. 'I don't know, sir. We been through most the fabric stores of Chicago already.'

'Is this something special?'

Æppel pulled Eugenie tighter by her side.

Mariel untangled their fingers and picked Eugenie up in her arms. 'Yes, kind of.'

'Can you describe it?'

Æppel took him over to a rack by the window. 'It's sort of like this… with a touch of this one over here…' She led him to a rack over the other side where summer dresses hung bright against a dark wood stand. 'And sort of that color there…' She pointed to one of the dresses. 'Sort of underlying the pattern like that. And it had little…'

'Madam? Please follow me.'

Æppel followed the man to a room at the back. She turned to look at Mariel, who waved her on with a smile. In the back room were floor to ceiling doors. The assistant slid one back and pulled out a bolt of cloth. Æppel's hand flew to her mouth in surprise. 'You have this?'

'Since around nineteen sixty-three. I think it's ideal for your little one. She will really look something at the vintage party in this.'

'It's for me.'

The assistant stepped back and looked her up and down. 'For the Madam? For some special occasion?'

'You could say that...'

'Wait... Here...' He reached up a hand towards Æppel's hair. She shied away from him and he clasped his hands in apology. 'I'm sorry. That was remarkably forward of me.'

Æppel stroked the cloth for reassurance, running her fingers over the little bumps and rills. 'We don't allow... No. That's not true anymore, but I'm still not used to being touched.'

'By men?'

'By anyone.'

'Then I apologize. And to say sorry, will you allow me... on behalf of the store... to get someone from the style department to fix your hair?'

Æppel ran her fingers through her hair, pulling out the tangles. 'Something wrong with it?'

'If Madam doesn't mind my saying so, it does look a little... uneven.'

Æppel studied the strands between her fingers, sifting the burned ends she'd not managed to brush out. 'Guess it does at that. Been too sore for a while to do anything with it. Not that I ever really did.'

'Then, may I ask, when is this special occasion?'

'Soon as I can arrange it.'

Mariel gathered up Eugenie and brought her into the room to see what was happening. The assistant rolled the bolt of cloth out onto the cutting table and looked at both of the women for confirmation of the length. Mariel shrugged. Æppel looked blank. Eugenie jigged up and down beside them. He reached down and patted her head, then rolled out another few yards before cutting across.

Mariel searched in her purse. 'Won't that be too much? Don't know if I brought enough money for that much cloth.'

The assistant folded the cloth and slid it into a paper bag. 'The little one will be wanting a matching dress. Should be enough to go around in there.'

Mariel leafed through the notes she'd got from Gradzynski, hoping there'd be enough left for a coffee at the station. 'How much is it?'

The assistant turned over the tag attached to the remaining bolt. 'Let me see… in 1963 it was three dollars and fifty-six cents a yard.'

'That was expensive back then.'

'It certainly was, Madam. Still is.'

'So how much is it today?'

'Three dollars and fifty-six cents a yard.'

'Are you sure?'

'Yes, Madam. Seventeen dollars and eighty cents including tax.'

'There must be ten yards of cloth there.'

'May I ask the Madam how much more of it she thinks we're ever likely to sell?'

#

'Well, I'm glad you don't need a photo ID to catch the train. Look at you girl. I never seen anyone scrub up like that with just a haircut.'

'Thanks, Mariel. And thanks for the trip… and the material. I just need someone to help me make it up now.'

'Just when I thought I'd finished.'

'You sew?'

'Used to, until Pav got his badge and I could afford to buy. Might still be able to get these fingers around it. Won't be easy though. That cloth is something else again.'

'I used to help my Mother sew.'

'Your mother sew that thing you're wearing?'

'Yes.'

'Hmm…'

#

'Have you thought of where we're going to live?'

'We'll make it somehow, Leroy. You always find somewhere.'

'That was okay when it was just us. You and me, we can make it work anywhere. But this kid's going to want some schooling soon. That means an address.'

'Does she have to go? All those rules again. I don't think I can do that.'

'School rules are meant to make everyone the same, not divide them up into who goes to Heaven and who doesn't.'

'An address means they can find us again.'

'Æppel. Stop shaking like that. Who's going to find us? There ain't none of them left.'

'My head knows. But my heart cain't shake the feeling. What if they were right 'bout things? What if it's just that Satan's decided not to take me yet. Maybe he's biding his time until I'm really happy. Maybe…'

'Æppel Passion. You hear yourself? How deep does this thing go? What do I have to do to make you believe in me?'

'You could put your arms around me… for a little while…'

'Won't that mess up your hair?'

'One more thing. I don't want no minister. Not from nowhere.'

'That's fine, Æppel. No minister. But then who's going to do the ceremony I don't know. Maybe we shouldn't bother at all.'

Æppel climbed across the bed to get out by the side of the dresser. 'I agree. We were fine the way we were. Is this schooling really so important?'

'Ain't you tired of moving around?' Leroy sat up against the pillows in thought, wondering how this conversation had become so turned around. 'And I thought this was your idea?'

Æppel sat by the dresser mirror, watching her fingers push her hair back into place. She moved them away and the small tower collapsed but the curls were still there and she knew it wouldn't take much to restore the way it had made her feel. If Eugenie slept a little longer.

'Maybe not all my ideas are good ones.'

Leroy stared at her reflection in the mirror until their eyes met. 'I thought this was one of your better ones.'

'So did I…'

'Until what?'

'Until you agreed so easily.'

'What's wrong with that?'

'I wanted to fight for it.'

'Æppel Passion! Where did that come from?'

'I don't know. Maybe it was there all along. Maybe it was just waiting for you to bring it out of me.'

'What you gonna to do about it?'

Æppel stood up from the dresser seat and lowered her arms. Her hair collapsed into a mess of waves around her head. She shook it from her eyes. 'Just throw that pillow on the floor.'

'Winner takes all?'

Present Tense

The doctor pushed in through the bar door and found Gradzynski. He took an envelope from his bag and threw it on the table. 'Present for you.'

'For me?'

'Well… not really but…'

Gradzynski fingered open the envelope and studied the official form inside. 'I can't take this to the County Clerk's office.'

'You have to, Pav. It's their only option.'

'If only I didn't know where you got it, maybe I could've kidded myself…'

'Hang on while I get a beer. Don't go making any rash decisions about this on your own.'

'And if I do?'

'I'll ring Mariel.'

'That's blackmail. Five to ten at a push.'

'How long do you want to spend in matrimonial purgatory, Pav?'

'Don't forget the third beer this time, I think I'm going to need it.'

'And don't forget to take the thirty dollars for the

marriage license...'

'You know how much that boy has earned this last few weeks?'

'You know how much more he's going to need?'

Gradzynski sat back into the soft cushion of the bar booth. His mind's eye clicked through the things he and Mariel had found necessary when they first set up home. Then multiplied it again for Eugenie.

#

'Pawel? Small conundrum. How come you told me to put Leroy Dubuque on our new Deputy's insurance record but his driver's license says Leroy Landry?'

'Slip of your pen, Joseph.'

'Yeah, but you said it was Dubuque, Pav.'

'Transmission problem, Joseph. Make it right.'

Gradzynski touched the envelope the doctor had slipped into his pocket the night before. His self-doubt roused itself from the gutter of his imagination and made him briefly consider second-guessing what he was about to do.

'While we're on the subject of transmissions, Joseph, get a hold of that sister of yours.'

'What she do this time?'

'Nothing yet. I want her to add something to the local social calendar. Complete with guest list.'

'After what she did last time?'

'No, Joseph. Because of what she did last time.'

Wind Storm

'There ain't enough room to jump a broomstick in here. So what you going to do?'

Æppel smoothed the creases out of a brochure. 'There's this one, Maggie. Leroy found it in a list on Ben's computer.'

'You're sure it's not too 'Churchy'? Don't want you running off at the last minute. I'd hate to have to stand in. That Leroy's a bit short on energy for me.'

'Well it is a 'church', sort of, but no gods and devils, only people. Leroy says they only care 'bout people.'

'First one I ever heard of. Give me that there brochure… Who's this Jenny Reynard?'

'She's a People's Minister, Maggie. Leroy says we need one for the ceremony. For the license. Looks kinda… sensitive looking.'

Maggie snatched the brochure out of Æppel's hand. 'Guess you could use that about now. Leroy found these people?'

'He looked real hard to make sure they weren't… you know.'

'How come you didn't want any ceremony for Eugenie, but it's different now when it's for you?'

'It's not for me, Maggie. I done ceremony for a lifetime. It's a catch-up for Eugenie... it's not her fault what happened to me... but most of all it's for Leroy.'

'You trust him with this?'

'Maggie! What kind of a fool question is that? I'm marrying him, ain't I?'

'Just asking. Sit down here and let me take a look at this.'

'I... Maggie... I think this is for me and Leroy to decide.'

'If I'm paying for this, I reckon on having some input at least.'

'You're paying for it?'

'Of course I am. Nobody ever tell you there's no pockets in a shroud?'

Maggie opened up the brochure between them on the table. 'Don't want that one with all the candles. Not with your Leroy, he's too good with fire... and anyway, that's Jewish.'

'I ain't anything, Maggie.'

'That's good then. It rules out the bullshit brigade. Let's take a look at this list.' She ran a finger down the page. 'This one's a doozy. It says... until Aliens, Zombies or Death do you part.'

'No, Maggie. I like this one here. It reminds me of our days out by the lake.'

'If you think you're planting an oak tree out in my back yard then forget it.'

'Don't you want to see something grow, Maggie? Something with new life?'

'Yeah, I want to see it. Feels like I waited a lifetime, but you know how long it takes to grow an oak? With what I got left I'd settle for a Geranium.'

#

'May your relationship and your love for each other be like this oak you have planted. May it grow tall and strong. May it stand tall during whatever storms… Sorry Ma'am, what was it you wanted to say? We're in the middle of a ceremonial practice here…'

'I never seen anything look less like an oak in my life. It's a Geranium for Heaven's sake.'

'Maggie. Don't interrupt the minister. I don't care what it is.'

'It's a rehearsal is what it is. Supposed to help get it right…'

'It will, Maggie.'

'And why are you wearing that dress out here where Leroy can see it if he comes home. What's he going to look at on the real day.'

'My heart, Maggie. I hope he'll be lookin' at my heart.'

The minister tapped the brochure. 'Can I carry on now?'

'Oh yeah, sure. Don't mind me. I'm just an old woman.'

'Thank you… May it stay strong through whatever storms may enter your… What is it now?'

'I always bring them inside when there's a twister.'

'Maggie! Please carry on, Miss Reynard.'

'Are we all sure?'

'Yes. We are all sure. Aren't we Maggie?'

'I guess.'

'…whatever storms may enter your life, and may it come through unscathed. Like this… plant… your marriage must be resilient…' The minister peered at Maggie over the page of script. 'It must weather the challenges of life and the passage of time and you must nurture one another as you will nurture this… plant.' She peered again at Maggie who was smiling. 'Something I missed, Mrs Gray?'

Maggie shuffled more comfortably into her chair. 'Nope. I'm just waiting for the bit about Aliens.'

'A little nourishment is needed every day so you can each grow and reach your fullest potential… just like this tree.'

'Geranium.'

'Gesundheit, Mrs Gray.' The minister avoided Maggie's glare. 'Are there any more bridesmaids? It might help if they were…'

Maggie plumped the cushion under her loose arm. 'There's only Maybelline.'

'You mean the neighbor with the theatrical dress sense?'

'Yeah, that's Maybelline. She was once an extra gust in 'Gone with the Wind'.'

Aliens and Zombies

'Do you, Leroy Landry, take Æppel Passion to be your wife?'

'I do, Ma'am.'

'Don't need the Ma'am, Leroy. This is your day, remember?'

'Yes Ma'am. Sorry Ma'am.'

Mariel pressed close against Gradzynski to get a better look while Eugenie shuffled in her arms.

'Doesn't he look smart, Pav? Whose uniform is that?'

'Joseph's Sunday best.'

'Think he can keep it after?'

'Maybe. If you keep feeding Joseph, he won't fit it anymore.'

'Pav!'

'Mariel. Step away a little. You're crowding my gun hand.'

'Don't know why you brought it anyway.'

'Mariel… If I say drop, you go down like a stone, wrapped around that kid.'

'In this skirt?'

'You do your best. Okay?'

The Minister caught Gradzynski's eye to silence him then

continued the service.

'Do you, Æppel Passion, take Leroy Landry to be your husband.'

'I do.'

'To have and to hold from this day forward, for better or for worse, for richer or for poorer?'

'I do.'

'In sickness and in health, to love and to cherish until death do you part?'

Maggie slid down a little in her seat. 'Ohhh.'

'What's the matter, Mrs Gray?'

'Don't mind me. Carry on.'

'Thank you, Mrs Gray. Æppel and Leroy, you may now exchange rings.'

Mariel rubbed the white space on the third finger of her right hand where her mother's wedding ring had lived for fifteen years.

She nudged Gradzynski. 'Look at all those rosebuds and pink bows on Æppel's dress, Pav.'

'I'm looking, I'm looking. Never seen you so artistic with a needle. Usually you're sticking 'em in me for something I forgot.'

'Mother would have loved this, Pav. It's so… rustic. She so hated the Church.'

Gradzynski turned slightly to free up his arm from Mariel's grip. 'Went every day I knew her.'

'She said it was God's punishment.'

'To go to church every day?'

'To pray for forgiveness.'

'For what?'

'She never would say.'

The minister thumbed a page in her book. 'Leroy? Is there anything you'd like to say to your wife while these witnesses are gathered here?'

Leroy fell to one knee. 'Æppel Passion, I promise to love you when you drive me crazy. To respect you when we disagree. To support you if bad times come our way. And to always remember how grateful I am to have you by my side.'

Æppel lifted his face and kissed him tenderly.

The Minister slid a hand between them.

'Æppel? Is there anything you'd like to say to Leroy while these witnesses are gathered here?'

With one hand under Leroy's chin, Æppel lifted him to his feet.

'Leroy Landry, you know me better than anyone else in this world and somehow still you manage to love me. You are my best friend and one true love. There is still a part of me today that cannot believe that I'm the one who gets to marry you. I promise to laugh with you, cry with you, and grow with you. I will love you when we are together and when we are apart.'

The Minister lifted high the plant pot beside her. 'May your relationship and your love for each other be like this flower you have planted. May it grow tall and strong. May it stand firm during whatever storms…'

Shirley sneezed twice, and loudly. Maybelline tried hard to stifle a giggle.

'Do you have a problem, Mrs Watson? May I take a moment to remind everyone that I am trying to conduct a solemn ceremony of marriage between two consenting…'

'Aliens…'

'Mrs Gray?'

'You forgot the Aliens…'

'You want the Zombies too?'

'In for a nickel…'

Bill Allerton

Rabbit Punch

'What can you see, Lucy? What can you see?'

By bouncing hard on the bed, Louise could catch a glimpse into Maggie's yard. She held Lucy up to the glass so the bright, black eyes could see across the way. Lucy had said that all kinds of people had been coming and going all afternoon.

'Who are they, Lucy?' Louise held the rabbit to her ear but for once it didn't talk to her. 'Do you know them, Lucy? Is Raymond out there?' She lifted the rabbit back to the window and turned its head this way and that. 'Tell me what you see! Is Raymond coming?'

The rabbit stared back at her with impenetrable black eyes. Deep in there were the only truths that Louise needed.

'You saw him, didn't you. I know you did. Look again.'

She lifted up the rabbit and this time she saw movement cross the reflective sheen of its eyes. She jumped up and down on the bed, each time managing a glimpse of the yard. Like a stop-frame animation, a man with dark hair and sunglasses was making his way softly around Maggie's shed, heading for the rear door.

'Lucy! Lucy! He's going to the wrong house! Why didn't

you tell me? How many times has he been here? He must know by now. It's that Maggie. She's stealing him. She's stealing Raymond! Oh, Lucy. Look and tell me it isn't true.'

She held the rabbit up to the window then slowly turned its head toward her. For an instant she saw something new in the depths of its eyes, something malignant in the indifference of its stare.

'If you won't talk to me Lucy... then I'll do this...' She ripped one arm clean away from the body. Stuffing showered the bed around her feet. 'And this...' She tore a second arm clean off and threw it through the open bathroom doorway to land in the tub. 'And this... and this... and this....'

Louise's hair was caught up with the fibers of stuffing that filled the air around her. The rabbit's body lay dismembered on the bed at her feet while Louise broke her fingernails scrabbling at the black, dispassionate eyes in the torn-off head.

'Oh, Lucy. Why would she steal Raymond? She knows I love him. Why?'

Lucy's head crumpled silently in her fingers. She threw it aside.

At the dressing table she crayoned on fresh lipstick after powdering her face the way she always did when she thought Raymond was coming. When she'd finished, she tried the bedroom door that she hadn't tried in months. It opened, but she'd never expected anything else. She dashed back to the bed and picked up the remains of the rabbit and clutched it to her chest as she stumbled up the stairs to the hallway. She wandered around a minute or so, looking into rooms she had completely forgotten.

She pushed her fingers inside of the rabbit's head and stared into the black, expressionless eyes. 'Where am I, Lucy? Is this Raymond's house?' Lucy's head remained silent on her hand. 'If you are going to be like that, Lucy, if you're just going to be like that, then I'll do this…' She punched the rabbit hard in the face. Its head spun away to the left and stared along the corridor. Louise spun in that direction. 'Is that where he is, Lucy?'

Daylight shone through the frosted glass pane in the door at the end. It was locked.

Louise threw the rabbit's head at the glass in disgust. 'You lie to me, Lucy! You lie! You lie! You lie!' The rabbit's head bounced back to land on the hall stable. Louise picked it up and began to scream at it until she saw, reflected in its implacable stare, a key on a hook.

She tried it in the door. It opened. She stared out across the yards, blinking in the bright daylight. She didn't know where she was, but she remembered Lucy had seen Raymond going into a house over the back. She remembered too whose house it was. It was Maggie's. And Maggie was stealing Raymond.

She ran out of the house and clambered over the low fence between the yards, catching her nightdress on the rail. She ripped it off with her free hand and ran as fast as she could towards Maggie's porch.

Satan Calling

In the corner of Gradzynski's eye, a face he didn't recognize appeared at the foot of Maggie's stairs. He didn't want to start a panic so he bit down on his immediate response until he could make out if the man was carrying.

The man caught sight of him and held up both hands. They were empty. Gradzynski grabbed Mariel by the arm and forced her behind him.

'Pawel! That hurt. What are you…' Then she saw where he was looking. 'Who's that?'

'Not a friend, Mariel. Stay behind me.'

'What about the others? You can't stand in front of them all.'

'I have to, Mariel. I'm all there is.'

'I thought Joseph was out front?'

'I don't want to think about that right now, Mariel. Remember what I said before?'

'Yes, but…'

'No buts.'

Mariel clung hard to his back. Gradzynski reached an arm between them and pushed her away. 'Drop.'

He slid his awareness into the man's perspective.

Shirley standing in front of the wheelchair… and by her face that was taking all she'd got. Doc standing behind her, hands cradling her elbows, absorbed in the act of keeping her upright. Ben? By the stairs and shading the gunman with his tall frame. Leroy and Æppel were covered from where he was standing. Maggie? Maybelline? Potential collateral. And why should he prove Bronski right about that? There must be a way through this…

He removed his hand from the butt of the gun where it had naturally fallen and held it up, empty. Too many lives in here to waste. And he couldn't yet see how to make this his call.

Shirley caught sight of Gradzynski's raised hands. Her head began to turn slowly in the direction he was looking, scar-stitched tissue stretching painfully, tugging a grimace from her mouth. Her eyes narrowed and without thinking she dropped a hand to her side. No gun. No uniform. Just an old dress of Maybelline's that Mariel had let out to fit.

She smiled crookedly. She'd studied that smile in the mirror that morning while Doc dressed her for the occasion, so no longer any fear, either. She turned her body slowly, keeping Doc covered as best she could, while from behind the tall, slender figure of Ben, a gun lifted towards her.

Gradzynski unbuttoned his holster. The leather seemed colder and harder than usual. Eleven people in one small room. How many funerals was he looking at here? He had to try to keep that to none. Or one at the most if he himself ran out of luck.

He stared deep into the sunglasses of the man he'd waited patiently for these last few weeks, trying to discern something… anything… behind them.

'These are good folks, Mister. Give 'em peace. Let's you and me take this outside.'

The gun swung towards him. 'An Eye for an Eye,

Gradzynski.'

Gradzynski held up empty hands. 'Had you figured for that Old Time Religion.'

'Truth is, Gradzynski, you never had me figured at all.'

'Only crazies are hard to figure. You're not crazy. You're just anger looking for somewhere to be.'

'And you want to make yourself the destination, right? Well, I'm sorry to disappoint you, Officer, but nobody paid me for that job.'

Gradzynski nodded towards the ceremony stilled on the hearth. 'Nobody's paying you for this one, either.'

'She's paying.' The gun barrel waved in the direction of Shirley who was struggling to stay upright and shield Doc. 'And she only has one coin left. Her last breath.'

'Where you gonna spend that?'

'This one's personal.' He lifted the sunglasses to show Gradzynski flame-red skin stretched around an eye socket. 'Nobody does this to me. I want her death rattle in my ear until my dying day.'

Gradzynski read the room again, sifting the little signs... who stood on which foot... which way they're leaning... anything that might clarify the unravelling of what happens next. 'Will this bring your eye back?'

Gradzynski chanced a look behind him. Mariel was a quivering shape in the shade of the furniture, skirt split to the thigh, Eugenie tight under her.

'Retribution, Gradzynski. Your little friend in the wedding dress learned all about that up at the squirrel cage. Go ask the expert.'

'Then I guess it's personal for me too. I'm a man has to stand up for his friends. What's that make me?'

The gun barrel swung towards him.

'Could be the first to die.'

The door burst wide open and Louise barreled

screaming across the room. Hurtling through the air towards the gunman came the head of a white rabbit, eyes staring wild and black. From reflex he shot and it exploded, showering the air with cotton threads.

There was a moment of silence in which Louise stood staring at her hand, naked now as the rest of her, before Eugenie burst out a loud scream. Mariel silenced her and held on until she stopped struggling. Gradzynski lifted out his gun but folks were stirring and milling around.

Leroy pushed Æppel and the minister to the floor and covered them with his body. Doc collapsed Shirley back into the wheelchair and came to stand in front of her.

Gradzynski snatched out his gun, shoulder high, tight in both hands. Ben began to move towards him. 'Ben. Stay put.'

'I can't. There's a guy here with a gun in my back.'

The gunman maneuvered Ben around so there was only wall behind them.

'Nobody else needs to get hurt here.'

'Put the gun down, then. Let's all walk out of here in one piece.'

'How about you put yours down first, Gradzynski, and then we'll see about that.'

'What you really after here?'

'Recompense, Gradzynski. Then I'm gone.'

'Which way you figure on going.'

'I've got options, Gradzynski. There are always options.'

'And Joseph outside? Give him any?'

'Sure. He don't owe me nothin'. He's cuffed to a rail out there. Head'll be sore in the morning.'

'Make your move then. You're doing too much talkin' here. You changing your mind?'

'Put your gun down, Gradzynski.'

'That would be real irresponsible of me.'

The gunman leaned out from behind Ben and waved the gun around the room.

'Be real irresponsible of you not to.'

'What's your name?'

'What's in a name, Gradzynski?'

'A man ought to know who's threatening to kill him.'

Shirley struggled up from the wheelchair. Her legs shook but she held up straight to stare down the gun.

'We read up on him, Pav. He uses lots of names but he always picks ones he can remember easy. Fact is, his whole life's one shit anagram. Once they were written out it didn't take long to find the one his father handed him, and you're wrong, Gradzynski, he really is one crazy son-of-a-bitch. Say hello to the Magpie. His name's Abrahams and you can forget about talking him down, you'd be the only one listening.'

'How'd you work it out?'

'I couldn't, Pav. Maggie did.'

Gradzynski thought hard about their chances. His own survival was no more than a slender edge to the argument but unless he made something happen soon, this stand-off was here to stay until many more died. Recalling how extreme the choice was that Leroy made up at the farm, he laid his gun slowly to the floor. He stood up and stared Abrahams in the eye.

The surgery was good, but not good enough to disguise the way one eye remained static when Abrahams glanced down at the gun. 'Kick it over.'

Gradzynski kicked it. It slid up to Ben's feet and stopped. The barrel of a gun pushed hard into Ben's kidneys. 'Pick it up.'

As Ben stooped to pick it up, Louise saw the gunman clearly for the first time and began to scream.

'You're not Raymond you're not Raymond your hair is

wrong you killed Lucy you're lying to me what have you done with Raymond did Maggie steal him?'

She tried to leap over Ben to get at him, face contorted in a grotesque parody of venal anger by the slash of lipstick across it.

Abrahams brought up his gun. Ben caught her and hugged her to him where he couldn't get off a shot.

'It's alright. I got her. She doesn't mean anything. Can't help it. She's confuse…'

The words caught in his throat as he recalled the day Jacob had given him the job of looking after her, along with an allowance. None of them could have known that he'd fall in love. Tears streamed his face, sticking to the fragmented stuffing in her hair as Louise shrieked and struggled in his arms.

'She can't… we can't… help it. Hey… Louise? What about that time I went for a haircut?'

He ran his fingers through her hair, combing out some of the cotton fronds.

Louise calmed down and clung to his chest, arms wrapped around him tight.

'I don't know, Raymond… when was that?'

Ben stroked her hair in a way that for some time now he'd tried hard to forget. 'Oh… maybe last week.'

She snuggled up against him while he held her tight. 'I… think I remember.'

'Sure you do, Louise. See?' He pushed the gun behind him.

Abrahams took it, pushed Ben away and leveled the gun at waist height. 'Alright. Nice and slow. I want everyone who can to make their way onto the stairs where you'll be good and safe. You first.' He prodded Ben with the barrel. 'Take your wife with you. Throw some clothes on her. Come on… the rest of you.'

Gradzynski lifted Mariel to her feet. Eugenie seemed absorbed by all the activity but remained silent, her flashing eyes missing nothing. Maybelline tried to help Maggie out of her chair but Maggie was just so much dead weight.

'No, ma'am. Leave her be. You take the stairs with the rest of them. You two… Leroy, Æppel, take her with you.'

Æppel stood her ground against the gun. 'Why don't you take me instead? Ain't I more to your taste? How many times you heard my name spoke out loud by now?'

'What?'

Æppel pushed Leroy out of shot so hard he staggered into Gradzynski's arms as she turned back to face the gun.

'I know who you are mister, an' you ain't who these folks think you are. You're Satan hisself an' I been waiting years for you to call. But don't think I ain't ready for you. I got happiness on my side an' Leroy's love comin' right down the line. You ain't gonna take me without a fight.'

He aimed the gun straight at Leroy. 'I already done that, and if that bunch of nuts up at the farm let you get away again that ain't my business. I got paid for my end of the bargain. Now shut up and move.'

Leroy dug in his heels and glanced sideways at Gradzynski who shook his head slowly by way of reply. He grabbed hold of Æppel from behind and pulled her reluctantly towards the stairs.

The gun swung away in the direction of Shirley. 'That's right. Now the rest of you, go. Minister? You take the old lady.'

Maybelline was looking around to see who he meant when the Minister took her by the arm and dragged her away.

'That means you too, Doctor.'

Doc and Shirley exchanged a long look.

'It's okay, Doc.' Shirley smiled at the face Maggie was

making behind him. 'Just help me back into the chair. It'll be fine.'

He lowered her gently into the chair. 'How can it be fine when this crazy...'

'Doc. Just go. I have this, okay? Some things come with the uniform.'

Abrahams took careful aim at Doc's legs. 'Move now, Doc, or it won't become an option.'

Shirley squeezed Doc's hand as hard as she knew how but could hardly make an impression. 'Just go. It's okay.'

Abrahams waited until they had all gone onto the staircase. Gradzynski stood at the bottom step, shielding as many of them as he could with his body, eyes searching for an opening through which to move.

Shirley settled back into the chair. 'Hey! Cracker! If you really want to hear this you'd better come close.'

Abrahams knelt in front of the wheelchair with his back to Maggie, gun aimed directly at Shirley's left eye. Shirley's mouth twisted around the words. 'You're a real cracker...'

'I'm a whole barrel.'

'No, you're not. You're just full of shit. And by the time they pump you full of tranqs in jail you won't know which end to put your breakfast in. You're going to die anyway, so go for it you bastard.'

'Nothing you want to say first?'

'Yes. Get your face out of mine.'

'I want to hear this.' He swung the gun around to encompass the room then back to Shirley. 'I want to hear you leave all this behind in one last, rattling breath.'

'Think you're going to have a memory? You're dead already, you son-of-a-bitch.'

Maggie shuffled sideways in her chair.

Abrahams whipped around to face her. 'Sit tight old lady. Know what's good for you.'

'What's good for me would be a pee right about now. What's good for you?'

'For you to shut up and get comfortable.'

Maggie shuffled again.

He turned back. 'That Minister of yours. She do funerals too?'

'Why? You want to book early? I'll try and get a rate. Seeing as you're already going downhill there won't be any of that heavy lifting.'

He swung the gun toward her. 'Stop shaking and start praying. I don't have all day.'

He turned back to Shirley, keeping the gun between them. 'Now... I want you to look into my eyes and repeat after me... I am about to die...'

Shirley leaned forward and grinned crookedly at him. 'Too right. And I'm gonna be the one that kills you, son-of-a-bitch.'

Maggie lifted the half bottle of rocket fuel from the stash that Leroy had built into her chair arm, leaned up and shattered it across the back of Abrahams' skull.

The gun dropped from his hand into Shirley's lap. She picked it up and aimed it into the top of his head from where she knew the bullet would travel the length of his spine, ripping and destroying in its wake.

Her aim was slow and deliberate. Over the past weeks her fingers had begun to quicken, but they hesitated long enough for Gradzynski to lift the gun harmlessly from them.

Maggie slumped back in the chair. One side of her face had fallen dramatically and she was unconscious.

Gradzynski touched the side of her throat. 'Doc?'

Doc held his fingers lightly against Maggie's throat and began to count. The beat slowed noticeably until he found himself pressing hard to feel anything at all. 'Looks like it took all she had, Pav.'

Gradzynski poked at Abrahams with his shoe. 'Looks like it was enough. Most folks never get to feel that way.'

'What way's that Pav?'

'Satisfied with what they did. No hope for her?'

'She's messed up inside. Been like that most of her life.'

'Messed up?'

'What folks did back then. You want me to go into detail so you can arrest some Nazi corpse somewhere?' Doc reached down to check Abrahams. 'He's still ticking, Pav. Better get him cuffed.'

'Keep the gun on him, Doc. I'll go get the ones off Joseph.'

Doc's hand wouldn't stop shaking. The gun in it was such an alien thing… 'Shirley?'

'Yeah, Doc?'

'Back there… I hardly dare ask. I mean… would you…? I mean… were you going to?'

'Sure I was.'

'How can you say that, Shirl? Is that any kind of an attitude to life?'

'It's one I grew up with. Want to teach me different?'

'You willing to learn?'

'Depends who's teaching.'

'What if it was me?'

'Well, Teach. Get a hold of that minister's diary and see what she's got. This could be a long lesson.'

'Zombies?'

'And Aliens.'

'The whole works?'

'I draw the line at Geraniums. They make me sneeze.'

Truth

'Doctor Schweitz? I have some sad news. I have to tell you that Magdalena Grau has passed away.'

'Ah… my friend from Chain O'Lakes. Was her passing peaceful?'

'Let us say it was as… as peaceful as we had come to expect.'

'And what have you done with her mortal remains? Just so the Museum can log this, you see.'

'Strange as it may seem, she already had a grave. My friend Pawel Gradzynski found a map reference on an old photograph in her chest of documents. We found some remains in a small coffin there so she won't be without company.'

'And all her worldly goods?'

'Not so much as was worth anything. A bottle of perfume arrived just after she died and we put that in the coffin with her, along with a pressed Geranium. There's the house, though. We had been hoping to swing that towards her friends Æppel and Leroy Landry.'

'Then her untimely death is indeed unfortunate, my young friend.'

'How is that? She managed way past her three score and ten.'

'That may be so, but who will now forge her Will?'

'I don't know. I'm a medical doctor. I try only to work with the truth.'

'Necessary lies need only belief to become truth. You believed in Magdalena Grau, did you not?'

'Guess I did at that.'

'Then Magdalena Grau is not the end of this tradition. Tradition never dies while one person remembers.'

'And are memories more or less than truth, Doctor Schweitz?'

'Memories are facsimiles, my friend, tinted by the ink of our individual perspectives. With your medications you will save many lives but with your pen you may also create new life for lost and broken ones. Forgive my presumption, but I hear in your voice that you have already begun to do so.'

'Then how shall I ever know the truth?'

'My friend, as you write, the truth shall come to know you.'